Bikini
SEASON

ALSO BY SHEILA ROBERTS

On Strike for Christmas

Bikini SEASON

Sheila Roberts

ST. MARTIN'S GRIFFIN

NEW YORK

BIKINI SEASON. Copyright © 2008 by Sheila Roberts. All rights reserved. Printed in the United States of America. For information, address St. Martin's Press, 175 Fifth Avenue, New York, N.Y. 10010.

www.stmartins.com

The Library of Congress has cataloged the first trade paperback edition as follows:

Roberts, Sheila.
    Bikini season / Sheila Roberts.—1st. ed.
      p. cm.
    ISBN 978-0-312-37080-0
    1. Dieters—Fiction.   2. Self-realization—Fiction.   3. Female friendship—
Fiction.   I. Title.
    PS3618.O31625 B55 2008
    813'.6—dc22

                                                            2008003146

ISBN 978-1-250-00046-0 (trade paperback)

Second St. Martin's Griffin Edition: June 2011

10 9 8 7 6 5 4 3 2 1

For Kimberly and Kathleen, my diet triage buddies.
Thank God for friends!

Acknowledgments

*P*utting out a book is such a team effort, and I am hugely indebted to mine. Huge thanks to my wonderful agent, Paige Wheeler, and my amazing editor, Rose Hilliard, for all their input. And speaking of input, what would I do without my critique buddies? Thanks to Rose Marie, Lois, Kate, the two Susans, Krysteen, and PJ! I'd also like to thank Jed Soenstrom, for his help with all things legal. Jed, you give lawyers a good name. Thanks, too, to Norma Smith, caterer and kitchen queen, for your invaluable help in figuring out calories per serving and other overwhelming food details for the recipes included in this book. By the way, no waistlines were hurt in the writing of this book.

Bikini SEASON

....

One

Was it a bad omen when you couldn't zip up your wedding dress? Erin Merritt looked over her shoulder at her reflection in the full-length mirror hanging on her bedroom door and sighed. A good two inches of skin peeked out between the zipper teeth, taunting, *Neener, neener, neener.* How had this happened in just a few weeks?

Don't play dumb, scolded her inner mother. *You know how this happened.* And then her inner mother gave her a little pat on the shoulder. *But it's understandable. You've been under a lot of stress.*

She had. Her job as an event planner was stressful enough. But in addition to being responsible for making all those fund-raisers and community festivals in nearby Seattle smashing successes, she'd been working on a shoestring for the most important event of her life, her wedding.

If Mom were still alive it wouldn't have been a shoestring. Mom always said, "What's money when you're making memories? Memories are priceless." Especially wedding memories, and that was why Erin wanted a storybook wedding.

But Adam Hawthorne, her Prince Charming, kept trying to mess up the story at every turn. "We're going to have some tight years at first. I don't want to rack up any more debt than we have to," he was always saying.

If she followed all Adam's cheapo suggestions they sure wouldn't have any debt. They wouldn't have any wedding, either. His mom had offered to spring for the cake, so there had been no need to argue over that. But they'd argued about everything else, from the flowers ("You don't need to budget so much for flowers, babe. My cousin could do them for us—she's big into gardening.") to the location ("Let's get married in your aunt's backyard."). Nice of him to volunteer her aunt, who had already done so much for her. Adam had no problem with volunteering people to do things for them to save them money. Erin, on the other hand, was reluctant to draft free labor. It was both tacky and dangerous. Just because someone liked to arrange flowers or take pictures, that didn't mean the person was any good at it.

Okay, she got that he didn't want her to spend fifty thousand dollars on a wedding, but he was carrying this broke med-school-student thing way too far, especially since he wasn't broke and his grandfather was taking care of his medical school bills. (It paid to be an only child with generous grandparents.) Anyway, it was their wedding, for crying out loud, and she was footing the bill for most of it.

Adam's argument to that was that he was going to get her maxed-out credit card bills right along with her. So what? She'd be the one paying them off. Anyway, how many times did a girl get married?

Only once, Mom used to say, and then a woman got smart. But Erin didn't want to get smart. She wanted to marry Adam. Wait a minute. That hadn't quite sounded right.

"We can put the money we save toward a down payment on a house," Adam kept saying. "You don't need a big party. Let's be smart about this."

Depressed, she slipped out of the gown, returned it to its garment bag, and hung it back in her closet. She could just imagine what Adam would say if he found out she'd outgrown the wedding gown he thought she'd spent way too much on.

Why had she been so dumb as to come home from work and try the thing on anyway? Oh, yeah, to cheer herself up after her crappy day. Well, cheers.

"You've got to quit stressing," Adam was always saying. Funny, considering he was one of her biggest stressors.

Erin sighed. Okay, everyone had their faults, and Adam's cheapness wasn't really a fault. He just didn't get how this all worked. Weddings cost money. And you had to plan ahead, far ahead. The Heart Lake Lodge was booked a year in advance, sometimes two. And she much preferred to use that idyllic location rather than make her aunt go crazy trying to get her house ready for a wedding. She could afford to pay her way. She didn't have to use people.

Adam didn't know it yet, but Erin had already reserved the lodge. Her friend Bev, who worked there, had told her there'd been a cancellation. Thank God for connections. Bev had ignored the waiting list and put their name on the event calendar. And when the time was right, Erin would tell him all about it and explain how lucky they were, and then he'd be as excited about it as she was.

It was mid-January now. The wedding was in June. Hopefully, the time for telling Adam would be right soon.

Erin suddenly felt a need for . . . something. She found it fifteen minutes later at the Safeway in the chips aisle. There was nothing like chips and salsa to make a girl feel better. Chips, salsa, and a margarita, she decided, and picked up some drink mix, too, to go with the half-full bottle of tequila she had stashed at the back of the cupboard.

Dan Rockwell was working the express checkout tonight. He smiled at her, then eyed her grocery items. "Party, huh?"

"Not really," she replied. She should have picked a different register. Then she wouldn't have had her brother's old buddy assessing her food purchases.

"Doctor McDoodoo must be coming over."

"That's McDreamy," she corrected him. "Like in *Grey's Anatomy*." If he was going to eavesdrop on private conversations people had every time they waited in line he should at least get the information right.

He nodded, pretending to be impressed. "Oh, yeah. I forgot."

Erin gave him a look that told him exactly what she thought of his faulty memory. The obnoxious crack was hardly surprising, though. Average-looking men like Dan always hated Adam Hawthorne because he was so incredibly gorgeous. With his ice-blue eyes and that square chin, those broad shoulders and perfectly sculpted abs (not to mention the rest of him), Adam could have been a movie star.

She supposed Dan could have been a movie star, too, a sidekick kind of movie star—the average-looking guy with the slightly crooked nose who did dumb stuff and said funny things and was always there for the hero, but never cool enough to be the hero.

Dan was a dork. He'd been a dork ever since she'd known him. Well, okay, there was that time when she was in seventh grade and he was in ninth that she thought he was really fabulous and had dreamed about his brown eyes and cute smile. And when a bunch of them were playing spin the bottle down in the basement at one of her brother Brett's dumb parties and Dan kissed her, it had given her a zing from her training bra to her toes. That zing turned to tingling mortification when he made a face afterward and said, "Yuck, I'm a pervert. I kissed a kid." She'd show him, she thought. He'd be sorry when she was older and really, really cool.

Then she got to high school and became a cheerleader, a cute blond cheerleader. Really, really cool. And it was payback time, payback for the times he'd teased her about needing to start shaving her legs, about that stubborn zit that suddenly appeared on her chin and kept appearing ever after every month like clockwork, about anything and everything that was none of his business. She got so cool she could freeze him with a look. Pretty soon his teasing became less confident and then it dried up, and when he came over to see Brett, he just mumbled, "Hi, Erin," and scooted off down the hall to Brett's room or out to the driveway to shoot hoops.

He never kissed her again until another one of her brother's parties in the basement. Brett had managed to become halfway cool, playing on the football team, but for some unknown reason he still stayed friends with Dan. That night, after a few illegal beers, Dan got her in a lip lock. She was no longer in training bras, but she had the same reaction. Scared by her lack of taste, she'd slapped him and informed him he was a dork (just in case he hadn't figured it out). And that was the last time he ever came near her. Which, perversely, pissed her off even more.

After high school everyone drifted apart and moved away and she only saw him when the holidays pulled them all home. And that was about as much as she cared to see of him. After all, who needed to see someone on a regular basis who had known you since you were a kid and could remind you of all the dumb things you'd done?

Now Dan had wound up living back in Heart Lake this year, like her. Only she wasn't staying. She was only here because Aunt Mellie was letting Erin stay in her rental house for next to nothing so she could save for the wedding. Once she was married she'd be living in Seattle.

Dan would be here forever, as frozen in time as the TV dinners in the freezer cases he stocked, destined to check groceries for the rest of his natural-born days.

She, on the other hand, planned to make a big splash in the world of event planning and own her own company ten years from now. And that was why Adam was a perfect match. He was going places, too. And really, except for his obsession over the cost of the wedding (which he was just going to have to get over), he was perfect. Women fell all over themselves to get him to talk to them, but he only had eyes (ice blue) for her. He was going to be rich and successful. They'd live in a beautiful house, have beautiful children (when the time was right), and take romantic vacations together. Life with Adam would be successful and secure. Perfect.

"You could get fat eating all those chips by yourself," Dan teased, giving Erin a severe yank back into the moment at hand.

Her eyes popped open wide. Fat? Yes, she'd gone up two sizes in the last six months, but . . . oh, God. It was really showing if grocery checkers were feeling the need to make comments. "Why did you say that?"

Dan's brow bunched in confusion. "Say what?"

"What you just said. About getting fat."

He shrugged. "No reason. I was just goofing around."

Being a dork as usual. Where along the way to adulthood had he decided he could start teasing her again? She'd obviously been too nice to him at Christmas. "Do I look fat?" she demanded.

He shook his head. "No, no. You look fine. I was just joking. Really."

Erin sliced her debit card through the slot on the little box at the checkout. "You should never joke about fat with a woman."

"Even when she isn't?"

"Even when . . . ever," Erin finished with a snap.

"Okay. Sorry. Chill."

"I don't need to chill. I just need to . . . not talk to you." She signed her name on the screen, then grabbed the receipt from him and marched out the door. As soon as she got in her car she ripped open the chip bag, filling her little VW Bug with the smell of deep-fried cornmeal. She pulled one out and bit down on it violently. Dan Rockwell was a dork.

She drove home, chomping on chips all the way. And all the way her inner mother scolded, *This is no way to fit into your dress.*

"I know," she agreed. "What is wrong with me?"

Her inner mother decided it was time to keep her mouth shut and said nothing.

Erin felt the sting from a surprise attack of tears. "Oh, Mom, I miss you so much." For a moment she considered going over to Aunt Mellie's house on the lake for some Mom-like comfort, but then remembered that this was dance lesson night. Aunt Mellie and Uncle Jake would be over at the Heart Lake Community Hall stepping on each other's feet.

So Erin went home and made herself a margarita to go with the chips and salsa. And called her friend Angela. She didn't bother with small talk or politely asking if Angela was busy. That would be a dumb question anyway. With two kids under the age of six Angela was always busy. Instead, Erin got right to the point. "My wedding gown doesn't fit," she wailed.

The words were barely out when she realized she'd heard more than Angela's voice on the other end of the line a minute ago. She'd heard a key in her front door lock. She looked over her shoulder and there stood Adam, wearing his old J. Crew jacket, the wool scarf and leather gloves she gave him for Christmas, and a stunned expression.

Angela Baker stared at her phone receiver. "What do you mean you've got to go? You just called."

"Adam just came in."

"Did he hear what you said?" If he did, how awful!

"Yep."

Angela wished she could think of some words of wisdom for her friend, but her mind was a complete blank. "Crud."

"Yep. I'll talk to you later," Erin said, and hung up.

Angela set the cordless on the end table, then restarted the Oprah show that she'd recorded and burrowed deeper under her afghan. Poor Erin. Adam would probably say something dumb and insensitive and then they'd get in a fight. If you asked Angela, Adam Hawthorne was what Dr. Phil called a nightmare groom. Here Erin was, trying to plan her big day, and all Adam did was pour cold water on everything she wanted to do. Saving money was one thing, but his ideas were off-the-charts bad. And selfish. *Bastardo*.

"That was quick."

She looked up to see her husband, Brad, leaning against the doorjamb between the living room and front hall. He'd changed out of his work clothes earlier and was clad in jeans and a sweater, the sleeves pushed up to accommodate postdinner bathtub patrol.

He looked like a Brad, with his fair skin and sandy hair—a contrast to her darker, Italian coloring. They had made one hot couple when they got married. Fortunately, she hadn't had to worry about her wedding dress fitting.

But that was a long time ago and now she was only hot from the neck up. And sometimes that wasn't so good, either. It was scary how quickly a woman could put on weight once she quit work and decided to stay at home with the kids.

"So, who kept you on the phone for only five minutes? Can we clone her?"

"It was Erin. Adam came over so she had to go."

"Yeah, well, he should enjoy that kind of attention while it lasts," Brad cracked.

"Very funny." Angela tapped her chin thoughtfully. "I'm not sure Adam is the right man for Erin. I just can't picture them together in the long run."

"They'll work it out. Hey, speaking of pictures, I almost forgot," he said. He opened the hall coat closet, then fished around in his coat pocket and came up with a handful of snapshots.

Hmmm. Where had he gotten those? They had their own printer here at home.

He sauntered over and joined her on the couch. It was a big, deep-cushioned leather number and it had cost a pretty penny, but Brad didn't care. He liked nice things. He didn't make a fortune working at First National's loan center in the city, but he never complained when she spent money. Unlike some people. Poor, poor Erin.

"By the way, the girls are all washed, but I told them they could play in the tub for five more minutes. They're soap-chalking everything."

"No big deal. It washes off," said Angela, reaching for the mystery pictures.

"Rachel made some copies of the shots she took at the office Christmas party."

Rachel. Angela's smile suddenly felt stiff.

"Ha! Look at that one of Jack trying to do the limbo," Brad said, looking over Angela's shoulder. "She's threatening to use it to extort money out of him."

I wouldn't put it past her. Angela began to look through the pictures. It was mostly people she didn't know and didn't care about. She stopped when she came to one of herself and a lithe redhead. Rachel, her husband's assistant. Her husband's single assistant. Single and looking assistant. Single and looking-to-wreck-a-home assistant.

Angela had seen women like this on *Oprah.* They had no heart, no conscience, no fat.

She studied the block with the dark-haired head standing next to Rachel. Herself. In her black slacks and one-size-covers-all black sequined top, she looked big, huge, mammoth, ready to be recycled, turned in for someone hotter. Like the bitch standing next to her.

Anger started simmering inside Angela. Rachel had given this to Brad on purpose, so he could compare the two of them side by side. It wasn't hard to see who was lacking. What a horrible, depressing shot!

"I look awful," she said.

Brad took the picture and looked at it. "No you don't. I like you in black."

Angela frowned. "That woman is a *puttana.*"

Brad raised an eyebrow. "I see you learned another new word in Italian. Do I even want to know what it means?"

"I bet you can guess."

She reached for the picture but he held it away, saying, "Oh, no. You'll probably tear it up."

She tried to reach across him and grab it. "It needs to be torn up."

"If you keep ripping up pictures you don't like of yourself pretty soon we won't have any in our albums." He grinned. "But then you won't spend a fortune on scrapbooking stuff, so maybe I should let you."

She stuck her tongue out at him.

"Daddy, Mandy just poohed in the tub," called their older daughter, Gabriella.

Brad grimaced and made a pretense of starting to get up.

Angela put a hand on his arm. "I'll take care of it."

He looked relieved. "Works for me."

She wasn't being that noble, really. She'd rather deal with the pooh in the tub than the pooh in the picture. She should never have let herself get so fat. The darned pounds had sneaked up on her one at a time, first hiding on her bottom and then spreading out to expand first an inch here and then an inch there. If she didn't do something about it soon she'd lose Brad to that redheaded home wrecker.

She fished the girls out of the tub and got them into their jammies, then sent them downstairs to play with Daddy while she cleaned up the mess. If only she could pull herself together as easily!

Brad had wanted her to see that picture, wanted her to see what she'd become. The other pictures were just cover. That one was where the real message lay. And it had come through loud and clear. She was a blob, a big, unsexy blob.

They got the girls to bed, and then watched some TV. Well, Brad watched. Angela only pretended to watch while she thought about how she'd let herself go. After the news they went up to bed themselves. She scrambled into her sleep tee while Brad was in the master bathroom brushing his teeth. She looked down at the thing in disgust. Rachel probably wore Victoria's Secret nightgowns to bed. Or maybe she slept in the nude.

Angela was safely hidden behind fabric when Brad came out of the bathroom, ready for bed in his boxers and T-shirt. He was still in great shape, not an ounce of fat on him. He slipped in between the covers. "Hey, baberino, why don't you lose that thing?" he suggested, nodding at her tee.

"It is getting kind of ratty." She needed to go shopping, get something new and sexy. But what was the point? She wouldn't look sexy in it.

He grinned. "No, I mean lose it now."

His words covered her smarting self-esteem like salve. She smiled at him. He still loved her. She was being silly.

She joined him in bed, losing the tee once she was under the covers. She never used to be so bashful.

He didn't seem to mind. He found her under there just fine.

But later, long after he was snoring happily, she lay in bed and thought about that picture. If she and Rachel had been cars, Rachel would have been a Maserati while she would have been an old, old minivan. What man would want a dumpy, old minivan when he could have a Maserati? Never mind that he'd had children with the minivan, that he still drove the minivan. He'd want the Maserati.

Next she got to thinking about Rachel, Brad's assistant, who worked late whenever he worked late. He'd stayed to work late just last week.

That didn't mean anything, she assured herself. Brad was a good man. He wouldn't cheat on her. Still, how many good men, surrounded by temptation every day, finally lost the will to fight? Just like a woman surrounded all through the holidays by cookies and chocolate, who finally couldn't take it anymore and dove mouth first into the Hershey's chocolate mint Kisses, a man could probably only go so long. Brad was human, after all. Everyone had an Achilles' heel. Was Rachel Brad's? Again, Angela thought of that picture.

Driven by a tsunami of panic, she slipped out of bed and went downstairs to the laundry room where she started digging through the bag for the dry cleaners, pulling out all his shirts. She sniffed each one and examined the collar for lipstick. She found nothing, but that didn't mean anything, really, just that things hadn't progressed too far yet. Brad and Rachel were still in the attraction stage, still flirting. She'd lean in close to him when putting something on his desk for him to sign. He'd sneak peeks down her blouse. Soon he'd be working late several nights a week. Soon the traces of lipstick would start showing up on his shirt collar. He wouldn't be able to help himself.

Then Angela would become like those poor, pitiful women who went on *Oprah* and insisted, "I had no idea my husband was having an affair."

No, she wouldn't be like them, because she'd have had an idea. And she knew right now that if she didn't do something drastic her husband was going to go Maserati hunting.

Okay, so she'd turn thirty in March, but she still had plenty of hum in her engine. She just needed a better chassis. And she needed to get one fast. Suddenly, she remembered the place on Oprah's Web site where a woman who wanted a new chassis could find the motivation and encouragement to get one. She padded into their little home office and got on the computer. Then she went to Oprah's Web site, drilling her acrylic nails on the desk as she searched for what she wanted. There it was, all the help and inspiration a girl could ask for. Good.

Rachel was going to end up on *Oprah* or *Dr. Phil* one day, no doubt about it. But Angela wasn't going to be there with her. She was going to go to booty camp and get hot.

Two

$\mathcal{E}$rin woke up with an anger hangover, still surrounded by the fumes of the previous night's fight. She and Adam had spent what should have been a romantic evening together shoving blame back and forth like a hot potato neither one wanted.

"You spent all that money on a dress you're only going to wear once and now it doesn't fit?"

"Why are you giving me a bad time when I'm already upset? If you'd quit picking fights over everything I want to do . . ."

"If you'd be reasonable and let me . . ."

"If you weren't such a cheap asshole . . ."

That was when Erin's inner mother jumped in. *You're not accomplishing anything by calling names, especially that one. I should wash your mouth out with soap.*

And she should have spanked Adam for being so insensitive.

"You know, maybe I'd better go back to my place tonight," he had finally suggested. Mom would have approved of that.

Erin certainly did. "Maybe you should," she'd agreed, turning her back on him. And so he had. And she'd had another margarita and finished off the chips. It was a small bag.

Anyway, she was going to make up for it and not have breakfast this morning. The idea of breakfast didn't appeal even remotely. Until she checked her messages and found no penitent message from Adam. Asshole. *He is, Mom. Really.*

Now, now, said her inner mother as Erin baked herself a Pop-Tart in her toaster. *It's a new day. You don't want to start it off in a bad mood, do you?*

As a matter of fact, she did.

She showered and dressed in the last clean clothes left in her closet—she had to get that pile of dirty laundry off the bedroom floor tonight before Adam said something. Except maybe he wouldn't come around to say anything. After their terrible fight maybe he'd decide he didn't want to be with her after all.

She tried to envision herself alone and adrift without him. She couldn't. She could, however, envision herself having another Pop-Tart.

She made a second one, fed Ariel her goldfish, then grabbed her purse and her car keys, shrugged into her coat, and dashed through the January drizzle to her car. On the way, she stepped in a stinky present from the neighbor's dog and had to turn right around and run back through the drizzle to the apartment to clean off her shoe. After first having to stop in the drizzle and rub off the worst of the mess on the grass. Wasn't this day just getting off to a fun start? But she didn't say a bad word. Mom would have been proud.

What would Mom have thought of Adam? She'd, of course, have proclaimed him a total hunk. And she'd have approved of his career choice. Very noble. And she'd have to have liked the way he took an interest in everything in Erin's life, from what happened at work or when she went out with her friends to her long-range career plans—he wanted to share it all.

But Mom would have been horrified by his cheapness. As a single parent, Mom had often had trouble making ends meet, but no matter how crazy their life or how tight their budget they had always found a way to splurge on celebrating life's important milestones. Erin remembered how much Mom had spent to help Brett and Carly get married in style, how she'd splurged on that crazy trip to Mexico for Erin's college graduation. She never had a surplus in savings and she died broke.

"But I've lived happily," she told Erin during their final visit. "You do the same."

Erin had tried, but it had been impossible to be happy without her mom. Until Adam had come along.

She'd call him and make up as soon as she got to work.

He called her first, reaching her on her cell just as she was getting back in her car.

"I'm sorry about last night," he said. "I didn't think before I spoke. I was just concerned about how much it would cost to replace that wedding dress."

It would have been nice if he'd been concerned about her. This was his idea of making up? She started the car with a forceful foot on the gas, making the engine roar. She did a quick check over her shoulder, and squealed away from the curb. "The dress can be altered."

Although having her wedding dress let out was the last thing she wanted. And if she was too fat for her wedding dress now, what would she look like on the beach in Hawaii in a bikini? She was going to have to bag the bikini. Maybe they should bag Hawaii. Maybe they should go to Alaska, someplace where she could cover up with lots of clothes.

"Do you really want to do that?"

Now he was probably worried she'd just keep swelling up—the incredible growing bride. "Of course not. I'll lose the weight. I just have to stop eating every time I'm stressed." She checked her reflection in the mirror. Her hair and makeup were fine. Was her face looking fuller than it had last week? Who cared about her face? She didn't have to fit her face in a wedding dress.

"Then don't get stressed. You're putting pressure on yourself about things that don't matter."

"What?" She was working hard to make their wedding a memorable day and he didn't even care. She gunned the gas and sailed through a yellow light.

That was red, said her inner mother.

No, it was orange.

"People will have a good time no matter what kind of flowers you have or what your bridesmaids wear," he continued. "You're worrying about stuff that's not important."

"It's important to me, Adam. This is a special day."

Adam let out an impatient sigh. "Are we building up to another fight?"

She hated when he did that sighing thing. It made her feel like she was being petty. But maybe she was. "No. I don't want to fight. It seems like that's all we've done since you asked me to marry you. I don't understand how two people who love each other and want to be together can find so much to fight about."

"We don't fight that much," Adam argued. "At least not about things that matter. The important thing is that we love each other. Right?"

"Of course. And I'm sorry I got so mad last night." Maybe Adam was right. Maybe she was stressing out about things that didn't matter. The wedding was important, and she wanted it to be as special as the man she was marrying. But it was only one day. What was that in comparison to the rest of their lives?

"Me, too," he said. "And don't worry. You'll get into your wedding gown in time. You've got months, and I'll help you."

"You don't need to. I can do it," she assured him. The last thing she needed was Adam's overzealous help in the diet department. They were still dealing with the after-effects of him helping her get organized.

In November, when she'd complained about her piles of papers, he had run out and found her a filing cabinet on sale at a discount office supply store. They'd spent the entire weekend sifting through her coupons and catalogs and bills. That had been embarrassing.

That had also been when Adam decided she needed his assistance with managing her money. She really didn't. She wasn't in debt.

He's only trying to help. Now back to the real problem: how are you going to lose the weight to get into your wedding gown? nagged her inner mother.

Drop it, Mom.

Her inner mother always knew when to shut up. She dropped it.

Kizzy Maxwell left the doctor's office wearing a frown. Okay, so according to the biopsy her problem probably wasn't cancer. That was the good news. But she was now going to be "monitored," which wasn't all that exciting. And the doctor wanted her to take off "some weight," which really meant about sixty-five pounds. Sixty-five pounds! He may as well have said a hundred. And how the heck was she going to diet with Lionel around?

She stopped by the Safeway store's deli on her way back to her kitchen shop and picked up a coleslaw salad. Coleslaw was good for you. Except for all the mayonnaise. But a little mayo probably wouldn't matter since coleslaw was all she was eating until dinner. She had salad makings in the fridge at home. She'd bake some chicken and make a salad for tonight. If he had meat, then maybe Lionel would be happy.

Until he found out there was no dessert. Lionel always expected dessert.

There was ice cream in the freezer. He could have that. She sure wasn't baking anything. Maybe she'd never bake again. How depressing!

But not as depressing as having cancer. She needed to get a grip on what was really important here. All she had was a thick uterus that hadn't properly sloughed its walls when she went through menopause. A thick uterus and a thick middle, both conspiring against her. Ugh.

Her cell phone rang and she fished it out of her purse. Of course, it was Lionel.

"So, what's the doctor say?"

"It looks like we dodged the bullet, but they're going to watch me."

"You don't have cancer."

"Nope."

"Then why are they going to watch you?"

"Just to be sure."

"That doesn't make any sense. What's the problem?"

"The doctor's pretty sure I just need some progesterone." Too much fat had turned into too much estrogen. And that was why she had to take off some weight. The fat was contributing to her estrogen-overload problem.

"So, if they put you on hormones does that mean your sex drive's gonna go up?"

"What's wrong with my sex drive?" she demanded, then realized that she had just gotten the attention of the deli counter clerk, two shoppers, and a stock boy. She lowered her voice. "As if you don't get enough, you big pig."

"Come on, girl, when it comes to you, you know there's no such thing as too much."

Kizzy shook her head. "You can sure dish up the sweet talk."

"And you love me for it. So, you want to go out to dinner and celebrate?"

"No, I've got dinner planned. Just come on home."

"Okay, then. See you later."

And when he did see her later, he came bearing gifts: champagne and a box of Godiva chocolates.

She turned from the pot of soup she was stirring and pointed to the candy. "Not with that we're not celebrating. I need to lose weight."

He set the candy and champagne on the granite kitchen island and gave her a hug. "Naw, you don't. I like a woman with some junk in the trunk."

"Well, I've got to empty my trunk. Dr. Stevens said so."

Lionel gave a snort of disgust. "A skinny white boy? What does he know about what looks good?"

Kizzy shook her head at him. "We didn't discuss my looks. We were talking about my health."

Lionel's scornful expression turned to instant concern. "I thought you were fine."

"Well, I am, but I still need to lose weight."

Lionel flipped back into scornful mode. He pulled her close and nuzzled her neck. "That doctor may know about your insides, but he knows nothin' about the rest of you. You look fine, Kiz. You really do."

She gave his cheek a caress. "You're sweet, Lion."

Of course, it was wonderful to have her husband love her just the way she was. But she didn't want to turn into some of the ladies at Zion First Baptist that she'd gawked at as a kid. It was one thing to have a body like Queen Latifah. It was quite another to have one like three Queen Latifahs put together. And she was already about a Queen and a half.

Lionel frowned at the soup and salad offering she placed on the oak kitchen table where they always ate. "Do I look like a rabbit to you? I hope this is just the first course."

She pointed her fork at him. "You could stand to whittle down a little, too, you know." He looked like an out-of-shape Emmitt Smith. A very out-of-shape Emmitt.

Gus, their King Charles Spaniel, sat nearby, watching them. At this, he cocked his head at Kizzy and whined as if fearing he, too, would get caught in her diet net.

Lionel wasn't any more receptive. He reared back his head and frowned at her. "Just because the doctor picked on you doesn't mean you have to go passing it on to me. I'm happy the way I am. And you should be, too." He forked the last bit of salad into his mouth, then he went to the fridge to forage. "I need meat."

"You had meat. There was chicken in the salad."

"And potatoes," he added, pulling out a bowl of leftover mashed potatoes from the night before. "Kizzy girl, we both work hard. We have got to eat."

"Not as much as we do. You sit at a desk all day, and I don't exactly run laps at the shop. That doesn't burn calories."

He stood in front of the microwave, watching the potatoes heat and shaking his head. "I don't know why they can't just give you some medicine or something. There's nothing worse than a stick-straight, skinny-ass woman."

Did Lionel have any idea how many pounds she'd have to lose to fit that description? "Believe me, I'll never be that."

He returned to the table and set the bowl of potatoes between them.

Kizzy's potatoes were never just plain mashed potatoes. They oozed garlic and butter and sour cream. Now the aroma of garlic danced around her nostrils.

"One bite won't kill you," said Lionel, as he heaped a carbohydrate mountain on his plate. He dug the spoon into the bowl then flicked a dollop on hers.

He went back into the bowl for more and Kizzy moved her plate out of range. "Lionel, you are not helping."

He let the spoon fall into the bowl and frowned. "I suppose you're not going to eat any of that candy I brought home."

"I'll have one piece," she said, just to please him.

He barely looked mollified. "Those are Godiva, you know."

It had been a nice gesture. She sighed. "I know, and I'll have one. But don't bring me any more after this. You understand?"

Beaming, he reached over and opened the box.

Three candies later, Kizzy was disgusted with both herself and Lionel. She was going to have to make some big changes.

And there was one way to start. After he left the kitchen she grabbed the half-full box and marched to the garbage can, Gus padding after her. She stomped on the pedal at the base of the metal can and the lid popped open like a giant Muppet mouth just waiting to get fed. All she had to do was dump in the candy.

She took her foot off the pedal, letting the lid fall back down with a disappointed clang. It was plain wasteful to throw out chocolates. She stood, looking at the garbage can. The only way she was going to stay out of these was to toss them.

Gritting her teeth, Kizzy opened the can again. She emptied the box into the garbage and the lid clanged shut. The moment felt depressingly symbolic. Life as she knew it was ending.

But at least she still had a life, she reminded herself, and she needed to do all she could to make sure it was a healthy one.

The first step to that would be getting some new mean, lean recipes into her repertoire. From now on her famous potato salad and fried chicken would have to be infrequent visitors in the Maxwell house. And those mashed potatoes Lionel loved so much would have to turn into salads. She sighed. Oh, well, cooking should always be an adventure, and it was time for a new one.

Cooking. Adventure. Oh, rats. She was probably going to have to disband her cooking club. It had started a year ago when Angela Baker, her neighbor up the street, had begged Kizzy to take her and some friends under her wing and turn them into kitchen goddesses. It hadn't taken too much begging, since Kizzy loved to cook. And she loved food. So, it turned out, did the women who came to her house once a month. They always wound up with something fattening on the menu.

First the chocolates and now cooking club. Life sucked.

Three

Each month the cooking club picked a meal theme, usually featuring cuisine from a different region or country, but tonight's menu was comfort food, and everyone was bringing her favorite. Angela had volunteered to make the main course. Her old friend Megan was making an appetizer and Erin was bringing bread. And for dessert Kizzy had baked a chocolate cake that could zap five pounds on a girl's hips simply for looking at it. That was going to be hard to stay out of.

Comfort food had been a good choice for tonight, she thought, remembering her chat with the doctor, a time traveler from the Spanish Inquisition. She needed some comforting.

"Start with a reasonable goal and take off twenty or thirty pounds," Dr. Stevens had said. "You'll be amazed at how much more energy you have."

Energy would be a good thing. It seemed like she was tired all the time. But that was because she was busy all the time.

"I know you work hard," Dr. Stevens had said, "and you play

hard. But try to exercise a little more and eat a little less and see what happens. And when you have company . . ."

"A lot of it." She had this cooking club, her church friends, family gatherings, and lots of neighbors dropping in, and she prided herself on always serving tasty goodies to everyone who came to her house. "What am I supposed to do, offer them carrot sticks?" she'd said in disgust.

Dr. Stevens had shrugged. "Find some new recipes and adapt the old ones. You don't have to starve yourself or your friends. Just eat differently."

Translation: torture yourself.

Tonight would be the equivalent of a last meal. After this she'd have to sit around and drool while everyone else ate.

She had just pulled a casserole dish of macaroni and cheese out of the oven when Angela arrived, bearing a plate of chocolate chip cookies and a huge pan of lasagna and the requisite recipe copies. "This is the last lasagna I'll ever put in my mouth," she announced, setting the pan down on Kizzy's stove. "After this, I'm getting serious about what I'm eating."

"I'm always serious about what I eat," Kizzy said. "I guess that's my problem. Oh, cute shoes," she added, pointing to Angela's peep-toe leopard-print pump.

Angela stuck out her foot. "They were on clearance at Stepping Out. But never mind me. What did the doctor say today?"

"Well, there's good news and bad news."

The blood drained from Angela's face. "Oh, no."

Kizzy shook her head quickly. "It's not that bad. The good news is it isn't cancer. The bad news is I have to lose weight."

"Me, too." Angela looked lustfully at her lasagna. "I hate dieting. I have no willpower."

Kizzy patted her ample hips. "Girl, I am the president of that club."

The doorbell rang and she went to let in the next guest.

There stood Erin Merritt, holding out French bread perfumed with garlic.

Kizzy eyed the carb temptation as Erin laid her offering next to the goodies collecting on Kizzy's granite-topped kitchen counter. She'd never be able to stay out of those.

Angela hovered over Kizzy's cake. "That looks incredible," she said, her voice practically dripping with drool.

"I can cut you girls a piece right now," Kizzy offered. "Life's uncertain, eat dessert first."

Erin shook her head sadly. "There's one thing certain in my life, and that's fat. I can't have any dessert tonight. In fact," she added, looking at the spread, "I can't have anything here."

"What?" Kizzy looked at her, shocked. "You've got to eat something."

"I know it's not comfort food, but could we make a salad of some kind?" Erin asked. "Have you got any lettuce?"

"Of course," Kizzy said, and started pulling lettuce, tomatoes, and onions out of the refrigerator. "If you can pass up Angela's lasagna, please give me a tiny helping of your willpower."

"I don't feel much like eating anyway," Erin said.

Kizzy dumped an armload of salad makings on the counter. "Is something wrong?"

Erin's lower lip began to wobble. "My wedding gown doesn't fit."

"Don't worry," Angela said, patting her shoulder. "Like I told you, you still have time to lose."

"Not if I keep eating the way I've been eating. I'm going crazy. I went through a whole bag of chips in one night."

That was nothing. Kizzy could have done it in one hour. She studied Erin. She was a pretty girl, with blond hair, stylishly highlighted, and striking brown eyes. Right now she looked worried. Maybe she was carrying a little extra weight, but Kizzy was sure she'd have no problem losing it. Now, having sixty-five pounds to shed—that was something to worry about.

"Are you stressed at work?" Kizzy asked diplomatically.

Angela wasn't quite so diplomatic. "It's more than work, isn't it? It's Adam."

Erin bit her lip.

Such a small gesture, but it said a mouthful. Kizzy felt righteous anger on her young friend's behalf bubbling up inside her. This Adam Hawthorne was a pain. Kizzy had met him when she and Lionel hosted an open house over the holidays and Erin and Adam had stopped by. He was an eyeful, Kizzy would give him that, and he had been friendly enough.

But Kizzy had met men like him before, men with a controlling streak half a mile long. He and Erin had been at the party less than an hour before he politely informed her that they needed to be getting on to the next party, and just like that Erin had agreed to leave. Kizzy was proud of her for not so quickly agreeing to all his cheap wedding ideas. Other than encouraging Erin to stand firm and fight for the things she wanted most, Kizzy had pretty much kept her mouth shut. It was one thing for a woman to complain to her friends about her man's bad behavior, but for a friend to diss that same man, that was a recipe for ruining a friendship.

The last member of their group, Megan Wales, arrived bearing a platter of little sausages rolled inside biscuits. "I brought pigs in a blanket," she said, and Kizzy tried not to think about the potential for symbolism lurking on that platter.

Megan was in her early thirties, an up-and-coming lawyer at a big Seattle firm, and was one smart cookie. She was also overweight, right up there in the high numbers with Kizzy. Looking at all of them, Kizzy couldn't help but notice that they had more in common than an interest in recipes.

Megan took in Angela's disapproving frown and Erin's sad face. "What's going on?"

"She's stressed," Angela explained. "Her wedding gown doesn't fit. Did Adam give you grief about that?" she demanded in a tone of voice that threatened to break his legs if he had.

"He did, but we've got it settled. He was only worried about where we're going to get the money for another if I can't lose the weight to get into this one."

"He should be ashamed," Angela said. "You're the one paying for the wedding gown."

"Aren't you footing the bill for everything?" put in Megan.

"I'm the bride. I'm supposed to. Anyway, his parents are getting the cake. And he's taking care of the honeymoon."

"*He's* supposed to," Angela said. "And I don't think he should be saying anything about things he's not paying for," she added firmly.

"He's afraid we're going to end up with a big pile of debt after we're married, and I can't blame him for not wanting to start off on the wrong foot."

"If you ask me, you already are starting off on the wrong foot," said Angela.

Kizzy pulled her vintage Vernonware plates from the cupboard and set them on the counter. "You're really not spending that much on the wedding, believe me," she told Erin.

"I know," Erin said. "He doesn't get how much weddings cost."

He didn't get a lot of things, if you asked Kizzy. The wedding gown wasn't the only thing that wasn't fitting.

"I think mine would fit you. You're welcome to wear it if you want," Angela offered. "God knows I'll never get into it again. And it would look really great on you. What size are you?"

"Ask me in another five months," Erin said miserably.

"Okay, here's the wedding special," Kizzy announced, setting a huge teak bowl full of salad next to the lasagna. "Let's eat. We've got white wine, sparkling cider, Coke, and, of course, chocolate milk to drink."

"I'll just have water," said Erin. "And salad."

"Salad won't keep you full for long," pointed out Megan.

Erin nodded. "Okay, I guess I'll get a little piece of lasagna."

The others followed her lead, taking tiny helpings of the lasagna or mac and cheese, large helpings of salad, and leaving the appetizer and bread untouched.

"This was not a success," Kizzy observed, looking around her dining room table at their itty-bitty servings. "I suppose no one's going to want chocolate cake," she lamented.

"I'll pass," said Erin.

"Me, too," said Angela.

"Me, three," said Megan. "In fact, this is my last meal with you guys."

What was this about? Kizzy wondered. Megan was normally happy to be at the cooking club, smiling and trying everything, often going back for seconds. And she usually had some interesting tale to tell about life at her law firm. Tonight she was sober as a judge who had just been asked to try her own child for grand theft auto.

"How come?" asked Angela.

Megan kept her gaze on her plate. "I'm quitting cooking club. I'm sure you'll be able to get someone to take my place."

"But why?" protested Angela. "It's only once a month. You've got to have time in your schedule for once a month."

Megan shook her head. "It's not working for me. Sorry."

"You never told me," Angela accused. "Since when?"

Megan didn't look her in the eye. "You guys are all great, but I just need to . . . do some different things in my life right now."

"Are you moving or something?" asked Angela. "That's sure the only way I'd quit."

Megan just shook her head.

And that made Angela's eyes narrow. She pointed a French-manicured acrylic nail at Megan. "It's the pencils, isn't it?"

"The what?" asked Kizzy.

"That's what she calls them," Angela explained. "They're total snobs who think they're better than Megan just because they're thin." She turned her attention back to her friend. "What happened?"

Megan shook her head. "I don't want to talk about it."

Kizzy sighed. "Well, I guess this is as good a time as any to tell you girls that I need to bail, too."

"What?" Angela gawked at her like she'd just uttered blasphemy. "But you're our leader."

"Our mom," added Erin. "Without you there wouldn't be a cooking club."

"I know, and I'm sorry to ditch you, but I can't keep eating like this. I have to lose weight. Doctor's orders."

"'Doctor's orders,'" Erin repeated, her eyes getting big. "Oh, no. What's wrong?"

"Don't worry. It's nothing that can't be helped by losing a mountain of weight," Kizzy said. "And let me tell you how well that's going over with Lionel."

"I hate how out of control I've been lately," Erin said with a sigh. "And I hate how I'm starting to look."

Angela frowned at her half-eaten lasagna. "Talk about hating how you look. Brad brought home pictures from the work Christmas party. Next to his hot assistant I look like a big, frumpy pig. Angela Porco," she added in an Italian accent. "If Brad's got a hot puttana at work and a fat frump at home . . ."

Kizzy pointed a fork at her. "Don't you be going there. You're the mother of his children. Anyway, not all men want a skinny woman." She frowned. "God knows Lionel doesn't. He's going to be no help to me at all. I'm going to need a support group."

Angela stared at her, like she was trying to digest something really profound. "Wait a minute," she said slowly. "We could be our own support group, our own Weight Watchers."

That got everyone's attention. "You mean weigh each other?" Megan asked, terror in her voice.

Kizzy couldn't blame her. Once a woman passed a certain point, she preferred to keep the numbers on her scale top secret. "Count me out," she said. "It's bad enough to have to go through that at the doctor's."

"No, no. No weighing," Angela said.

"Okay, so what did you have in mind?" asked Megan.

"Well, I'm just thinking," said Angela. "Everyone here has pretty much said she needs to lose weight, right?"

The others nodded.

"So, why not try to help each other? I mean, the only reason Kizzy was going to drop out was because she's got to get serious, and our monthly pig-outs won't help. And Megan, is that the same reason you were going to bail? I mean, it's not because you don't like us. Right?"

"No. You're all great," Megan said. "In fact, this is the first time in years when I've been with other women who aren't either judging me or competing against me."

"Well, then," said Angela. "We all want to lose weight. Why not stick together?"

"Hmmm," said Erin. "That's not a bad idea."

"Oprah's got great diet advice on her Web site," Angela continued, warming to her subject. "Maybe we could all do an Oprah booty camp."

"That would only help me if Oprah stayed at my house, followed me around, and slapped me every time I got into the fridge," said Kizzy. "I need something a little more hands-on."

"That's where cooking club comes in," said Angela. "We can collect recipes that are good for us, and we can help each other eat right."

It was a great idea, but . . . Kizzy shook her head. "Once a month won't keep me on the wagon."

"Me, either," said Megan.

"Well, what if we met once a week?" Angela suggested. "Would Lionel mind?" she asked Kizzy.

"Not as long as he got to eat the leftovers," said Kizzy. Although he probably wouldn't be real excited about leftover salads. Still, Lionel could stand to take some pounds off, himself. Heck, even Gus needed to slim his doggy figure.

"Bella," said Angela, beaming. "Let's do it. If we started right away maybe I could lose twenty pounds in time for my birthday."

"Okay, so who else wants to do this?" asked Kizzy.

"I will," Megan said with a decisive nod.

"Me, too," said Erin.

"Then we're all in," said Kizzy, and the others nodded, smiling.

"We should have a plan for how we're going to make this work," Megan suggested. "Maybe start with some research."

"Stay out of the chips," said Erin.

"Sign up for booty camp," added Angela.

"Set goals," said Kizzy.

"I can already tell you what mine will be," Angela said. "I want to be in a bikini by summer. Brad's volunteered to host the office picnic out here in August and I'm going to outhot the office hottie."

Kizzy made a face. "I haven't been near a bikini in over twenty years."

"I've never worn one." Megan said the words so softly, Kizzy wasn't sure she'd heard her.

"You've never worn one?" repeated Erin.

Megan shrugged. "Let's just say I never really had a bikini kind of body."

Megan needed to loosen up, live a little, Kizzy decided. Yes, she was packing a chunk of extra pounds, but even so, with her green eyes and stylishly cut chestnut hair, Megan was still a pretty girl. There was more to life than being a support system for a great mind.

There was also more to life than being a support system for a spoiled stomach, Kizzy realized, thinking of the way she'd been living the last few years. She looked out her dining room window at the lake, tucked in under the cover of night. She could almost see herself lolling around on her dock in a cute little bikini, then . . . "I'd love to be able to jump off my dock and swim across the lake," she mused.

"I could go for just sitting on your dock in my new bikini and drinking girly drinks," said Angela.

"And I'd love to have to take in my wedding gown," said Erin, "and be able to take a bikini on my honeymoon."

"Are you going someplace where you can actually wear one?" teased Megan. "For all you know, Adam could be taking you to the Motel Cheap in Tukwila."

"I'll have you know we're going to Hawaii. Adam got a deal."

At least Adam had done something right, Kizzy thought. "Well, then, let's do it," she said.

"This is great," said Erin. "I feel better already."

"Me, too," said Angela, smiling. "*Bene.* This is going to be fun." Everyone looked at her like she was nuts. "Well, sort of," she amended. "More fun than trying to lose weight alone. And ninety percent of the time when you've got a goal you've got a fifty-fifty chance of succeeding. I think I read that somewhere," she added.

Kizzy couldn't imagine where, but she kept her mouth shut.

"We should name ourselves," Angela decided.

Megan looked disgusted. "Why do we need a name?"

"Just for fun," Angela said. "How about the I-Hate-to-Diet Club?"

Erin rolled her eyes. "That's positive."

"Let's think of something more inspiring," Kizzy suggested.

Angela snapped her fingers. "I know! The Bikini Club."

"No," Erin corrected with a grin. "The Teeny Bikini Club. And when it's bikini season we'll all celebrate on Kizzy's dock wearing them."

"Oh, I like it!" cried Angela. "We could do it on the Fourth of July."

"Independence Day," Erin said with a nod.

"I'll still look scary in a bikini by July," Kizzy said. Angela frowned at her and she added, "But I'll do it."

"I don't know," said Megan.

"It's just going to be us girls," Angela said. "Come on, it will be fun."

"We'll see," Megan said.

Kizzy knew what those words meant. She'd used them often enough over the years to placate her kids when she had no intention of giving in. She understood Megan's reluctance. Megan probably had the most weight to lose. She wouldn't be bikini-ready by summer. But maybe, if she lost some weight, she'd at least feel encouraged.

Kizzy raised her glass of chocolate milk. "So, here's to the Teeny Bikini Diet Club. Starting tomorrow, we toss out all our chocolate stashes left over from the holidays."

"And dump the cookies," added Angela.

"And everyone finds a diet book and brings it to the first meeting," Megan added. "We can set goals."

Angela sighed. "I'm already going through baking withdrawals and we haven't even started."

"You can make up something nonfattening for us," Megan suggested.

"I like it," Angela said with a nod.

"And we each have to start an exercise program," added Erin, who was getting pumped.

The mention of exercise threw cold water on Kizzy's enthusiasm. It was one thing to imagine herself fit and fine, swimming the lake, but in reality she wasn't really a sports fanatic or a fitness freak. As far as she was concerned, gyms were places of torture. "I hate treadmills and bicycles."

"You just have to find something that's fun," Erin told her.

Kizzy grimaced. "There is no such thing."

"Don't worry," said Erin. "We'll help you find something to get you buzzed about exercise."

That settled, they spent the rest of the evening brainstorming possible menu themes for future meetings, and by the time they were done everyone was excited.

"We are going to be hot by bikini season," Angela crowed, doing a little boogie in her seat. "Totally bella."

"I'm going to fit into my wedding dress," said Erin, smiling.

"And we're all going to feel better, which is the most important thing of all," added Kizzy.

"Now we just have one thing left to do," said Megan.

"What's that?" asked Kizzy.

"We need to toss the cookies and cake and the casserole left-overs."

"We can't toss out perfectly good food," Kizzy protested. And besides, Lionel had left the house fantasizing about the treats he was going to enjoy when he got home from his bowling league. He'd be disappointed.

"If you send those cookies home with Angela you'll sabotage her," Megan reasoned. "And if that cake stays here can you resist it?"

It was one thing to talk the talk, but Kizzy was already backing up from the idea of walking the walk. "Why don't I freeze it? Then we can eat it later in the year when we're all fit and fine."

"I don't know about you, but a little thing like a freezer wouldn't keep me out of chocolate cake," Megan said.

"She's right," Angela said, her voice steely. "It all has to go. No gain, no pain."

"That's no pain, no gain," Megan corrected her absently.

"I made that cake from scratch," Kizzy protested.

But Megan and Angela were already on their way out to the kitchen, Erin in hot pursuit.

Kizzy trailed them miserably. There were people starving in the world. It seemed so wasteful to throw away good food.

Who was she kidding? That had always been her excuse for not getting rid of things she shouldn't be eating. What not wasting food usually translated into was saving treats for future indulgence, and if she was going to carve a healthy new body for herself she was going to have to lose that kind of faulty thinking.

Gathered in the kitchen, they were just about to begin the food disposal ceremony, starting with the chocolate cake, when Kizzy got inspired. "Wait!" she cried, throwing herself in front of the garbage can. "I know a much better way to dispose of all of this. We can take the cookies down to my neighbor Faith to take to the homeless shelter where she volunteers. And Linda Isaacson just had foot surgery. Her kids will inhale all these leftovers."

"Oh, great idea," said Angela, clapping her hands. "Let's deliver them right now."

"That works," said Erin, grabbing the plate of cookies.

Five minutes later they were parading down the street, bearing foil-wrapped offerings to the neighbors, Erin and Angela giggling and singing the chorus to the Pretenders' "Brass in Pocket" loud enough for the whole neighborhood to hear that they were special.

"Gonna lose my arms," Erin sang, improving on the original lyrics. "Gonna lose my legs."

"Gonna lose my butt," added Angela, off-key.

" 'Cause we're special," they chorused.

Kizzy couldn't help smiling. Yes, they were.

Linda's family was excited over the food offering, the younger kids jumping up and down as their dad and oldest sibling took the goodies with grateful smiles. And Faith promised to put the cookies to good use.

"That felt good," Erin said as they walked back.

"And it proves we're serious. From now on we start becoming different women," Kizzy said.

"Better women," added Megan.

Would losing weight make them better? Kizzy wondered.

She was still mulling it over when Lionel came home from bowling and started snooping around the kitchen for leftovers. "So where are the goods?"

"Gone." Kizzy put her Fitz and Floyd salt and pepper shakers back on the counter next to the stove, then returned to the dining room and pulled her grandmother's old floral tablecloth off the table.

Lionel leaned dejectedly in the doorway. "You ate everything?"

"No," she said, and started for the laundry room. "We gave it all away."

"To who, and why?"

"To people who really could use it," she said over her shoulder. "Some is going to the shelter with Faith tomorrow and some went to the Isaacsons. And as for the why, I don't want the temptation in the house."

"People who could use it. Humph. I'd have used it," he grumbled. She put the soiled tablecloth in the hamper and Lionel watched her morosely. "Here I come home hungry and you don't even give me my props."

She came up to him and slid her hands up his chest. "I can give you your props right now if you want."

He smiled, his irritation over the vanishing leftovers forgotten.

Kizzy couldn't help smiling, too, as Lionel started helping her out of her blouse. Men were so easily distracted.

If only women were, she thought later as she lay in bed, remembering that chocolate cake. She hadn't even gotten a taste of it, and there wasn't so much as a crumb left in the house.

She sighed and turned over onto her side. There was a reason diet was a four-letter word.

Erin left Kizzy's house with visions of bikinis dancing in her head. She could do this. She didn't have that much to lose. Getting into her wedding dress by June was doable.

She stopped off at the Safeway and loaded her shopping basket with lettuce, tomatoes, celery, low-fat salad dressing, and chicken breasts. And she hurried past the snacks aisle, trying not to think about chips and salsa and margaritas. The express checkout lane was closed and there was no sign of Dan Rockwell anywhere. Good. At least she wouldn't have to put up with a running commentary from him. She went to an empty checkstand manned by a woman.

But then, just after she'd unloaded her groceries onto the conveyor belt, there was a changing of the guards, and the current checker left to be replaced by . . . not him again.

"Hey, there," he said cheerily as he reached for the head of lettuce. "Belated New Year's resolution?"

"No." She sounded defensive and snotty. Okay, no reason for that. He was only making conversation in his usual clueless manner. She tried for a lighter tone. "Just trying to eat right. You know I don't always sit around eating chips," she couldn't help adding. What business was it of his if she did? Why had she felt the need to say that?

"Sometimes you're just in the mood for chips. Nothing wrong with that."

"There's not," she agreed. "And there's nothing wrong with eating salad to balance out the chips."

He looked at her seriously. "You're not fat, you know."

How embarrassing that he'd remembered their last conversation. He couldn't remember her fiancé's nickname, but he could remember talking about her fat.

Cut him some slack, he's trying to be nice, whispered her inner mother.

Well, he could go be nice somewhere else. There were other people around, and she didn't need him talking about her weight with the entire store listening.

"Do you mind?" she said between clenched teeth.

"Having you come through my checkout? Nope."

"Well, I'm not going to if you don't stop talking about my weight every time."

"Sorry. Just thought you'd like to know. I mean, you were so pissed last time."

"I was not pissed, I was . . ." She stopped. "Okay, yes I was pissed. It really had nothing to do with you." Other than him being a dork, which he couldn't help.

"I figured that out," he said as she swiped her debit card. "Next time you come through you should buy some chips," he added. "Good for the soul."

"They may be good for the soul but they're not good for the hips," Erin informed him as he gave her the receipt.

"Yeah, that's the problem with a lot of women these days. All they think about is their hips." He handed over the bag. "Yours are fine, believe me."

What was this, some sort of grocery line shrink session? "Thanks, Dr. Dan. I'll remember that," she said, and took the bag. As she left the store, she found herself trying to remember if Adam had actually ever said her hips were fine.

He hadn't, she was sure. But, so what? She'd never asked him. Anyway, he told her he loved her, and that was what counted. He loved her and she loved him and they were perfect for each other. And life was perfect. And by June, her hips would be perfect. And then her wedding would be perfect. Perfect.

Four

*M*egan was actually smiling when she drove back to her condo after cooking club (cooking club it was going to stay—no way was she going to think in terms of teeny bikinis!). She had a plan, she had support, and, for the first time in a very long time, she had hope.

And that was a big change from when she'd first arrived at Kizzy's house. She had come home after work and almost thrown out the stupid appetizer makings, almost thrown out everything in her refrigerator. Almost. But then she'd felt so depressed that she'd wound up eating half the refrigerator, which was even more depressing.

That was when she had her now-or-never moment. She could either continue feeling invisible at parties when men drifted past her to talk to the pencils, keep shoring up a shaky I'm-smarter-than-anyone façade in front of her shoddy self-esteem, or she could do something. To do something, of course, was the smart choice. And the first something that came to mind had been to quit the cooking club. Belonging to a club that centered on food was like being a diabetic and working at a candy factory.

She'd almost called and canceled, but the need to be with women who actually appreciated her had driven her to go one last time. Anyway, it was gutless to bow out over the phone. And when Kizzy had opened her door and smiled at Megan like she was a long-lost relative it had been salve to the smarting wound she'd received at work, the wound that had turned her into a ravening refrigerator beast.

Her day at the firm of Weisman, Waters, and Green (referred to by the younger members of the firm as Wise Ass and Greed) had started okay. She'd spent almost the whole morning in her windowless office on the forty-first floor—the firm occupied both the forty-first and forty-second floors—of the First Orca Trust Tower, putting together a brief in support of a motion for summary judgment that had at least a reasonable chance of success. By eleven she was feeling restless, so she'd slipped down to the little coffee shop on the lobby floor for a mocha and muffin. Back on the forty-first floor she'd gotten as far as the hallway, lined with bookcases of leather-bound legal journals, when she passed Pamela Thornton and Ashley Paine, two of the pencils. They looked sharp in their black business suits with their white blouses discreetly unbuttoned to show a hint of cleavage, and their slender little feet in heels, their long shiny hair, and perfect makeup. She, of course, was dressed for success, too, and her long hair was stylishly cut, but compared to the pencils she looked like SpongeBob SquarePants in a suit. They smiled as they chatted, showing off professionally whitened teeth. They could have been models or actresses posing as lawyers—Julie on *Boston Legal*. Neither one of them was a Harvard Law School graduate like she was, and Megan knew neither one had graduated in the top percentile. Yet here they came, prancing down the hall like a couple of goddesses out slumming. Pamela Pencil carried a cup of black coffee. Of course, it wouldn't have anything fun or fattening in it. Goddesses didn't do fun or fattening. Goddesses didn't need food. They fed on their own conceit.

She'd barely gotten past them when Ashley said in a quasi-undervoice to Pamela, "The poor whale. She'll be here a million years and never make partner."

Megan Wales, whale. Ha, ha.

Oh, I'll make partner someday, Megan thought as she kept walking. But I won't have to do it lying on my back.

She could have easily voiced her thought, but why sink to their level? Anyway, her barb would have been nothing more than a pin-prick which they would brush off their golden selves much as they brushed rain off their expensive cashmere coats when they first came to work every morning. Megan, on the other hand, knew she would struggle with her wound all day long.

And a little voice whispered that Ashley was right. In a society that prized beauty, nobody wanted to save the whales. The world treated you differently when you were fat. It was the last socially acceptable discrimination.

But that was all B.C., before cooking club. Now Megan felt like she'd found new evidence or the key witness to turn a trial around. She was going to change, and so was her life. If Wise Ass and Greed wanted a hot *Boston Legal* babe to put in first chair on defense, they'd get one. Brains and looks. The pencils couldn't compete with that. "We'll see who's pretending to feel sorry for whom then," she said, and the green eyes peering back at her from her rearview mirror narrowed in determination.

It had been forever since Erin had exercised. How pathetic, considering how much she used to get, she thought as she entered the Heart Lake Health Club Saturday morning. Cheerleading in high school, tennis in college. And then she'd gone to work and turned into a slug. Actually, she'd turned into more of a slug after meeting Adam. They hadn't played tennis since August. And since Adam wasn't all that into dancing, most of their clubbing consisted of drinking and playing trivia games at the Last Resort, their favorite watering hole. Which was okay, but it didn't exactly get the heart pumping.

She climbed onto a stationary bike, set it for a medium difficulty workout level, and then began to pedal off toward the land of Thin.

She smiled and pedaled faster. She could do this. *We've got it, we've got it, we've got it, got it, got it, got it. Goooo, team!*

She was just working up a sweat when she saw—oh, no!—Dan Rockwell striding toward her. And oh, no!—looking at him in his workout grubbies gave her a zing, the same kind of zing she got every time she went to a movie and Leonardo DiCaprio walked out onto the big screen. Dan sure wasn't dressed like Leo. No movie star would be caught dead in those Goodwill cast-off shorts and that faded T-shirt sporting a picture of Homer Simpson. But the body inside the clothes looked movie-star good—thick pecs, legs corded with muscle, beautifully sculpted biceps peeking out from under those tattered sleeves. It was a lot more of him than she saw when he was working the checkout stand.

Okay, so he looked good in a pair of shorts. Big deal. What did she care how he looked? She was a happily engaged woman. Maybe she could pretend she hadn't seen him. She slipped off the bike, ready to sneak to a far corner of the gym.

But too late, he'd spotted her. He got a goofy grin on his face and started her way. Great.

Be polite, said her inner mother.

She smiled. Politely.

"I didn't know you came here," he greeted her.

"I just joined."

"Getting in shape for the big day, huh?"

The last thing she wanted to do was talk about her upcoming wedding with Dan Rockwell. In fact the last thing she wanted to do was talk with Dan Rockwell. Period. Just because he hung out with her family at Christmas and she'd come through his checkout line a few times, it didn't make them buddies. "Something like that."

He nodded.

"I'm done here if you want to use the bike," she said. Then she turned and hurried away.

But she couldn't escape him. As she made her way around the gym using the different pieces of equipment, it seemed she saw him everywhere. It felt like he was following her. Of course he wasn't, and it was only coincidence when he wound up running on a treadmill right next to her.

"You're in pretty good shape," he observed as they jogged along.

Couldn't he see she was listening to her iPod? She kept running and pretended not to hear.

He kept on talking like she could. "All that running probably relieves the stress," he commented.

She frowned at him. "What stress?"

He gave a half-grin like he'd known all along she was hearing him. "They say planning a wedding is way up there on the stress charts."

"They who?"

"I don't know. I just heard that somewhere. Not surprising, though. It's a big commitment. What if you get it wrong? Then you've got all that grief, a messy divorce. If you've got kids . . ."

"I'm not getting it wrong," Erin said. "Adam is perfect." She'd had enough of this. She turned off the treadmill and hopped off.

Dan kept running. "Yeah?"

"Yeah," she said, leaving the polite completely out of her voice. She grabbed her towel and started to mop the back of her neck.

"How come you never smile, then?"

"What?"

"If he's so perfect how come I never see you smiling?"

"You hardly see me enough to know whether I smile or not," Erin snapped.

"When I do see you, you're not."

"Maybe that's because when you do see me you're always saying something to tick me off."

"If you were really happy, maybe I couldn't do that," he said, looking straight ahead.

She marched around to the front of his treadmill. "You could make Mother Theresa mad. And you don't know anything about me."

He raised an eyebrow. "I watched you grow up."

"That was a long time ago, and seeing me at Christmas when Brett's home or in the Safeway checkout doesn't exactly count for much. You don't know me now."

He grinned. "Yeah. Kind of too bad, isn't it?"

"Not for me," she said, and left him there, running nowhere.

Adam called her on her cell as she was walking out the door. "How are things at the hospital?" she asked.

"Busy. I just wanted to let you know I won't be able to do anything tonight. I really need to study."

Her spirits fell. She'd been looking forward to having some time together. But becoming a doctor wasn't easy. Adam needed her support. "No problem," she said.

"You sure? You're not out buying something fancy for dinner right now, are you? If you are, I could probably manage dinner."

"Always time for a free meal?" she teased. "Well, too bad. I'm not shopping. I'm just leaving the gym," she added, hunching her gym bag over her shoulder. "I was working out."

"You didn't tell me you were going to join the gym." His tone of voice sounded pleasantly accusing.

"You're not going to give me a bad time about that, are you? I so need to lose weight."

"No, of course not," he said. "I'm proud of you for wanting to get in shape."

"Good," she said with a smile. "Thanks for not giving me grief about spending the money."

"Oh, come on. I'm not that bad," he said, now sounding pleasantly irritated. "But I did think we were going to discuss any big-ticket items before spending any more," he added.

Erin frowned. "I didn't think the gym counted as a big-ticket item."

"That's because you're not good with money, babe."

Her frown deepened. "I wasn't living on the street when you met me." She opened her car door and tossed in her gym bag with more force than was necessary.

"And you don't want to be. Look. Everybody has stuff they're good at. Managing money isn't your thing. I don't think you get how much you're spending . . ."

Oh, boy. Here they went again, back to the wedding. "We can't do this for nothing, Adam. We really can't. Weddings cost money."

There was silence on the other end of the phone. Had the call been dropped? "Adam?"

"I'm here." Some of the pleasantness had fallen out of his voice.

She scowled and started her car. "Well, say something."

"I'm trying to figure out what to say that won't make you mad."

"That's easy," she said, trying to keep her voice light. "You say, 'It's your day, baby. I want you to be happy.'"

"If I say that we'll end up with a fifty-thousand-dollar wedding bill. I'm just trying to keep a lid on things."

Is that what he called it? "I'm not going to spend fifty thousand dollars, Adam. I plan events for a living. I know what I'm doing. Why can't you just trust me to do it?" Why was this the one thing they fought about?

He sighed. "I never said you didn't know what you're doing, but you're not planning this for some corporation that has unlimited funds. And if I'm part of this, too, why don't I get any say in it?"

"It seems to me you've had a lot of say in it, and mostly you've said no. I'm beginning to think that if it was up to you, we'd just go to the courthouse and get married in our jeans."

"I'm not that bad," he insisted. "But I don't think we need to try and compete with Paris Hilton. And you're wanting to keep spending money we don't have like it's water. Now you're going through enough chips and salsa to stock a restaurant. I'm starting to worry that you're spinning out of control."

Out of control? She was out of control? Out of whose control? "Adam, I just exercised my butt off so I could fit into my wedding gown and not rack up any more expenses. You know I'm not going to see the inside of a bag of chips for months. I am not spinning out of control."

"Then how come you're yelling?"

She was. She never yelled. This was not the way it had been when they were first together, when he was her rock, her shoulder to cry on, her best friend. What was she saying? He still was.

A sudden terrible thought burst into her mind. Maybe he wanted out. "Adam, do you still want to marry me?"

"Of course I want to marry you."

Well, good. But if he did he shouldn't be such a wedding wet blanket. "Then quit trying to ruin our wedding day! I can do this if you'll just quit stressing me out."

"Okay, fine," he snapped.

"Fine," she snapped back.

Fuming, she shut her cell phone and stuffed it in her sweatshirt pocket. Why did they have to fight every time they talked about the wedding? Why, why, why? She gunned the motor and backed out of her parking place. And something went thump against her car.

What on earth? She slammed on the brakes and looked over her shoulder and her heart stopped. *Oh no, oh no, oh no!*

Five

Erin jumped out of her car and ran around to the back where Dan Rockwell was picking himself up off the ground after bouncing off her rear bumper. "Oh, my God, are you all right?" she cried, taking his arm.

He gave his head a shake and examined his palm. It was shredded. Looking at it, Erin felt suddenly woozy.

"I think I'll live." He started brushing off the back of his sweats.

She looked around at the back of him. She could see his skinned-up thigh through the rip in his pants. Heaven only knew what he'd have looked like if he'd only been wearing the shorts he'd had on inside the gym. She could have cracked open his head. Just the thought of it—now her head was spinning. "Oooh."

He put his one good hand to her back and bent her over. "Here, put your head down."

"I'm so sorry. I didn't even see you back there," she said to his feet.

"Well, I put on my invisibility cloak on the way to my truck."

If only he hadn't been walking to his truck. If only he'd already been in it. She straightened up and that didn't do much for her head, either. He grabbed her arm to steady her and the kind gesture made her start babbling. "Dan, I'm so sorry. Have you broken anything? Sprained anything?" He needed medical attention. She tried to tug him toward the gym. "Let's go back in. They've probably got a first aid kit."

"It's okay. Really," he said, resisting her efforts. "I'll go home and dump on some hydrogen peroxide and I'll be good as new."

"You could get infected before you get home." She gave another tug. She'd almost squashed him. The least she could do was make sure he got immediate medical attention.

"Okay," he said and finally quit resisting.

All the way, she kept talking. "I feel terrible. Are you sure you didn't break anything? Does it hurt much?"

"Only when I laugh." She made a face and he sobered. "Seriously, it's not that bad. You sent me flying, but I'm tough."

"Sent you flying. Oh, God," she whimpered.

"Don't worry. I'm not going to sue you," he teased.

She hung her head. "You should. I was mad. A person should never drive when she's mad."

They were inside the gym now and the man at the reception desk took one look at Dan's hand and grabbed the first aid kit. "I'll let you know how the surgery goes," Dan cracked as the man led him away.

Erin's shaky legs deposited her onto the nearest chair. She would never drive angry again. Never.

That meant, at the rate they were going, she would have to never talk to Adam before getting into a car again as long as they both lived. Her cell rang and she pulled it out of her sweatshirt pocket and checked the caller ID. Adam, of course. She was surprised it had taken him this long to call back. She couldn't deal with him right now. She returned the phone to her pocket unanswered and settled in to wait for Dan.

Five minutes later he was back with his hand wrapped in gauze.

Her phone had rung twice more while he was gone and she'd finally set it to vibrate . . . which it was now doing about every thirty seconds. At the sight of him, she jumped up like a relative in a hospital waiting room, anxious for the doctor's report.

He smiled at her and held up his hand. "All better."

"Take care, man," said his honorary doctor.

Dan nodded, then turned his attention to Erin.

"I am so sorry," she repeated. "I shouldn't have even started my car with the mood I was in."

"Maybe you need some anger management training," he joked.

"Maybe I do." She'd never thought of herself as an angry person before. Was she?

"I suggest a session right now over coffee."

That's suspiciously like a date, cautioned her inner mother, *and you are engaged.*

I almost killed him, she argued, and it's the least I can do. She should probably offer Dan free morning coffee delivery for life. Or at least the next year. She nodded. "Okay. Are you sure? You don't want to go home and ice your hand, take a pain pill?"

"Nah. Like I said, I'm tough." He smiled. He'd always had a cute smile. It wasn't as gorgeous as Adam's, though. Nobody's was.

It went without saying that they'd go to the Coffee Stop, which was right around the corner on Lake Way. She got in her car, backed up—carefully—and followed Dan to the ivy-covered brick cottage that housed one of the community's favorite gathering spots. It had started to rain, and they dashed across the parking lot and into the coffee shop. Warm air and the aroma of freshly ground coffee greeted them.

As always, the place was doing a brisk business, with friends chatting at the many small tables and a couple of stray older men hiding grizzled beards behind newspapers. Dan pointed to a table in the far corner by the gas fireplace. "Why don't you stake us out a place and I'll get the coffee."

"This is a shrink session. I'll buy the coffee," she said. He opened his mouth to argue and she added, "It's the least I can do after trying to run you over. Please."

He smiled. "Okay. A tall Americano."

She watched as he threaded his way among the tables. A couple of women smiled at him as he passed, then kept right on checking him out. Obviously not everyone in Heart Lake thought Dan Rockwell was a dork.

She got his Americano and a white chocolate latte for herself, then hurried after him, anxious to sit down and give her nerves time to settle. "Are you sure you're okay?" she asked as she set the drink in front of him.

He smiled up at her. "I'm fine. And thanks."

"Pretty cheap shrink session, if you ask me," she said, "especially since I almost killed you in the parking lot."

He leaned back in his chair, long legs sprawled in front of him, and took a sip of his coffee. "Well, I like to take a charity case now and then. So, tell me. Why were you so angry?"

She took a sip of her latte. Geez, the adrenaline was still bouncing around in her. She could tell by how jumpy she felt. *So let's add some caffeine and sugar to that.* She set down her cup. "I was having a bad morning, that's all. It happens."

"Yeah, sometimes it does." He raised his cup in salute. "Well, here's to your day getting better. Mine already has."

She couldn't help but smile. "That was a sweet thing to say."

"It's true." He grinned at her. "I'm drinking coffee with a hot woman. It's a hell of an improvement over sweating on a treadmill."

Now he's complimenting you, observed her inner mother. *Remind him you're engaged.*

He already knows, Erin replied. She decided she needed that caffeine and sugar after all and reached for her cup.

"I haven't had much chance to talk to you since you moved back," Dan said. "Why did you? I thought you were happy living it up in the big city."

"My aunt offered to let me live in her rental house for free. It gives me a chance to save for the wedding." *There. Now he's been reminded. Happy, Mom?*

"Oh, yeah. The wedding. How's that coming? Got all the champagne ordered?"

"We're going with sparkling cider."

Dan gave a snort. "Since when don't you like booze? Oh, wait, don't tell me, let me guess. McDoodoo doesn't drink."

"It's McDreamy, and he drinks," Erin said, irritated. "But champagne is expensive. We may do champagne punch," she added, suddenly inspired. That would be a nice compromise.

Dan nodded slowly. "Good idea. When you're doing a big wedding all those bottles of champagne can get pricey."

"Well, it's not going to be all that big."

Dan nodded again. "Anyway, you don't have to drink. People just take advantage of the free booze and get all sloppy. Sparkling cider goes with anything. Come to think of it, I went to a wedding just last year where they served sparkling cider. The food was so good nobody seemed to care. Well, not much anyway. They had those jumbo shrimp and little egg rolls and for dinner they served salmon and . . ." He slowed to a stop and studied her. "No jumbo shrimp and egg rolls and salmon?"

"Tortilla appetizer wraps and fruit platters?"

"Fruit's good."

She sat up a little straighter. "It is. Anyway, we don't want to start out with a lot of debt. What we save on the wedding we can put in savings toward a down payment on a house."

"True," Dan said diplomatically, and suddenly became fascinated with the contents of his coffee cup.

What was he doing, reading her future in there? "What are you thinking?" Erin prompted.

"Nothing." He appeared to give himself a mental shake. "You don't need a lot of food anyway. Everybody's dieting these days. They won't miss it. They'll be busy dancing and stuff. Got a band yet? I know these guys . . ." He stopped, eyebrows cautiously raised. "No band?"

"Well." She still hadn't told Adam about getting the Heart Lake Lodge for the reception. Maybe she could tell him she'd gotten the band along with the lodge—a package deal.

"Of course, you don't need a band," Dan said. "Most people have DJ's these days anyway."

She nodded.

"When are you getting married again?"

"June. We have lots of time." She hoped she sounded convincing.

"Oh, yeah. Sure. Um, so, who's going to give you away?"

"Brett." Her dad hadn't been a part of their lives since she was four. And Brett was excited to have the honor.

"And my uncle is marrying us," she added. Uncle Jake had been better than three dads. If she asked him, Uncle Jake would pay for enough champagne to fill Heart Lake, but she wasn't going to ask him. He and Aunt Mellie had done enough for her over the years.

"He's a cool guy," Dan said, nodding approvingly.

"And I was able to get the Heart Lake Lodge," Erin offered. "I'm going to surprise Adam with it."

"Ah-huh."

"I've always wanted my wedding there," she rushed on.

"Then you should have it there."

She bit her lip, and Dan cocked his head. "And will Mc . . ." He caught himself and switched gears. "Will the groom be cool with that?"

Erin suddenly found she was the one staring into her coffee cup. She looked up to see Dan studying her. "He will be when I explain to him how lucky we were to get it."

Dan didn't say anything. Instead he nodded and took a long drink of his coffee.

"Okay, this is a pretty crummy shrink session I'm getting," Erin cracked. "What are you thinking, doc?"

He gave her a lopsided grin. "You don't want to know."

He was probably right, but she still said, "Yes I do."

"I think your mom would have found a way to have the champagne and the shrimp and the salmon. And the band."

"But she wouldn't have wanted me fighting over all that with my fiancé."

"You're right. She'd tell you to keep the band and find a different fiancé."

His words knocked the breath right out of her.

He gave a shrug and got up. "Forget I said that. It was a shitty thing to say. You know I've always been good at putting my foot in my mouth. Thanks for the coffee," he added, and left her there, wishing she had flattened him with her car.

What did he know about what her mom would have done? What did he know about anything?

Erin left the coffee shop intending to go home, shower, call Adam and get her head on straight—get both their heads on straight. Instead, she found herself on her aunt Mellie's doorstep, holding out a box of vanilla tea, her aunt's favorite.

"Hi, there. I was just thinking about you," said her aunt, hugging her. "Come on in. Let's have some of this. You know you don't have to bring me something every time you stop by."

"But I like to. You're my favorite aunt."

"Also your only aunt," Aunt Mellie teased.

"Favorite even if I had a million." Erin stepped into the entryway and was greeted by the faint aroma of lemon, her aunt's favorite candle fragrance. She followed Aunt Mellie into her big kitchen and parked on a barstool at the granite counter, swiveling to look at the lake, framed by a big picture window. Even on a gray day, it was beautiful. In fact, Erin decided she liked it best on days like this. It was fun in the summer to see people out playing with their boats and Jet Skis or lazing around on those colorful blow-up mats, but on a drizzly day like this when the lake lay quiet she found it settled something deep inside of her. It had been fun living in the city, but she'd missed this.

Aunt Mellie, who didn't know the meaning of the word "fat," set a plate with freshly baked scones in front of her. "How are the plans for the wedding coming?"

Erin moved the plate out of reach. "Rotten. I can't fit in to my wedding dress."

Aunt Mellie patted her arm. "Well, you've got an aunt who is the queen of alterations, so not to worry," she said, but she kindly took the plate away, replacing it with a cup of steaming water, the box of teabags, and a pottery dish filled with packets of sugar substitutes.

Erin opened a vanilla teabag and dunked it into her cup. She could feel her aunt watching her, but she kept her gaze on the darkening water in the cup.

"You know, everyone gets nervous before her wedding."

Since when did her aunt turn psychic? Erin occupied herself with pulling out the teabag, putting it on the saucer, watching the stained water pool out around it. "I'm not nervous, I'm just stressed."

"You're planning a wedding single-handed. That's enough to stress anyone." Aunt Mellie paused a moment, then added, "Remember, I'm here to help. Free labor."

Erin smiled at her. "I think you're doing enough with the free rent."

Aunt Mellie shrugged. "That's not much, not for my favorite niece."

"And your only niece."

"Favorite even if I had a million," Aunt Mellie quoted back to her.

Just like Brett was her favorite nephew. She and Uncle Jake had three kids of their own, but they'd had no problem adding Erin and Brett to the mix. Aunt Mellie had sometimes even treated Mom as if she were one of the kids. It had been hard on Aunt Mellie to lose her baby sister, and her blond hair had frosted over during Mom's final battle with lupus.

She leaned on the counter and cocked her head at Erin. "So, what's really bothering you, sweetie?"

This antsy, weird thing growing in her was hard to put into words. And maybe she shouldn't. Like her aunt said, everyone got nervous before her wedding. "I guess I'm just jittery."

"I was a mess before your uncle and I got married. I almost called the whole thing off two different times."

"Why?"

Aunt Mellie shrugged. "Oh, this and that. He wasn't making much when we first got together and he was a bit of a miser. I thought we'd spend the rest of our lives eating beans and tearing paper napkins in two to make them last longer."

Looking around at her aunt's big house with her state-of-the-art kitchen, her Pottery Barn pretties, and her expensive art, it was hard to imagine money ever being an issue. "I guess he turned out not to be cheap."

Aunt Mellie smiled. "I wised him up. Anyway, once he started moving up the corporate ladder and making good money, he stopped worrying about every penny."

"So, he changed." That was encouraging to hear.

"We all do."

"Was that the only thing that worried you?"

"There were others. Where we wanted to live, for one. He wanted to go live in some big city. I wanted to stay here, near my family. I gave him a chance to find out how wrong he was." She smiled at the memory. "Before we got married he had an opportunity to work in L.A. and I encouraged him to take it. He hated it down there, missed everybody. The poor man could hardly wait to get back here. And then there was the little matter of the wedding night. Your grandma and grandpa were great sticklers for making sure your mother and I behaved ourselves. I was pretty inhibited."

Her aunt, the karaoke queen? "Um. You don't exactly strike me as inhibited."

"Well, in some things I was. And I was actually worried about the great unknown, so we took care of that after the rehearsal dinner." Aunt Mellie's cheeks flushed pink. "After that I could hardly wait for the honeymoon. So, you see, things have a way of working out."

Her mother's marriage hadn't. "How about Mom? Was she nervous?"

Aunt Mellie sobered. "She should have been. I think she always knew, deep down, that she was making a mistake, but your mother could be stubborn."

"So, if you're nervous, you're doing the right thing. If you're not, you're making a mistake?" That sounded ridiculous.

Aunt Mellie shook her head. "There are nerves and there are nerves. You know how sometimes you just shiver a little when you open the refrigerator or you look outside and see it's snowing? And then other times, you're shaking like crazy because you're in the middle of an earthquake and the ground underneath you is shifting? You're shaking both times. One you should simply shrug off. The other? You should move someplace where they don't have earthquakes. Figuratively speaking," she added with a grin. "It's been years since we've had an earthquake in this area and I'm not going anywhere."

Erin sighed and took a sip of her tea. "I guess I'm just seeing snow."

"Probably," her aunt agreed. "But keep in mind, if the ground starts shaking, it's never too late to run away."

"Thanks, I will," Erin said. And all the way back to her place she kept asking herself, Would I know if the ground started shaking?

Erin pulled up to find Adam's car parked outside. As soon as she'd stopped in the driveway he was out of it and striding toward her like a man with a purpose. Uh-oh.

But what was this? He was carrying a greeting-card-shaped envelope. He barely gave her time to get out of her car before he caught her by the shoulders, crushed her against him, and kissed her. What was this about?

She found out as soon as they came up for air. "We are not going to fight any more," he informed her, and handed over the card. "Read it."

She tore open the envelope and pulled out a card sporting a picture of a donkey wearing an old-fashioned dunce cap. Inside the caption read, "I'm a dumb ass." She couldn't help smiling. Then she read what he'd written and she almost cried. *No more fighting over the wedding. It's your day, baby.* She looked up at him. "You mean it?"

He nodded. "Absolutely."

"Oh, Adam!" She threw her arms around his neck and kissed him. "I do love you."

"And I love you."

"And don't worry. I promise I'm not going to spend a fortune on this wedding," she couldn't help adding.

He nodded. "I just want to be kept in the loop. That's all."

"Of course," she said. "I want this day to be special for both of us."

"It'll be special for me no matter what," he assured her.

That was what he was doing, wasn't it, assuring her? Or was he trying to encourage her not to spend money? She decided not to ask. There was no sense ruining a perfect moment.

Angela had awakened on Saturday with the best of intentions. She would get breakfast for everyone, and then jump-start her diet with a trip to the gym. All the teeny bikini dieters would be so amazed when they all met next Friday and she announced that she'd already started working out. Maybe she'd even drop a pound before her first diet book arrived. She got out of bed and pulled on her sweats. Hmmm. She'd sure have to get some better-looking workout clothes. Maybe she should go shopping before she went to the gym.

While she'd been deciding which to do first Gabriella climbed the counter in search of the Twinkies, which were now hidden,

and fell in the process, giving herself a nice goose egg on her forehead. This required ice and much rocking, comforting, and a little
bit of scolding, followed by a story. Angela then made breakfast
(you shouldn't work out on an empty stomach—she'd read that
somewhere): French toast with strawberry jam, which she'd promised the girls the day before. She boiled herself an egg and had half
a grapefruit. And the little bit of leftover French toast from Mandy's
plate. But she'd work it off when she went to the gym.

She'd been about to put on her tennis shoes when Rhonda, her
fellow committee chair, stopped by to discuss the fund-raiser for a
Big Toy gym set for the preschool playground. And, of course, Angela had to offer her a cup of coffee.

After Rhonda finally left it was time to get lunch. Grilled cheese
sandwiches and apple slices and chips for Brad and the girls and a
salad for her. And the leftover bite (okay, two) of sandwich that
Mandy had left on her plate. Well, she'd get to the gym in just a little bit.

But first it was time to supervise Gabriella while she changed
her gerbil's cage. Then it was time to find Happy, who, with the
help of Mandy, managed to escape during the cage cleaning. Then
it was time to chase after Mrs. Fields, the cat, who had found
Happy. Now it was time for more rocking and consoling, followed
by a trip to the pet shop.

Next, Brad, who was balancing the checkbook, had required
her presence to explain some of her checkbook entries—he claimed
they were cryptic. Why he always said that she had no idea. She always knew exactly what she was doing.

Finally, she had to run to the grocery store, something she often
did on Saturdays so she could leave the kids with Brad and be able
to actually hear herself think.

By the time she got home she could have cared less about the
gym. She could have cared less about anything. She had just set
the last bag on the kitchen table when Brad wandered into the
room and asked, "What's for dinner?"

"McDonald's," she decided. "An early dinner would be great. That would give any calories she collected plenty of time to burn up before bed. Although she was just going to have a salad, and there weren't any calories in that.

At McDonald's, she did, indeed, get a salad. But then she finished off Mandy's ice cream cone. It was dripping everywhere.

Kind of like her fat. "That was not good," she told her reflection in the mirror later that evening. "You have to do better."

She would. And like Rhett Butler said, tomorrow was another day. She'd do better tomorrow.

Except tomorrow was Sunday, and they always did something fun as a family on Sundays. Going to the gym was not fun.

Well, then, she'd go to the gym on Monday. She smiled, pleased with her decision. Rhett Butler would have approved.

Six

PRACTICALLY SINLESS
CHOCOLATE CHIP COOKIES

....

¼ cup oil
1 cup unsweetened applesauce
1 egg
2 cups whole wheat flour
1 teaspoon salt
1 teaspoon baking soda
⅓ cup carob chips

Mix oil, applesauce, and egg. Sift dry ingredients and . . .

Angela dipped a finger in the bowl of cookie dough for a sample. "Then toss the whole mess," she concluded with a scowl, lifting her kitchen garbage can lid and disposing of the failed experiment. She crumpled the sheet of paper with the failed formula and hurled it in after. Who wanted to be practically sinless, anyway?

She got two cubes of butter out of the fridge, then set them in a bowl in the microwave and melted them. Quick as a cat burglar, she pulled brown sugar, salt, and baking soda from her baking cupboard and dug out fresh measuring cups. She knew this recipe by heart. It didn't require much time to magically take eggs, flour, sugar, and butter and turn them into cookie dough. And then add some baking soda and salt, a whole bag of chocolate chips, and, voilà, you had . . . heaven.

She'd never hear the end of it if any of her teeny bikini club members got wind that she was already a diet dropout, cheating only three days after vowing to change her wicked eating ways. But it wasn't really cheating when they hadn't had their goal-setting meeting yet. That wasn't until Friday and this was only Monday. Anyway, she was only going to eat one.

Mrs. Fields the cat wound around her legs as she worked, begging.

"Chocolate will kill you," she told the cat. Or maybe that was dogs. "It's probably not good for you, either. And besides, you don't deserve anything after what you did to poor Happy." Hopefully, Happy was living up to his name up there in that great gerbil cage in the sky.

Mrs. Fields, unrepentant for her cat behavior, continued to rub against Angela's legs until Angela caved and fed her. Canned cat food, of course—no cookie dough. The cat settled down and began to delicately lick it.

Speaking of licking. Angela dipped a finger in the dough and sampled it. "Now, that's what cookie dough ought to taste like."

What a pain, she thought as the first batch baked, filling the house with the scent of chocolate. It was completely unfair that women had to go through so much suffering to look good when men could eat and eat and never get fat.

She sighed. "Yeah, I know," she said to Mrs. Fields, who was now on the counter, watching her lay the cookies out on a rack to cool. "I shouldn't be doing this, but I just need a taste. I can't quit cold turkey. I'm only going to eat one, then I'll give the rest to Brad when he gets home." And that would make him happy. Whoever said the way to a man's heart was past his stomach sure knew what she was talking about.

Angela picked up a warm cookie and took a bite. That glorious combination of brown sugar, butter, and chocolate hit her taste buds and she moaned in delight. "Better than sex, and they last longer," she informed the cat. "But don't tell Brad I said that."

The doorbell rang and Angela gave a guilty start. She wasn't expecting anyone. Who would be stopping by in the middle of the afternoon? Her mother, maybe? Hopefully, no one who knew she was dieting. She ran on tiptoe to the door and put her eye to the peephole.

Erin! What was she doing here? The psychic cookie connection, of course. Erin always seemed to know when Angela was baking. Except Angela wasn't supposed to be baking.

The doorbell rang again and Angela raced to the kitchen to hide the evidence. She grabbed the bowl with the leftover dough and the rack of cookies and looked frantically around her. She couldn't hide them anywhere in the kitchen. That would be like leaving the murder weapon at the scene of the crime.

The doorbell continued to summon her. What was Erin doing here, anyway? Why wasn't she still at work?

Angela raced to the laundry room, dropping cookies as she went, then yanked open the dryer which, fortunately, was empty, and stuffed the whole mess inside. On her way back, she picked up the two that had fallen on the floor, calling, "Coming!" For only a nanosecond she thought of tossing them in the garbage. That would be a terrible waste. She ducked into the bathroom and stuffed them in the medicine cabinet.

Another cookie had rolled into a corner to hide, and Angela caught it and stuffed it in her mouth. Chewing frantically, she ran back to the kitchen, grabbed a can of Lysol from under the sink, and sprayed her way into the living room. Then she ditched it behind a chair and went to let Erin in. She almost choked swallowing the big lump of cookie in her mouth.

"I was beginning to think you were dead in there." Erin stepped inside, holding what looked like a white plastic mat.

"I was in the bathroom. I wasn't expecting company."

"Sorry, but I had a miserable diet day. I thought I'd stop by for moral support."

Moral support was good, but the timing sucked. "Why aren't you at work?" It was only two in the afternoon. The girls were still napping. No one should have been around to catch her. Did she have chocolate breath?

"I had to run errands for Gregory the tyrant out here and I got done early and decided to call in sick for the afternoon. Which was no lie," Erin added. "I'm sick of Gregory micromanaging me. Plus he's given me a workload that should be getting done by two people. Between him and planning for the wedding, I feel like my head's going to pop off."

"I'm sorry he's turning out to be such a pain to work for," said Angela. *But not half as sorry as I am about you showing up right in the middle of my baking binge. Darn, darn, darn!*

"So, aren't you going to ask what this is?" Erin pointed to the mat she was carrying.

What Angela really wanted was to ask Erin to scram so she could finish baking. But she'd be a terrible friend if she did that. Left on her own in this kind of mood Erin might do something crazy like dive headfirst into a bag of chips to drown her sorrows.

So Angela pretended she wasn't a cookie criminal and put on her best welcoming face. "What is it?"

"Something fun for us. I think I've found a way to . . ." Erin stopped talking and pointed to Angela's mouth. "You've got something stuck in the corner of your mouth."

Angela pressed her fingers to her lips. Oh, no. Chocolate! Evidence right there on her guilty face.

Erin's expression turned suspicious. "Wait a minute." She sniffed. "What's that I smell?"

Angela popped her eyes as wide open as they'd go. "What's what?"

Erin wrinkled her nose. "It smells like Pine-Sol and . . ." She dropped the mat and, like Sherlock Holmes on the trail of a villain, marched to the kitchen.

"I had a scented candle burning," Angela said, trotting after her. "Maybe that's what you smell. Go on out in the living room. I'll bring us a diet . . ."

"Chocolate chip. It smells like chocolate chip cookies in here."

"That's just the candle scent," insisted Angela. "You're hallucinating, having food flashbacks. Very common among dieters."

They both saw it at the same time, the one thing that, in her panic, she'd forgotten to hide. There it sat on the stove, the murder weapon left at the scene of the crime.

Erin picked up Angela's WearEver AirBake cookie sheet. "Still warm." She narrowed her eyes. "Okay, where are they?"

"Gone," said Angela, forcing herself to look innocent.

Erin's face collapsed like a bad soufflé. Angela might as well have said, I stole your Lotto winnings and ran away to Vegas. "You ate them all?"

No, and she wasn't about to share her last meal. Or, worse yet, have Erin toss it out in a misguided effort to save them both.

"You're not supposed to be eating cookies," Erin scolded.

"We haven't set our goals yet." That excuse had about as much substance as cotton candy. Angela felt her face warming.

Now Erin was opening cupboards. "Okay, what'd you do with them? You know, it doesn't do any good to get rid of everything on Friday night and then make more on Monday."

"It doesn't matter now. They're gone." Was her nose growing?

Erin pointed a finger at her. "You're a terrible liar."

She was, but she kept up her bluff. "Okay, search every cupboard," she said with a careless flick of the hand. "You're not going to find anything."

Erin got a knowing smirk on her face. "Maybe they're not even in the kitchen. Maybe you hid them somewhere. Maybe that's why it took you so long to answer the door."

Uh-oh.

"That's it, isn't it?" Erin crowed. "Where are they?"

Angela scrunched her lips together. No way was she telling.

"Come on," Erin said, her voice softening. "I'm only doing for you what I hope you'd do for me."

It would be really immature to keep lying. It was time to give up. "Oh, all right." Angela led the way to the laundry room. She opened the dryer and dug out the incriminating evidence.

"Great hiding place," said Erin, pulling out the cooling rack. She picked up a cookie from the bottom of the dryer and set it on the rack, then licked chocolate off her fingers. "Except it could be a little hard on your clean clothes."

"I had to think fast." Angela looked at the pile of crumbled cookies now sitting on the plate. "You know, I did start out trying to make something good for all of us."

"What happened?"

Angela shook her head. "It wasn't good. Anyway, I was going through withdrawals. I just wanted one." She gave a helpless shrug. "I think I'm addicted to sugar. Can you be a sugar addict?"

Erin sighed. "Probably."

"This is going to be harder than I thought," Angela confessed. She gave a reluctant smile. "Thanks for coming in time to save me from myself. I'd have probably wound up eating half the bowl."

Erin smiled and gave her a consoling hug. "More cookies for the shelter, I guess."

"You'd better stay while I finish baking them. I think I need a bodyguard."

Erin's smile widened. "I've got your back."

So, Angela thought, as she poured Diet Cokes for them, that takes care of today, but who's going to have my back tomorrow?

"And now for the surprise," Erin said. She retrieved the mat, then handed it to Angela. "Here, spread these out in front of the TV. I'll get the rest of the stuff."

"What is this?"

"Be right back," Erin called.

The mat turned out to be two. With all those circles, they reminded Angela of the old Twister game.

Erin returned with a PlayStation. "Are we going to play Twister?" Angela greeted her.

"No. We're going to move it. I borrowed this from my cousin. She said we could use it till she gets home from college in June."

Angela watched as Erin began hooking the box up to the TV. "Have you heard of Dance, Dance, Revolution?"

"Oh, yeah," said Angela, suddenly excited. "I've been wanting to try that."

Erin turned on the big-screen TV, stepped back, and started pressing different parts of the mat with her toes, setting up the program.

Now Angela was interested. "We really are going to dance?"

"Sort of. It's mostly jumping around, putting your feet to the side or the front as the screen prompts you. We stand with our feet on these circles," she said, positioning herself on the mat, "and then we do whatever it says. The goal is to keep up. I'll show you." She selected a song. "We'll do beginner level."

"Drop the Bomb" began to play, and the TV turned psychedelic with a punked-out skateboarder doing acrobatics while arrows started to glide up the screen. Erin demonstrated. "See? When the arrow points to the side you've got to step to the side. Up means in front of you, down in back of you."

"Oh, fun!" cried Angela. "I can do this."

Almost. It turned out to be a lot harder than she imagined, and she felt like a fool as she stumbled and bumbled along next to Erin, who was, like her, letting out a series of "Eeks." But it was fun. "This is great," she said after they'd finished.

"That's what I thought. I figured we could do this a couple of times a week, then maybe graduate to some dance workout DVDs."

"Ooh, I saw the *Dancing with the Stars* workout DVD for sale on eBay. Maybe I'll get that for us."

Erin grinned. "Great idea. Now, what do you say we get those cookies baked and packed up and do a little more DDR?"

They finished baking the cookies, then went at it until Angela finally collapsed on the couch. "I am so out of shape it's pathetic. Forget the DDR. I need R and R," she moaned.

"Oh, no you don't," Erin said, hauling her to her feet. "You've got to work off those cookies."

"I'm never baking again as long as I live," Angela decided. "It's not worth the pain."

They went at it some more, then, both rubber legged, they agreed it was time to quit with the exercise already and flopped on the couch.

"We have to have lost at least a pound, don't you think?" Angela asked.

"Probably not," Erin said regretfully.

"Oh, well. Greece wasn't built in a day," Angela told her. "Or something like that."

"Something like that," Erin agreed.

"Mommy, what are you playing?"

They both turned to see Gabriella coming down the stairs, wiping the sleep from her eyes, dragging her favorite teddy bear. "Looks like it's time for you to get on the treadmill now," Erin teased. Then she called, "Who's this cute thing?" to Gabriella.

That woke her the rest of the way up. "Aunt Erin!" she squealed, and came running.

Erin picked her up and swung her around. "Oh, look how big you're getting!" She set Gabriella down and pretended to examine her back. "Okay, where are you hiding your wings today?"

Gabriella giggled. "Aunt Erin. You know I'm not an angel. I'm a girl."

"You're a girl angel," Erin told her.

"Can I play what you were playing?" Gabriella asked.

"Not right now," Angela said. "Mommy needs to rest."

"I can leave it here for later," Erin said. "Would you like that, Gabby?"

Gabriella was now starting the steps to a dance that every mother of small children recognized. "Right now you need to fly off to the bathroom, girl angel. Hurry up. Make it in time and I'll give you a treat."

Gabriella ran out of the room, dark curls bouncing.

"And that is why half the women in America are now struggling with their weight," observed Erin.

"She can do some DDR with Mommy after dinner," Angela said. "If Mommy's legs ever stop feeling like cooked spaghetti."

"Tell me about it. Okay, I'm going to go. You sure you'll be okay here with the cookies?"

Angela nodded. "They won't be here much longer, anyway."

She said good-bye to Erin, and then cut up apples for Gabriella and Mandy, who also had decided it was time to come back to life. After their snack she and the girls walked down to their neighbor Faith's where Angela unloaded the fat bombs she'd baked earlier. Erin had wrapped them in foil for her so she couldn't look at them and be tempted to eat one. Or two. Or six. When they got home she and the girls cuddled on the couch and watched *Sesame Street,* and then Angela made dinner and tried not to think about the chocolate chip cookies that got away. Think, instead, about how you beat the cookie monster, she told herself. Well, sort of, with a lot of help from her friend. She had inhaled some before Erin stopped her. But she could have eaten the whole batch. It was a victory, she decided.

So she couldn't help bragging a little when Brad came home.

He'd taken a minute to appreciate Gabriella's latest preschool artwork. Now he smiled at Angela and asked, "And how about you, babe? How was your day?"

"Perfecto," Angela replied. "Erin came by and we exercised."

"Way to go," he said. He lifted Mandy from his lap and loosened his tie. "Do I have time to take a shower before dinner?"

"Sure," she said, giving their tossed salad a final toss.

He was back five minutes later, looking hunky in jeans, his chest bare. "Do I have any more deodorant?"

Brad's Right Guard—she'd meant to pick that up when she was shopping for the goodies for the cooking club meeting. "Oh, I forgot to get it. Just use mine for tonight," she said, pulling the chicken breasts out of the oven.

"And smell like baby powder?" he protested.

"Well, there might be some in the downstairs bathroom." The words were barely out of her mouth when she had a flashback: herself stuffing chocolate chip cookies in the medicine cabinet. "I'll go check," she said. Then later she'd destroy those damning fat bombs.

But Brad was already ahead of her. "Don't bother. I can look."

"I can find it faster," she insisted, trying to slip past him.

He gave her a funny look. "It's not like I don't know where the medicine cabinet is."

"I don't think it's in there. I think it's under the sink." She ducked into the bathroom and pulled open the vanity door. "You just go on upstairs and I'll bring it up to you."

It was too late to head him off. He was right there. He leaned over her and opened the medicine cabinet and started rummaging around. Two chocolate chip cookies jumped out and dove into the bathroom sink.

He picked one up and looked down at her, eyebrow raised.

Uh. "Surprise?"

"For me?" Brad teased.

Gabriella, who seemed to have antennae for finding juicy moments, had followed them and her eyes lit up at the sight of the cookie. "My treat!" she cried, jumping up and down.

Angela took the cookie from Brad and handed it to her. "Here," she said, pulling the other one out of the sink. "Give this to your sister." So much for giving them healthy treats.

Gabriella took the cookies and scampered off.

"I gave the rest of the batch away," Angela said.

"All except for those two? They didn't want to leave so they ran and hid?" He smiled and shook his head. "I swear, Ang, being with you is like living in a sitcom. I never know what kind of crazy thing I'm going to come home to."

She wasn't sure that was a compliment. "Okay, when Erin came over I didn't want to get caught, so I hid the evidence. But she caught me anyway. So that's why there aren't any cookies. We really did give the rest away," she finished. That sounded so lame. Rachel probably never hid cookies in medicine cabinets. Rachel never baked cookies. That was why she was hot.

"Next time, don't give away all the evidence. I'll help you get rid of it." Brad said, searching the medicine cabinet. He found a surplus can of deodorant. "Thank God. Now I don't have to smell like baby powder."

"I really was good," Angela insisted as he turned to leave.

"Ang, I'm not your keeper. If you want to bake cookies it's fine by me. I like cookies."

"But you don't want a fat wife," she told him. Enough of this terrible cheating! She was not only sabotaging her diet, she was sabotaging her marriage. If she wanted to keep her husband she was going to have to get serious about dieting. "I have to be good."

Brad pulled her against him. "I like you better when you're bad."

"You'll like me more when I've lost forty pounds," she assured him.

"I like you fine the way you are."

Of course he was just saying that to be nice. She thought of Rachel the hottie. No more cookies. Ever. And for sure not before Friday.

Seven

*I*t was Friday night, the night of the first official meeting of the Teeny Bikini Diet Club. Everyone showed up bearing salads and diet and exercise books.

"Cabbage salad with shrimp," Kizzy announced, setting her teak salad bowl down on the granite counter. "And that looks good," she said, pointing to Angela's tomato, basil, and mozzarella mix.

"It is," Angela said. "I tried some before I came."

Kizzy nodded at the carrot salad in the glass bowl. "And this is the salad you said you were going to make?" she asked Megan.

Megan nodded. "I'm calling it Practically Perfect Salad. Carrots for carotene, green peppers and celery and onion for seasoning, and tuna fish for protein. Just a little low-fat mayo to hold it together."

"So what keeps it from being perfectly perfect?" Kizzy asked.

Megan picked up a small bowl filled with chow mein noodles. "These are the culprit. You're supposed to put about a cup worth in the salad, but I think just sprinkling a few over our plates will do the trick as well."

"I think you're right." Kizzy surveyed the growing selection of salads, well pleased. "It looks a lot different than the last time we met, doesn't it?"

Erin nodded. "It sure does."

"This really looks impressive," Megan said, pointing to Erin's seafood salad contribution.

"It's one of my aunt Mellie's recipes," said Erin. "She's like Kizzy. She makes cooking look easy."

"Cooking is easy," said Kizzy. "It's controlling how much I eat that's hard. And, speaking of eating, let's try these salads."

"And then we can talk about our diet plans," said Angela.

"Lifestyle changes," Kizzy corrected her. "I'm done dieting. I've got to change the way I live. Period. And maybe change husbands if Lionel doesn't shape up," she added.

"What's Lionel done wrong?" asked Angela.

"He keeps bringing home things I can't have and telling me one bite won't hurt me."

"And do you bite?" asked Megan.

Kizzy frowned. "More than I should." She squared her shoulders. "But no more. I need to take care of me. The next time Lionel brings home something bad for us I'm going to let him have it good. He needs to respect what I'm trying to do. Come to think of it, so do I."

"What do you mean?" asked Erin.

"I'm just thinking that if I really respected myself I'd have taken better care of me over the years. I mean, if I don't care about me, who will?"

"Good point," said Megan.

"You're off to a good start tonight," added Erin, digging into her seafood salad.

"This looks awesome," Kizzy said as she dished up Angela's Italian salad. "If I get enough recipes like this maybe eventually I won't miss potato salad."

"Oh! I know a way you can still have it," Angela told her. "I learned something really awesome when I was at the store yester-day. I met this woman in the produce department and she told me how you can make potatoes calorie free."

"Do tell," said Kizzy, sounding doubtful.

"You know how when you boil them, you get that kind of frothy stuff?"

"Yeah."

"Well, that froth is the sugar in the potatoes. You pour that off before you mash them and then all the sugar is gone."

Kizzy raised an eyebrow. "I always pour the water off before I mash potatoes. Trust me, it doesn't take out the sugar."

Angela looked disappointed. "It doesn't?"

"The woman who told you that, what did she look like?" asked Megan.

Angela's cheeks turned frosting pink. "Um."

"I rest my case," said Megan.

Angela shrugged. "It sounded good."

"You know, what you said a minute ago about respecting your-self really resonated," Megan told Kizzy. She dropped her gaze. "I could sure think more highly of myself."

"Top ten percentile of your class, up for partner at your firm? How can you not think highly of yourself?" Kizzy wondered.

Megan gave a little one-shouldered shrug. "It's pretty easy, es-pecially on a Saturday night when it's only me, my sudoku puzzle, and a DVD."

"That has nothing to do with being a good lawyer," Erin in-sisted.

But everything to do with life, thought Kizzy. A woman could have all kinds of successes, but if she didn't feel good about herself everything else rang hollow.

"It has a lot to do with becoming a partner," said Megan. "A big firm like mine wants partners who can bring in clients. I'm no rain-maker. I'm not exactly the queen of the cocktail party; I suck at working a room."

"Once you start feeling better about yourself, don't you think that will all change?" Kizzy suggested.

"Maybe. I hope so."

"You're a smart woman," Kizzy said. "You'll find your way. If you can learn to work a courtroom I bet you can learn to work a living room. After all, you do fine here with us."

"That's because you guys always make me feel so welcome."

"Maybe you just have to see yourself as welcome wherever you go," Kizzy told her. "Because you are, I'm sure."

Megan spooned up some carrot salad. "I guess."

"No, you *know*," corrected Erin.

Megan almost smiled. "You're so full of it."

"Once a cheerleader, always a cheerleader, I guess," Erin said. "But really, Kizzy is right. You have to have a little faith in yourself. You can do whatever you set your mind to. We all can."

Megan nodded and drifted out to the dining room.

Kizzy sure hoped Erin was right. At fifty-five she needed to get serious about taking care of herself.

"So," Angela said once they were all assembled. "What books did you guys find?" She pulled out two from the shopping bag at her feet and held them up one at a time. "I've got Dr. Phil, and this cool exercise book."

"I can top that," said Kizzy. "Look what I found at the bookstore." She held up a book titled *The No Sweat Exercise Plan*. "How's this for good?"

"I want to borrow that when you're done," said Angela. "I hate getting all sweaty."

Next Kizzy took out a cookbook. "And this is great. The good news is they even have some dessert recipes in here."

"Is that pizza I see on the cover?" asked Angela, leaning forward.

"It sure is," said Kizzy. "They claim the plan is flexible and I'll never feel deprived."

"I need that," said Angela. "I'm already feeling deprived. I wish someone would invent a chocolate diet."

"And a no-exercise diet," Kizzy muttered. "Has anyone started exercising?" she asked.

"Erin and I already started," Angela bragged, "and I've got our exercise plan in my car. Do you want to try it?"

"Is it hard?" asked Kizzy. "I was planning on easing into the exercise thing." After all, she didn't want to drop dead of a heart attack before she'd barely gotten started.

"It's very fun," Angela assured them. "I'll go get it."

"Okay, is this really fun or is it some weird thing. Angela thought up?" Megan asked Erin after Angela had rushed from the room.

"It's nothing Angela thought up, and I think you'll like it." Erin assured her.

Angela brought in the equipment and Erin helped her set it up.

"I've seen this," said Megan. "They played this in *Music and Lyrics*. It looked dumb," she added under her breath.

"It's not dumb," Erin assured her. "It's fun."

And it was. After their food had settled, they took turns hopping around the DDR mat while the others sang along with the songs and laughed at every misstep. Megan surprised them all by catching on quickly and keeping up the best.

"You're a natural," Angela told her. "You could probably dance your way to skinny."

"That would be a lot of dancing," Megan replied. Like Kizzy, she had a lot of weight to shed.

"What the heck? You've got nothing to lose," said Angela.

"I wish."

By the time the party broke up everyone was pumped and ready to take down the weight giant. "Okay, ladies, same time next week?" asked Kizzy as they gathered up their salad bowls.

"I'm in," said Erin. "Thanks for not breaking up the club and abandoning us," she added, giving Kizzy a hug. "This is going to be great."

The other two echoed her. "And let's wear workout clothes next week and do some more fun exercising," said Angela.

"A DDR sock hop," joked Kizzy.

"That sounds good to me," said Erin. "And tomorrow I'm hitting the gym."

"I'll make it in on Monday," Angela pledged.

"I'm walking on Monday before I go to the shop," vowed Kizzy.

They all looked expectantly at Megan, whose face turned pink. "I'll . . . think of something."

"Do they have a gym in the First Orca Trust Tower?" asked Kizzy.

Megan looked like Kizzy had just threatened to shove her off the First Orca Trust Tower. "I . . . couldn't."

Angela grimaced. "The pencils are there, aren't they?"

Megan bit her lip. "That gym, it's just not me."

"How about joining Curves? I've heard it's pretty nonthreatening," Kizzy suggested.

Megan nodded slowly.

"There's probably one not far from where you work downtown. You could hit it on the way home," put in Erin.

"I'll check into it tomorrow," Megan decided.

Kizzy nodded. "Good. We've all got a plan. Let's work it."

A plan. It was a good beginning, she thought as she waved good-bye to her guests.

She shut the door and went to the kitchen to finish cleaning up while waiting for Lionel to come home from his bowling league. That might have been a mistake. She walked past the fridge and heard something call to her from the freezer compartment. *Kizzy. Kiiiizzzzy.*

It was the Ben & Jerry's Cherry Garcia ice cream, locked in there and wanting to come out, of course—Ben & Jerry's Cherry Garcia, her favorite, which Lionel had dragged home a few days ago.

No, she told herself firmly. *That is not the way to get healthy.*

But there was only a little left, no more than a dab.

She could almost feel a tiny angel with wings poking out of her warm-ups, jumping up and down on her shoulder. "Don't do it! You got such a great start tonight."

Of course, for every little angel, there's a little devil, and a chocolate one popped up on her other shoulder. "Like you said, there's only a dab left. How fat are you going to get on a dab? All you had tonight was salad, so you can afford a dab. And a little taste of something sweet now and then will keep you from feeling deprived. That will actually help you stay on your diet."

She moved toward the fridge, the little angel shouting, "No, no, steer away. Danger, danger!" while the devil snarled, "Shut up, will you?"

Kizzy opened the freezer and pulled out the container.

"Just take one bite," suggested the little devil.

She opened the container and looked inside. There really wasn't much there. And she'd been so good. She'd eaten salad and exercised. Just a bite, that was all she needed.

She got a spoon out of the drawer and dug in. Just a bite turned into two and then three.

"What are you doing?" screamed the angel.

She looked in disgust at the last remaining quarter cup of ice cream. It was almost ten o'clock. If she ate that it would go to bed with her and start a new fat settlement on her waist as she slept. This was no way to get healthy, no way to respect herself and treat herself right. She set her jaw in determination and slapped the top back on the container.

"Oh, come on. There's still some left," said the devil.

She forced her feet to march to the garbage.

"You're not going to throw that away, are you? That's wasteful," cried the devil.

"Better wasteful than waistful," Kizzy told it, and tossed the last of the ice cream.

She could almost see the little devil wailing, "I'm melting," and sinking into a brown pool. Hopefully, soon it would be her fat that was melting.

She smiled and dusted off her hands. There. Took care of that. And she couldn't believe how empowered she felt by that one small victory.

Jazzed, she got out her Aretha Franklin CD. She put it on full blast and started dancing. Gus wagged his tail and gave her an encouraging bark.

She was still dancing when Lionel came home. "Check it out," he said. "It's a party."

He sidled up to her and started dancing, too. "What are we celebrating, Kizzy girl?"

"Feelin' good," she said, still grooving.

"Yeah?" Now he was in back of her, running his hands up her arms. "You should feel good more often. Were you thinking about your daddy coming home?"

"No, I was thinking about that ice cream sitting in the garbage instead of on my waist."

Lionel stopped dancing. "In the garbage? You threw out the ice cream?"

"There wasn't much left." She kept rotating her hips and smiled at him over her shoulder. "Come on, Lion, celebrate with me." She bumped him with her hip.

"That stuff ain't cheap, you know."

She turned around and faced him and did a little bump and grind against him. "Do you really want to talk about ice cream right now?"

He didn't, and half an hour later they both went to bed feeling good.

Yeah, but can you keep it up? taunted a new little devil.

Kizzy folded her pillow over her ears. She was going to win the battle of the bulge or die trying.

Die. She sobered. She had to stay serious about this if she wanted to live a long, healthy life. Her kids weren't even married yet. She wanted to stick around to meet her future son- and daughter-in-law and her grandbabies. Oh, yes. She could keep it up.

Angela returned home stoked. She was going to be so hot that the office hottie would look like warm leftovers compared to her. She would be beautiful . . . bella, bellisima—worthy of the long line of Italian beauties in her family. Of course, she'd have to e-mail Oprah about their diet club. Maybe they'd all get flown to Chicago to go on *Oprah*. That would be so awesome.

The kids were in bed when she came in and the house was quiet, all except for the sound of laughter coming from their home office. She wondered how long Brad had been in there working. The poor guy worked a ton of overtime, both at work and at home, but being salaried, he never got paid for it. Which was totally unfair if you asked her. Not that he ever asked her, but she told him anyway.

She kicked off her shoes and padded down the hall. She'd sneak up on him and surprise him with a kiss on the back of the neck, remind him what a happily married man he was.

"No, she doesn't suspect a thing."

Her husband's words floated out into the hallway like some evil genie, stopping Angela in her tracks and squeezing her heart. Hard. This wasn't right. She had to have heard wrong, or walked into the wrong house.

But no, that was Brad's voice saying, "You're the best."

Who was the best? She'd always thought it was her.

"Ang'll be home any minute. I'd better get off."

Well, he wasn't going to get off with her!

She marched into the office. "What don't I suspect? Who were you talking to just now, Bradley?"

He jumped at least two feet off his chair. "Ang. You scared the shit out of me."

She crossed her arms in front of her and drummed her finger-tips. "What don't I suspect?"

"What makes you think I was even talking about you?"

"Woman's intuition. And you said you had to get off because I'd be home any minute."

"You misheard."

There was nothing wrong with her hearing. She pointed a finger at him. "You're having an affair. Right in front of my back."

He looked like she'd just accused him of being an axe murderer. "What? How can you even think a thing like that?"

She glared at him. "Easy after hearing what you just said."

He left the desk and came and put his arms around her. "Look, I wasn't even talking about you. We're planning a surprise party for someone at work who's retiring. That's all."

"Then why did you have to get off the phone because I was coming home?"

"When you're planning a surprise, the less people who know the better. I thought you might accidentally let something slip."

How dumb did he think she was? "If you don't want me to know, why aren't you doing all your planning at work?"

"We just had something come up that needed to be dealt with tonight. No big deal."

She narrowed her eyes. "We who?"

Brad's face got red.

She pulled out of his arms. "Ha! It's Rachel. I knew it. You were talking to Rachel."

He threw up his arms. "Okay, I was talking to Rachel. So what?"

So that was the end of their marriage. She didn't even have time to get skinny because the other woman had already won. She burst into tears. "You're having an affair. With Rachel!"

"Oh, baby." He drew her back to him and cradled her head against his chest and started stroking her hair and she tried not to think about how good it felt. "I'm not having an affair. I promise."

Angela was really crying now. "That's what every man says when he's lying."

He cupped her chin, forcing her to look at him. "When have I ever lied to you?"

Off the top of her head she couldn't remember any specific time. But that didn't mean he hadn't. She caught up a sob and wiped her eyes.

"I'm not cheating," he repeated. "I don't even know what would put that idea in your head."

That picture of Rachel that he'd brought home, for starters.

"And frankly, it pisses me off that you'd think I am. I have never cheated on you."

That was a long time to be faithful considering they'd been to-gether since high school. She bit her lower lip and dropped her gaze. She hadn't meant to insult him. Still. "Well, what was I sup-posed to think when I heard you telling Rachel the puttana that I don't suspect a thing?" she demanded.

He made a face. "That I'm talking about someone else."

"Oh." Well, that was a possibility.

He smiled that tender Brad smile that always made her go gooey inside. "I love you, Ang. You've got to know that." He gave her a long, sexy kiss, sliding his hands down her back to her bot-tom. Her big, fat bottom.

"Even though I'm a porco?"

"I don't think you're a porco," he said, and kissed her again. This time his hands wandered up to her breasts. "I think you're hot," he whispered, and pulled her snugly against him.

And there was the physical evidence. Hmmm. Maybe she'd been wrong.

Next thing she knew they were in the desk chair naked and Brad was gladly showing her just how much he wanted her.

Okay, she thought later as she went upstairs while he checked to make sure the doors were locked, maybe she had jumped to conclusions. In the bedroom mirror she gave herself a serious ex-amination. Brown eyes. They were okay. But her nose was too turned up. It made her look like she was twelve. Her lips were great, though. She knew that. The neighborhood kids had teased her about them when she was little, calling her monkey lips, but those monkey lips became an asset after puberty hit. Angelina Jolie had nothing on her.

She made a face. Monkey lips were okay. A gorilla body wasn't. She'd always been a little on the curvy side—when you grew up in a family that celebrated its Italian roots that was bound to happen. But now she had about as much shape as a pile of pasta.

Rachel had a perfect body.

Angela suddenly remembered Brad's guilt-red face when she asked him who he'd been talking to. Why would he go all red like that if he had nothing to hide? *She doesn't suspect a thing.* Angela's postsex feeling of security vanished, stolen by a hottie with red hair. Now she wanted to cry all over again. *She doesn't suspect a thing because she's a stupido porco.*

No, don't go there, she told herself. Brad was still only on the edge of that slippery slope that led to the No-tell Motel. She had time to pull him back. And maybe he really was planning a surprise party for someone. *Don't go loaning trouble. Have a little faith in your husband. Have a little faith in yourself.*

She'd have a lot more faith in herself once she'd lost some weight.

Eight

$\mathcal{M}$egan had managed a carb-free weekend, and she'd joined Femme Fit, a girls-only gym. Monday morning she arrived at the firm feeling like a woman who had just won the case of her life— on the inside, at least. But the day had gone steadily downhill from there. She spent the whole morning toiling away in her windowless office, reviewing a new stack of paperwork in search of that one important bit of information Tanner Hyde needed for *Newton* v. *Owens* and had gotten nowhere. She hated discovery. It was the bane of her existence.

No, Tanner Hyde was the bane of her existence. He reminded her of her stepfather: impossible to please, rarely smiling. And when he did smile, it was sardonic. Of all the partners to be assigned to work under! Why was he so damned hard on her, anyway? Maybe he was resentful that he hadn't been given one of the pencils. Well, she'd like to see Pamela come up with anything.

She dug out the little plastic bag she'd filled with carrot sticks from her lunch sack, removed one and bit down violently. No one told you when you were in prelaw, dreaming of living a *Law & Order* life, that you would grow up to get buried in a windowless office with a pile of paperwork and told to spin straw into gold. And even if she managed that feat, it probably wouldn't help her make partner. She needed to prove she could bring in clients. She needed to turn herself into a rainmaker. How was she ever going to do that cooped up here? How was she ever going to make partner? She closed her eyes and saw herself winding up working for someone like Vernon Black and Associates, the ambulance chasers who advertised on late-night TV. Her life couldn't come down to that. It just couldn't.

A knock on her door made her jump. She didn't even have time to call "come in" before Tanner stepped into the room and started sucking out all the oxygen. He had the kind of body that could model suits in a catalogue, and a perfect, adversarial lawyer's face, with sharp features and eyes like a hawk. And he had an air about him that just automatically made criminals squirm and lawyers bristle. He was in his middle forties and rumor had it he'd gone through two wives. He'd probably scared them to death.

Megan took a deep breath and raised her chin. She refused to be intimidated by this man.

"How are you coming?" he asked.

"Rotten, thank you." She shouldn't have said that. What a non-team-player thing to say!

Half his mouth lifted. Only Tanner could manage to smile in a way that made a person not want to smile back. "This is called paying your dues, so don't bitch. I'm sure I don't need to remind you that we go to trial in sixty days." And with that, he turned and left her office, shutting her prison door with a snick.

Who did he think she was, Criss Angel in drag? Was she supposed to say, "Abracadabra," and make something appear out of nothing? Damn the man!

She threw a carrot stick after him in a postencounter fit of rebellion and it hit the door and bounced down onto the carpet with a soft plop. "No problem," she grumbled. "I have no life. Maybe I'll get a sleeping bag and move in here." She laid her head on her desk and blinked back tears of frustration. What she needed now was a little man to suddenly appear and promise to help her turn this crap into gold. She'd gladly promise him her firstborn child in exchange for the help, just like the woman in the old fairy tale had done. That would be a contract she'd never have to honor since she'd never have a child. She was never going to get married anyway. Who'd want a whale?

"Stop that," she ordered herself. She sat up, rubbed her eyes, and put an end to the pity party. Then she dug out another carrot stick and got back to work. There was gold in here somewhere and she was going to find it.

By Sunday night Angela had convinced herself that she was being silly. Of course Brad wouldn't cheat on her. But then this morning she'd called the office just because, well, maybe she needed to pick up a gift.

She'd gotten Marion the receptionist. "Brad asked me to get a present for the big surprise party coming up," Angela had told her. "What would the guest of honor like?"

"What big surprise party?" Marion had asked.

Dread unfurled itself inside Angela's chest, pushing hard against her heart, but she gamely soldiered on. "You know, the office surprise party? Brad was talking about planning one for someone, but he didn't give me very many details."

"Oh," Marion had said. And that was all she said.

"You don't know about any surprise party?"

"No, but that doesn't mean anything. If it's a surprise, there are probably just a few people planning it."

Yes, of course, that made sense.

Almost. Except if anyone would know about a surprise party it would be Marion. She knew everything that went on at the office.

Angela's woman's intuition went on red alert. Someone was being very sneaky, and it wasn't her.

"Want me to ask him?" Marion offered.

So he could make up another lie? "No, that's okay. I'll ask him when he comes home tonight." Or maybe she'd just kill him when he came home.

Anger stewed inside Angela the rest of the day. She helped at Gabriella's preschool, which involved dropping Mandy at her mom's, then picking Mandy up at her mom's, which meant staying for a quick lunch at Mom's and acting as if everything was fine. And the pressure built. In the afternoon she hosted a scrapbooking party and sat around pretending everything was fine while she and five other preschool moms turned pages with family pictures into works of art as their children ran around the living room in dress-up clothes. She found an old picture of herself and Brad in her over-flowing shoebox. They were at a Halloween party, all dressed up like Batman and Catwoman. There they stood, fake cartoon characters, posing and yucking it up. They'd long since lost the costumes but they were still fakes, pretending to be a happily married couple, solid and devoted. Well, one of them was devoted. The other was a no-good bastardo. Anger possessed her hands and she began cutting the picture into tiny pieces, starting with a strong snip right up the middle of Brad's crotch. And all the while Josh Groban warbled "You Raise Me Up" in the background.

"Oh, that was a cute picture," chided one of her guests, bringing her back to the moment at hand.

Of a stupido wife and her bastardo husband. Cute. "It was a bad one of me," she lied, too embarrassed to confess the real reason behind her scissor mania to women she was just getting to know.

After the party ended it was time to pick up the house and start dinner, although she wasn't all that hungry after spending the afternoon noshing on cheese and grapes and veggies with dip. She'd originally planned to serve tiramisu cake, but now that she had to get hot, tiramisu had to be a thing of the past.

As she worked, she kept thinking about the picture she'd destroyed. Their life had been fine when she'd been skinny. All she had to do to put it back together again was to look good. She could do this. She could get her husband back.

But maybe she didn't want him back, she thought after he came home from work that night and gave her a big, old sloppy kiss like he was the world's most loyal husband. He clowned around for the girls at dinner as though they were one big, happy family. This, she'd heard, was how it was in Italy. The men had their family and then their mistress on the side. The tangy sauce from her chicken parmesan (the diet version, no breadcrumbs) suddenly felt like acid on her tongue. Why did she want to go to Italy anyway? Why was she learning Italian? So she could commiserate with other women whose husbands were cheating bastardos?

She shoved aside her plate and watched Brad through narrowed eyes while dancing an angry staccato on the table with her fingernails.

He stopped in the middle of pretending to dangle broccoli spears from his ears like earrings and gave her a "what's wrong" look.

Oh, yes, she should have been playing along and smiling, saying things like, "Silly Daddy." Well, excuse her if she didn't want to play. She pushed away from the table and took her plate to the sink.

"Baby?" Brad said from the table.

Baby. Did he call Miss Hottie "baby"?

"I'm not hungry," she said, and left the kitchen.

Behind her she heard Brad say, "Finish your dinner, girls. Mommy and Daddy will be right back." She was as far as the living room when he caught up to her. "Ang, what's wrong?"

"Nothing," she said stiffly, and kept going.

He dogged her all the way through the room and up the stairs. "Well, something's wrong. What'd I do?"

What did he do? Was he serious? "What did you do? You have the nerve to ask me that, you big, fat liar?"

"Well, yeah, since I don't know. And I don't appreciate being called a liar."

"And I don't appreciate being lied to," she retorted, and stormed into the bedroom. She tried to slam the door after her, but that didn't work since Brad was right behind her, pushing it open. She turned and glared at him, putting a hand on her hip. "You can quit playing dumb. I called the office today."

He threw up both hands. "And?"

"There is no surprise party for anyone."

He looked at her like she was one of the girls and she'd just done something naughty.

He had a lot of nerve. She wasn't the one being naughty. "I was going to get a gift, so I called Marion. And guess what? She didn't know a thing about any party." Angela stabbed a finger at him. "So, that means you're lying."

His jaw began working the way it often did when he was ticked and trying hard not to blow up. "Well, guess what. Marion's the one the party is for."

"Marion?" squeaked Angela. Oh, no. She plopped onto the bed. *Oh, boy.*

Brad shook his head, looking thoroughly disgusted. "Ang, will you just trust me? Please?"

She bit her lip and nodded.

"Daddy," Gabriella called from downstairs. "We're done."

"Okay," Brad called back, "I'm coming." To Angela he said, "I'm going to go back downstairs to our daughters now. Then, after they're in bed, I'm going to go have a big friggin' affair with my damned La-Z-Boy." With that he marched out of the bedroom.

Angela fell back on the bed. That had been bad. But at least she didn't have to worry about her husband. She let out a sigh of relief. Okay. She'd been silly and insecure all along. Brad loved her and she loved him and everything was fine.

Except, wait a minute. Friday night he'd told her he was planning

a party for someone who was retiring. Marion was forty. Who re-
tired at forty?

"Lion, I'm trying to finish making dinner here," Kizzy said, and gave
Lionel's hand a playful slap.

He unclamped his hands from her breasts, but continued to
peer over her shoulder at the pots on the stove. "Okay, Kizzy girl,
where are you hiding that fried chicken? I smelled it as soon as I
came in the door. Got it stuck in the oven?"

"There *is* chicken in the oven," Kizzy said.

"All right." Lionel rubbed his hands together.

"But it's baked."

Lionel made a face. "Baked? Baked?"

"And we're having acorn squash to go with it."

"And garlic potatoes?" Lionel asked, lifting the lid on one of the
pans. His frown got a little smaller. "Okra. Well, that's something
good. What's over there?"

"Green beans with bacon bits."

"That's okay. Except the bacon's probably fake."

Kizzy made no comment.

"But where are the potatoes?" Lionel continued.

"No potatoes tonight."

Lionel grunted. "Are we ever going to have mashed potatoes
again? Or potato salad. Why can't we have potato salad?"

"Because I don't want to tempt myself," Kizzy said simply.

Now Lionel was actually pouting. "Kiz, you're going way over-
board with this thing."

"Not really."

He disappeared from the kitchen, then returned a minute later
with a plate laden with . . .

"Cheesecake." Kizzy's taste buds started doing the happy dance.
She frowned at Lionel. "Now, what are you doing with that?"

"Carol brought it in to work today. I told her it was your favorite and she insisted on me bringing it home. And it's a good thing I did," he added, "since there's nothing good to eat around here."

"There's plenty good to eat," Kizzy informed him. "We're changing our definition of good, remember?"

"No, you're changing our definition of good. And girl, your definition stinks."

"Well, you can eat that, but I'm not going to." Kizzy said, and turned her back on the cheesecake.

"I'm sure not letting it go to waste," he said. "You can go ahead and be miserable if you want. I'll eat your piece and mine."

"Fine. You go right ahead."

But she knew it was there. And she thought about it as they sat at the kitchen table, eating her nutritious, nonfattening meal. And afterward, when Lionel helped himself to a piece and forked a huge chunk of it into his mouth she really thought about it. One little bite, how much harm could one little bite do?

As if reading her mind, he said, "Here, have a bite of mine before you drown in drool." Then he softly added, "Anyway, I brought it home for you, Kiz."

One bite turned into two, then three, and before she knew it, he'd fed her two thirds of the dangerous stuff. She scowled at him. "You let me eat almost that whole thing!" No, she'd let herself eat almost the whole thing, and that made her even angrier. She walked over to the dishwasher and shoved in her plate. Then she turned and pointed a finger at him. "I swear, Lionel, if you bring home anything else I can't have I'm going to club you with a rolling pin."

He held up both hands. "What? You've been working hard at this. I was just bringing you a treat to reward you."

She suddenly remembered something she'd read in one of the diet books she'd just bought. "No," she said slowly as she processed her revelation, "you were sabotaging me."

He reared back. "What?"

"You don't want me to succeed on this diet. Even if it kills me, you'd rather have me fat."

"You're not fat, you're big. And that's a rotten thing to say."

"But it's true, isn't it?"

"Well, I don't want you to be a twig. If I wanted a twig I'd have gone and married some skinny girl."

"Skinny can be pretty," Kizzy pointed out. "Look at Oprah's friend Gayle."

"I don't want Oprah's friend Gayle. I want a woman with some junk in the trunk and something on the front end, too."

Kizzy pursed her lips together. There he was, her husband, her friend, the man who was supposed to always want her best. She was trying to lose weight and what was he thinking about? Himself. "The doctor told me to lose weight, Lionel. If I don't, I can't get healthy. Is that what you want, for me to be sick?"

His bluster fell away and he looked stricken. "No. Good God, no."

She walked over to him and poked him in the chest. "Then you'd better quit trying to mess me up. 'Cause if you don't stop, I'm going to go live with my sister and leave you to eat KFC until you grow feathers and a beak."

His jaw dropped. "You'd do that? You'd leave me, Kiz?"

"For as long as it takes to get these pounds off, yes. Remember those wedding vows you took? Well, they said in sickness and health—and that means skinny or fat. You've had the sickness part with a big, old wife who can barely walk a block without getting winded. In another few months you're going to have a wife who you are going to have to run to keep up with. You'd better get used to it." She picked up the plate with the last of the cheesecake.

"Oh, no. You wouldn't."

She did. Into the garbage can it went. "Don't do that to me again, Lionel. I mean it. I need to get healthy."

Lionel scratched the back of his head. "Well."

"Well, what?" Kizzy demanded.

He heaved a big sigh. "I guess Oprah's friend's not so bad looking."

Kizzy smiled. Now that was the Lionel she knew and loved. "Come here, you."

And he came, like a man running for his last meal.

Erin decided it would be best to go to the gym weekday evenings, when Dan Rockwell was working. She didn't want any more gym encounters or coffee counseling sessions. No more contact. Period. Dan Rockwell was developing upsetting her into a fine art.

Before going to the gym tonight, she had an appointment with Hope Walker, the owner of Changing Seasons, Heart Lake's new flower shop, who was staying open late just for Erin. Hope was supposed to be a genius with flowers. Maybe she could be a genius on a budget.

There was something about flower shops, Erin thought as she walked through the door, that made you want to have a party. Everything was so festive and pretty. And this shop really said party. Refrigerated cases held arrangements of all sizes: large ones in antique pitchers, tiny ones in teacups. Buckets bloomed with long-stemmed roses, carnations, baby's breath, and mixed bouquets. In one corner sat what looked like the world's largest Christmas cactus, still blooming and housed in a fat yellow pot supported by ruby slippers. A little sign next to it said, "Feed me, Seymour." A collection of helium balloons danced above one corner of the counter, ready to grab for a last-minute birthday present or get-well gift. Potted plants of every variety decorated shelves, and in the window a huge Valentine display complete with both flowers and heart-shaped candy boxes reminded passersby that February 14 was right around the corner. Erin sniffed. Something in here smelled really good. And then she saw the little, foil-wrapped pots of hyacinths, all dolled up with pastel bows. She would have to take one of those home with her.

"Hi," Hope greeted her. She looked a little like a flower herself, with her ruffled long-sleeved pink top spilling over her jeans—a pale flower, the kind you might just walk past and not see at first. Except for her hair. The extreme short growth on her head practically screamed post-chemo grow-out. She looked to be somewhere in her late twenties or early thirties—way too young to have to cope with something so awful.

"I love your shop," Erin said.

Hope looked around and smiled. "So do I. It's been a godsend."

"That's some plant," Erin said, pointing to the cactus.

"That's Audrey, the shop mascot," Hope said. "I've had it for years."

"I've never seen such a big plant," Erin said. "You've sure got a green thumb."

Hope smiled. "Plants are my thing. So is doing flowers for weddings," she added, motioning Erin to a small wrought-iron patio table where she'd laid out an album full of sample pictures of floral arrangements.

They settled in, Erin with the photo album, Hope with her laptop.

The minute Erin started looking at the arrangements she knew she'd come to the right place. They were gorgeous—striking and modern: delphiniums and some kind of unusual greens in a tall vase, passionate pairings of reds and oranges in an arrangement that made you think of sex, tranquil arrangements of light shades of green, misty blues, and other cool hues.

"Where are you having the wedding?" asked Hope.

"At the Heart Lake Lodge."

"Oh, lucky you," breathed Hope.

"It's going to be perfect," Erin predicted. In spite of all the corners they were cutting. Anyway, it wasn't how you got married that counted. It was who you married.

"What are your colors?"

"Brown and green."

"Nice." Hope began typing. "I could make you a bouquet with white and chocolate roses, baby's breath, and plumosa."

"There's such a thing as a chocolate rose?"

"Absolutely. Do you have a favorite flower, by the way? Something you'd like to incorporate?"

"Well, I like daisies," said Erin. "But they stink," she added, wrinkling her nose.

"Daisies are sweet, though. You know they symbolize innocence."

"Bag that, I guess," cracked Erin.

Hope grinned. "Maybe you won't want white roses then. They symbolize purity."

"I still have a pure heart. What do chocolate roses symbolize?"

"You know, I don't know," Hope said, still typing away. "We could incorporate some stephanotis in the arrangements up by the altar. For good luck. And carnations. A lot of people don't like to use them. They don't have the cachet roses do, but you can do a lot with carnations. And they're affordable."

"Affordable is good," Erin said quickly.

"So are huckleberry branches and salal, and they look great in a big arrangement. Chocolate mint is nice, too. Is this an evening wedding?"

"Yes."

"So you'll want candelabras?"

Erin nodded. She closed her eyes and envisioned herself in her wedding dress, walking toward Adam in a romantic haze of candlelight. Thank God he'd finally come to his senses and turned over the creative control to her.

"Oh, I know something really cool we could do for your centerpiece on the refreshment table." Hope's typing got faster. "A big platter piled high with limes and Granny Smith apples and pears."

"Wow," Erin breathed. She'd never thought of using fruit as a table centerpiece. In fact, she hadn't thought of much of anything Hope was suggesting. She made a mental note to file Hope's number in her computer so she could use her for events in the future.

She was a little less excited after Hope had entered all the information into her computer and printed out prices. Even with the carnations it wasn't cheap. But Hope was creative, and she would be more affordable than any of the other florists Erin had checked into.

Still. "I'd better think about this," Erin said. "I think I'll probably have to scale back some. Can we finalize this in a couple of weeks or so?"

"No problem," said Hope. "We've got plenty of time. And don't worry if you have to cut a few things," she added. "We'll make it nice for you no matter what you decide on."

Erin thanked her and bought a hyacinth. It was just one little flower, but it was sweet and it made her feel good. And that would be her motto when making her final decision on flowers for the wedding. She didn't need to go on flower overload for the wedding. She would think small but tasteful. Less was more.

"And if you want to bring your fiancé in . . ." Hope began.

"Oh, that's okay," Erin said quickly. "He trusts me." Anyway, the last thing she needed was the man who had wanted his cousin the happy gardener to do their flowers helping her make her final decision.

Outside the shop, she closed her eyes, took a sniff of her hyacinth and smiled. Hope would help her make the wedding beautiful. Everything would be perfect. This day was perfect.

Until she opened her eyes and saw Dan Rockwell coming down the street.

Nine

£rin wanted to turn and run somewhere, anywhere—across the street, back into the flower shop. But it was too late. He'd seen her.

The sudden halt in his step indicated he was feeling the same way. She watched as Dan mentally gathered himself and moved forward, giving her a salutary nod. "How's it going?"

He sounded as stiff as she felt.

Be polite, said her inner mother.

"Fine," she said. "I was just looking at flowers for the wedding."

He pointed to her hyacinths. "Pretty small bouquet."

"The bouquet will be gorgeous," Erin said. "This was just a little something extra to make me feel good."

"You just ordered flowers for your wedding. You should feel great."

"I do," she insisted. "But who can resist hyacinths?"

"Someone with hay fever? Here, let me smell it." She held the flower up to his face and he took a deep sniff, then produced a huge, fake sneeze.

"Very funny," she said, trying not to smile.

"No, that does smell good. Are you having some of those?"

"I'm not sure they'll be in bloom in June. Anyway, I'm happy with what I'm getting."

"Glad to hear you're getting what you want."

"Well, within reason," she qualified, and then realized she'd just opened the door for Dan to insult McDoodoo. McDreamy, she quickly corrected herself. Grabbing for something to turn the conversation, she pointed to Dan's grubby jeans, speckled with paint and the tattered tennis shoes. "You're not working at the store?"

"They give me a day off once in a while for good behavior." He looked down at his jeans. "I was working on a project. Just came to town to pick up some dinner."

Good. At least he wouldn't be going to the gym. Her curiosity got the better of her and she couldn't help asking. "What kind of project?"

"I'm fixing up a house on the other side of the lake."

She cocked her head. "I didn't know you moonlighted as a carpenter."

He grinned. "Like someone recently said, 'You don't know anything about me.'"

Okay, he was starting to irritate her.

He began speaking again before she could tell him. "I bought a little place that I'm going to fix up and flip."

He wasn't staying forever at the grocery store, checking groceries and stocking the freezer? Who'd have thought it? "Are you going to be one of those guys who makes his fortune in real estate?"

He smiled. "Maybe. Got a lot of things I want to do. Money'll help 'em happen."

A lot of things he wanted to do. He was right. She didn't know him.

And you don't want to; you're engaged, her inner mother reminded her.

Happily engaged. "Well, I'd better get going," she said. "Good luck with the house."

"Good luck with the flowers," he said.

"Thanks," she murmured, and hurried away. But partway down the street she grew thoughtful and slowed down. Was that man with the plan really Dan Rockwell? And, more to the point, why, when he wasn't irritating her, did he interest her? She half turned and looked back down the street. No sign of him. He'd vanished, like an angel.

She frowned. Or a ghost. She firmly shook Dan Rockwell out of her mind and continued on. She was only interested because he was a childhood . . . something. Who cared about Dan and his get-rich plan? She had plans of her own, weight to lose and a wedding to pull together. *Have a nice life, Dan.*

She sped to the gym and jumped on the treadmill. And started running. And running. And running.

It was Tuesday, lunch hour, and Megan finished her chicken salad in record time. It was filling. She wasn't hungry, really. But her taste buds were just itching for trouble. If she didn't get out of this office, she was going to wind up down at the lobby coffee shop that doubled as a muffin land mine. Maybe a change of pace, a change of place, would be good. She needed to do something to keep herself from falling off the wagon, and she needed to do it quickly.

She looked at her commuter tennis shoes that she wore for her bus ride into the city every morning, sitting in a bag under her desk. A walk. She could take a lunch-hour walk. Why not? It beat sitting here fantasizing over muffins.

She picked up the bag and opened her office door. Then she looked to see if anyone was coming. Like it mattered if anyone was coming? What did she care if someone saw her waiting for an elevator with her tennis shoes in a bag? Ridiculous. She yanked open the door and strode out into the hallway.

She had just pushed the down button when Pamela Thornton pranced up behind her. "Erin, off to get some lunch?"

Coming from any other person that would just be a conversation starter. Coming from Pamela the Pencil it was an opening shot.

"Just out to run some errands," Megan said, and kept her gaze on the closed elevator door. She felt rather than saw Pamela leaning over to look in her bag, and moved it away.

"Running. Literally?" She arched an eyebrow.

"Walking. Literally," Megan snapped. The elevator doors slid open and they both stepped inside.

"Walking off your frustrations? Having a bad day?" Pamela taunted. "How are things going on *Newton* v. *Owens*?"

"Okay." *Brilliant answer, Wales.*

"I hear Tanner is a bastard to work for."

"He's successful and driven, and he's a man."

Pamela rolled her eyes. "He's going to break you, you've got to know that."

Oh, now she got what was going on. "And then, when he breaks me I'll scuttle away and no longer be an embarrassment to the firm? Is that it?"

"No, of course not," said Pamela. "I just meant—"

Megan held up a hand. "I know what you meant. And what are your chances of making partner?"

Pamela's mouth turned down and her eyebrows dipped—as much as Botoxed eyebrows could. "Damned good. I do my part for the firm."

"Yes, you do," Megan agreed. "You keep up . . . morale."

"Hearsay, darling. You should know you can't build a case on that. But here's something you can build a case on: facts. Fact: there are only so many partnerships available this year. Fact: the firm wants rainmakers. Who are they going to choose, a bitter big girl who couldn't bring in a new client unless she kidnapped him or someone with legal brains *and* a personality? I wonder." The doors swished open and Pamela gave her long hair a shake, then stepped out.

It was all Megan could do not to kick her in the butt and help her on her way. She followed Pamela out the elevator into the lobby, then marched toward a grouping of chairs and sat down to put on her shoes. Bitter big girl? Who did that pencil think had made her bitter? Women like Pamela!

Shoes laced, she steamed out of the First Orca Trust Tower and down Second Avenue, her mood a perfect match for the gray Seattle sky. *Bitter big girl. Humph!* Talk about someone living in a glass house throwing stones. Pamela wasn't all sweetness and light.

Megan swallowed and realized that she actually had a bitter taste in her mouth that had nothing to do with the fumes from the diesel bus roaring by. *Bitter big girl.* Was she?

Of course she was. She thought back to her first taste of bitter. She'd been eight. Paul, her new daddy, had just shooed her away from the potato chips at the neighborhood barbecue. She'd grabbed one last handful and he'd given her a swat on the bottom to help her on her way. That had been humiliating.

But not half as humiliating as hearing Paul say to Angela's dad, "That kid is such a pig. At the rate she's going she'll be the size of the Goodyear blimp by the time she's twelve."

Well, she showed him. She didn't turn into the Goodyear blimp until she was fourteen. And every year along the way she missed her real daddy who died when she was six. Her real daddy would put her on his feet and dance with her and call her Peanut and Princess. Paul only called her fat.

Someone must have told him not to do that, because he finally stopped. But by the time he did it was too late. She knew what he thought of her. And although she tried to salve the hurt with contraband cookies and chips, she never succeeded. The times when they clashed she found herself wondering why a man who smoked three packs of cigarettes a day got to defy statistics and keep living when her real dad had to get in a car accident and die. All that resentment helped her build a chip on her shoulder the size of an eighties shoulder pad, and she'd worn it right into Wise Ass and Greed.

Her steps slowed as she remembered the first time she'd met Pamela Thornton and her friend Ashley Paine, Megan's competition at the firm. It had been at a cocktail party that Grant Waters had hosted for some of the new members of the firm. She'd walked into that elegant drawing room with its ancient carpets and Queen Anne furniture and tried not to gawk at the Chihuly glass. Pamela and Ashley stood by the fireplace, drinks in hand, talking to Jonathan Green. Instead of joining them, Megan had frozen in her tracks. The only thing that saved her was Tanner showing up at her elbow and saying, "Isn't this your dream come true? Why do you look like you're in a nightmare? Go mingle."

She'd tried, she really had. She drifted to the edge of the group and pretended like she belonged. But she didn't. She knew it and they knew it. They gave her a crumb—fleeting smiles—then turned their rapt attention back to Green. She'd broken off from the magic circle and drifted toward the bar, stopping on the way to put some caviar on a cracker.

"Way to have them hanging on your every word," Tanner said at her elbow.

She took in a deep breath. He'd been one of the partners who interviewed her. He'd probably recommended her to the firm. He was invested in her success, although why, she had no idea. Why was she here at all? She clearly wasn't what they wanted.

"They're too busy getting their noses brown to want to listen to anything I've got to say. Their brain size probably isn't any bigger than their bra size," she'd added under her breath.

Tanner had let out a bark of laughter that turned heads in their direction. "Oh, you ladies are going to get along well," he predicted.

As the night wore on, Megan felt the womens' assessing gazes on her. Once Pamela even smiled at her, but she hadn't been able to smile back.

Would things have turned out differently between them if she'd smiled? Megan sighed. Probably not. She was pretty sure someone had overheard her comment to Tanner and went running to Pamela and Ashley with it. Whatever had started the nasty rivalry, they'd been shooting barbs back and forth practically from the beginning. And with each encounter the barbs had gotten sharper.

Bitter big girl. Maybe she was. What did she have to be bitter about, really? Nothing but her weight. And whose fault was it that she was fat? She could blame it on a lot of things, a lot of people—especially her stepfather—but the truth was she was the one who had forked all that food into her mouth. A woman could only go so long blaming her childhood for her problems as an adult. It was time to stop.

She picked up her pace and walked down the hill toward the Seattle waterfront where ferryboats, shops, restaurants, and seagulls all vied for attention. Down here the air took on the salty tang of the sea. Megan took a deep breath, filling her lungs with it. A weak winter sun found a small corner of sky and brightened the gray just a little. This was a beautiful city. She had a great job. She could have a great life. And she didn't have to be big or bitter. It was really her choice.

A woman in jogging shorts and a sweatshirt with an iPod plugged into her ears ran past her. Megan stopped and watched the woman. She looked so graceful, so in control of her world.

Running. That was a goal to work for. Megan would like to become a runner, jogging about the city in cute little shorts, a ponytail swinging. She took some experimental jogging steps and found herself quickly winded. Okay, maybe not quite yet, but soon—maybe by summer. Perhaps even by spring. She didn't have to run a marathon. She could start by running a block and work up from there. She turned and started back to the First Orca Trust Tower. On the way she went into the Hallmark store and picked up a card. It was time to stop feuding with the skinny women of the world. If you couldn't beat 'em, join 'em. She was ready to join the club.

It was Friday night, and the members of the Teeny Bikini Diet Club showed up with tales of both diet tragedy and triumph to share.

Angela had come up with a new diet idea, and she shared it as they sat around Kizzy's dining room table, sampling Angela's ham and asparagus antipasto. "When you're out to eat, have someone in your family order dessert. Then, when they're eating it, you chew along with them, and it's almost like you're getting to eat it."

"Did you read this on the Internet?" Megan asked suspiciously.

"Well," Angela hedged.

"Have you tried it?" Megan persisted.

"Not yet. But it sounded good. And I thought it might help me next time we take the kids to McDonald's."

"Ordering a salad next time you go to McDonald's will probably help more," Megan suggested, dishing up an Angela offering that she'd interestingly dubbed Italian stir-fry.

"I don't know," said Erin. "If somebody sat down next to me and started chewing on chocolate cake I'd strangle her."

"You're right," Angela decided. She pushed her vegetables around her plate. "I hate my life. And I only lost one pound this week. Every time I feel bad I eat something bad."

"If that's the case, be glad you lost even one pound," Megan told her.

"And at least you lost a pound," added Erin. "You're on your way. Pretty soon you'll be so hot Brad won't even want to leave for work."

What should have made Angela smile instead set her lower lip to wobbling.

Kizzy laid a hand on her arm. "Angela?"

"Uh-oh," said Megan. "What's wrong?"

"Brad is having an affair," Angela wailed and started crying.

"Shut up," scoffed Erin. "He's Mr. Family Man of the Century. No way."

"Well, he is," Angela insisted. She gave a red pepper in her stir-fry a vicious stab. "I overheard him."

"What?" Erin dropped her fork. "You're delirious."

"When did you hear him and what did he say?" asked Megan.

"I heard him last week when I came home from our meeting. He was on the phone with Rachel the puttana and he said, 'She doesn't suspect a thing.'"

"You don't know he was talking about you, though," said Megan, arguing for the defense. "Did you confront him?"

"Yes. He said he was planning a surprise party for someone who's retiring."

"Well, then, there you have it," said Megan.

Angela shook her head. "The woman's only forty." She waved a hand at the array of diet fare represented around the table. "Look at this," she said wildly. "All this diet food. What good is it going to do us? What good is it to even try when men are such bastardos. I don't know why I'm even bothering to—"

Kizzy clamped a hand over her lips. "Don't say it. We need to have a talk right now. All of us."

Everyone tensed, watching Kizzy like so many parishioners bracing for a hellfire-and-brimstone sermon.

She looked around at them, eyes flashing. "We are not doing this for any man. We are doing this for ourselves. We are doing this for our health, because we want to look and feel the best we can. The men can come along or not."

They all sat silent, staring at her. Finally Angela spoke in a small voice. "But I don't want to lose Brad."

"If his love depends on the size of your waistline you've already lost him," said Kizzy. "We marry each other for better or for worse, that's what the vows say. Let's just concentrate on improving and feeling good about ourselves. Anyway, that's a lot of pressure to put on yourself when you're dieting," she said to Angela.

"You can't make saving your marriage depend on the success of your diet or you'll make yourself crazy," Megan added.

"I already am," Angela muttered.

"One step at a time," Kizzy said, giving her a hug. "You first. Get healthy. That's the cornerstone. You build from there. If you don't care for you, how can you expect anyone else to? Got it?"

Angela bit her lip and nodded.

"Now," Kizzy said firmly, "let's enjoy our meal. Let's work on living today and not go borrowing trouble from tomorrow."

Angela sniffed. "You're right. I need to stay in the second."

"And you need to not jump to conclusions," Megan told her. "You could be wrong."

Angela didn't say anything, but from the grim set of her mouth it was plain that she was convinced she wasn't.

The women began eating again, but the ambiance was gone from Kizzy's cheery yellow dining room. Instead a somber mood reigned.

"This antipasto you brought is really good," Erin said to Angela in an attempt to lift her spirits.

"I love the Italian stir-fry," said Megan.

"I just wish we had some garlic bread to go with it," Angela grumbled, still not in the best of moods.

"I could sure go for some ice cream," said Erin.

"Tiramisu," Angela said with a sigh.

"Nothing tastes as good as thin feels," Megan said. "Come on. Let's do some DDR."

"Good idea," Erin seconded.

Two hours later they had stomped the food monster into the ground.

"We did it!" Angela crowed. "You know, I feel so much better. I really needed this tonight. Thanks, guys. For everything."

"That's what friends are for," Kizzy said. "Let's make sure we e-mail each other this week. And if anyone is having problems, call one of us. We're all in this together."

"Thank God," murmured Erin.

Adam had come in while Erin was gone. She found him waiting for her in the living room, medical books spread out on the coffee table. "Hi, there," he greeted her. "I fed your fish for you."

He'd also reorganized the house. The kitchen counter was cleared, which meant she wouldn't be able to find anything for a week. It looked like all her magazines had been banished to the recycle bin, including her latest issue of *Bride*.

Adam hated clutter.

He is so perfect for you, cooed her inner mother. *Think how organized your life will be.*

"How was your meeting?" he asked.

"Good. Nothing but healthy food."

"Sounds like a drag to me," he said.

She cuddled up next to him on the couch. "But by the time I'm done I'll have no problem fitting into my wedding dress."

"I can hardly wait to see you in it," he said, putting an arm around her shoulder. "You're going to look incredible. So, how are the plans coming?"

This was encouraging. Now was the time to tell him about the Heart Lake Lodge. "Great. I was able to get the Heart Lake Lodge for the reception. Can you believe it?" she rushed on. "That place is always booked a year ahead, but they had a cancellation and Bev saved the date for us. I still can't believe we lucked out. I've dreamed of getting married there ever since I was a little girl."

Adam's smile tightened and she braced herself for him to say the E word. He didn't.

"You're not going to ask how expensive it was?"

He took a moment to answer, like a doctor searching for the best way to deal with a difficult patient. Then he shook his head. "No. I told you, it's your day."

And now he sounded like he regretted ever saying that.

She searched those beautiful ice-blue eyes in vain for a spark of excitement. "All I have to do is say the word and it's unbooked." And there went her fairy-tale wedding. But if he asked her to let the lodge go, she would. *You'll still have Prince Charming*, she reminded herself. She held her breath and hoped anyway.

"What does renting it do to the budget?" he asked.

"It puts me over."

You're not good with money, babe. She'd hated hearing those words when he first said them to her. She didn't like them any better as a memory.

"How much over?" Adam asked.

Erin felt like a woman preparing to jump across a canyon. She braced herself. "Two thousand five hundred and ninety-five dollars. Actually, make that two thousand ninety-five dollars. Bev is waiving the five-hundred-dollar event supervisor fee as a wedding present. I know we want to save for a house," she rushed on, "but we can do that and still have a nice wedding. This is a one-time event in a woman's life and it's important to me." And she wasn't that bad with money, damn it. He just expected her to do this for nothing.

He took a deep breath and nodded. "Then that's where we should have it."

She stared at him, almost afraid to believe her ears. "You mean it? Really?"

He nodded.

He was a new man. She threw her arms around his neck. "Oh, Adam, you're the best. Thanks for understanding."

"I want you to be happy," he said, but he sounded more like he was trying to convince himself than reassure her.

She slipped onto his lap. "I've found the perfect florist, too."

"You don't want my cousin to do the flowers?"

"This woman is affordable," Erin assured him, and immediately started a mental checklist of all the places she could cut back on the flowers.

"So is my cousin, and I already told her she could."

"Adam, we didn't decide for sure."

"Come on, babe. It's only flowers," he said, and kissed her. "And you got the lodge."

"This florist is amazing. And the flowers won't cost much. I promise," she added, and nibbled on his lower lip. He ran his hands down her back and she reached for the top button of his shirt.

"Okay, fine," he said as he settled her down among the couch cushions, his mind obviously on something other than flowers.

But it isn't really, a voice whispered at the back of her mind. *And you know it.*

The voice sounded a lot like Dan Rockwell. She squeezed her eyes shut and mentally hummed the wedding march. It almost drowned him out.

Angela returned home to find Brad sacked out on the couch with a copy of *Sports Illustrated.* Lying there on the couch in his jeans and stocking feet, he didn't exactly look like a man who was having an affair. But would she know what a man having an affair looked like?

He smiled at her over the top of the magazine. "Hey, babe. How was Bikinis Anonymous?"

She stuck her tongue out at him. "Go ahead, make fun. You'll be sorry when I'm looking hot in a new bikini."

"No I won't, believe me." He threw the magazine aside and patted the couch and she went and squeezed in next to him. "Hey, I know a way to burn some calories," he said, pulling her on top of him.

It wasn't hard to tell what he wanted. A man just couldn't have this much energy if he was having sex with another woman, could he? But what if he could? What if he was? The thought of him kissing Rachel's bare skin seared her heart. How could a man share that kind of closeness with two women? How could Brad, her Brad, do that?

A new thought spun her from devastated to terrified. What if he gave her an STD? She slid off him.

"Hey, where are you going?"

"To bed. I just started my period," she lied.

"Oh." He sounded disappointed.

Well, that was nothing compared to how he'd sound if she caught him cheating on her.

Ten

Megan stepped on her scale Monday morning and almost screamed. Four pounds. She'd lost four pounds! One of them just since meeting with her fellow dieters on Friday. She hopped off the scale and started jumping up and down and whooping—until the person in the apartment under her hollered something indecipherable.

She stopped the jumping, but kept the buzz going, dancing her way out to the kitchen and singing while she made her morning omelet, "I lost four pounds, I lost four pounds." She danced to the bathroom and showered, running her hands down her waist. Did it feel slimmer? Not yet, but who cared? She was on her way. "I lost four pounds!"

As she boogied to the closet, she caught sight of the card she'd bought the week before, the one she'd had every intention of giving to Pamela, the one with the scary blank page inside. Now the woman on the front of the card seemed to be watching her. *I'm waiting for you to give me words.*

Megan put on her bra.

Still waiting.

She wriggled into her panty hose.

Still here.

She pulled on her blouse.

Still . . .

Okay, okay. Megan snatched the card from the dresser. She padded out to the kitchen, grabbing a pen from the glass of pens and pencils sitting by her cordless, then sat down at her drop leaf oak table and opened the card. And stared at the blank page. "I have no idea what to write," she muttered.

She gnawed her lip and tapped the tabletop with her pen. It was easy to argue a case. Easy to argue, period. You didn't buy this card to argue your case, she told herself. Just be honest.

Megan took a deep breath, shook the nerves out of her hand, and scrawled, "You were right. I was a bitter big girl. But not anymore. I hope we can start out on a new foot." She took another breath and signed her name. And her heart started pounding as if she was running. She shut the card and shoved it in the envelope, then put it in her purse.

The card wasn't done with her. *Don't forget where you put me.*

It was still reminding her when she stepped into the elevator at the First Orca Trust Tower forty-five minutes later. The ride up to the forty-first floor felt like Stephen King's Green Mile. And when the door opened and she got off, it was all she could do not to bolt for the security of her windowless office. But she forced herself to turn to the right and walk down to Pamela's office. She lifted a shaky hand and knocked on the door, her heart knocking right along, too. A moment later, the door opened, and there stood Pamela, tall, thin, and icy.

Words, where were the words? Megan's brain and mouth both went on strike simultaneously. But the card tugged on her hand, raising it up, up, up. And then there it hovered between them, an invitation.

Pamela raised an eyebrow and took the card.

"I have to get to work," Megan stammered. Then she did a quick about-face and tried to walk as slowly and confidently down the hall as she could. Safely inside her office, she closed the door after her and leaned against it and let out her breath. *Did it.* And suddenly, miraculously, she felt lighter than air.

"I'm going out to the shop to work for a while," Lionel announced after dinner Monday night.

He'd been disappearing into the garage to his makeshift workshop every night after dinner for the last two weeks. What he was doing out there Kizzy had no idea.

"What are you making, Lion?" she asked.

He shrugged. "Nothin' much. Just puttering."

She'd read the Mars and Venus book. She knew men had to go into their cave and get some downtime. But Lionel sure seemed to need a lot of it lately. And, come to think of it, he was starting to look a little like a bear. His love handles had expanded and she saw more belly hanging over his belt. How could this be? He hadn't brought anything bad for them home and she was feeding him good food, but it seemed lately that every pound she lost he found. Did he have a stash at work?

Curiosity burned in her as she loaded the dishes and stowed leftover salad in the refrigerator. Finally she decided to douse the flame with a little visit to the garage. Maybe Lionel was thirsty. She'd take him a Diet Pepsi to sip on while he worked.

Pop in hand, she opened the door and slipped into the garage to find him leaning on his workbench, poring over his January issue of *Handyman* and eating a Twinkie.

"Lionel!"

He jumped and whirled around, dropping the Twinkie on the cement floor. His eyes got big as golf balls. "Kizzy."

She made a face. "What are you doing?"

He picked up the Twinkie and set it on the workbench in back of him as if to shield it. "What are you doing out here?"

She held up the glass. "I came to bring you something to drink."

"Oh, well, thanks." He walked over to her and took it.

"And I thought I'd come out and see what you were working on," she added, her tone of voice accusing.

"Oh, uh, nothing yet. I haven't decided."

"So, you've been out here every night just . . . ?"

"Thinking," he supplied.

"And eating." She walked past him. What else was over there besides Twinkies?

He fell in step with her. "Hey now, what are you doing?"

"I'm wondering what else you've got out here." She stopped in front of the row of shelves where he kept his supplies. It wasn't hard to spot the can of Pringles trying to hide behind the glass jars of nuts and bolts and nails.

She grabbed them and held them in front of him, both eyebrows raised.

Lionel looked like a kid at the principal's office. "That's for in case someone stops by, like one of the neighbors."

"Uh-huh." She flipped open his toolbox.

"Now, Kizzy Girl, what you want to go snoopin' in my toolbox for?" he protested, trying to reach around her.

But he was too late. She'd already found the stash of candy bars. "Uh, uh, uh. Lionel Jefferson Maxwell."

Lionel was pouting now. "Don't go climbing all over me, Kiz. I haven't brought a single thing into the house to tempt you."

"No, you've just been coming out here tempting your own fat self," Kizzy retorted.

He scowled. "Woman, I am not the one on a diet and I want something good to eat once in a while."

"So, you just sneak out here and pig away," Kizzy said in disgust.

"Well, you won't make anything for me. What am I supposed to do?"

Suffer right along with her, of course. Although it wasn't really fair to ask him to, even though it would be good for him to shed some pounds. Still, a person had to want to do this for himself. Getting healthy wasn't something someone, even someone who loved you, could decide for you. She'd been wrong to force her diet on him.

Lionel dropped his bluster. "Anyway, I'm eating it out here because I don't want to make you feel bad."

"I appreciate that, Lion, I really do. And if you want a stash out here then I guess you should be able to have one." She was tempted to warn him that if he kept this up he, too, would soon be having an unpleasant chat with the doctor like the one she'd had, but she resisted. Deep down he knew.

His jaw came unhinged. "You're not going to tell me to get rid of this?"

She shook her head. "No. I'm not going to be your enabler and feed you things that are bad for you, but I'm not going to ride you, either." She slipped her arms around him. "I want us both to be healthy, Lion, but what you eat is your decision. I shouldn't have come snooping out here. I'm sorry."

He heaved a deep sigh. "I shouldn't have come sneaking out here. Sorry, Kiz."

She patted his broad belly. "Well, you stay out here and plan your project. I'll see you when you're done."

He picked up the Twinkie and shot it basketball style into the big waste can he used for his garbage. "I'm done now."

She wasn't sure exactly what that meant, but she decided not to ask. She wasn't going to be Lionel's diet conscience. She had her hands full being her own.

"I'm doing awful," Angel typed to her online chat group. "I'm thinking of trying that new diet pill."

"I wouldn't," logged on another woman. "I tried it and spent the whole afternoon in the bathroom. I thought I was going to die. It was awful."

Another dieter chimed in. "I found something. It's called Quick Fixx, and it's great. I've lost ten pounds in two weeks and I've got tons of energy. And it's herbal, so it's totally safe."

A totally safe way to lose a lot of weight in a hurry—talk about your perfect timing! The woman had just started selling the stuff, and she sent Angela to the Web site where Angela ordered a bottle of pills and had it sent express mail. She could have bought two weeks' worth of groceries with what she spent on the pills and the shipping, but if they worked, they'd be worth every penny.

And, as it turned out, they were. They worked great. The first day she took them her appetite vanished. And she had sooo much energy.

"And I've lost three pounds already," she bragged to the Bikinis.

"Wow, that's great," said Erin. "I need some of that."

"I'd read the fine print first," Megan said. "You don't know what kind of side effects these could have. Ever hear of fen-phen?"

"But these pills are herbal," Angela said. "Totally safe." She took a little sandwich bag containing one of the miracle pills from her purse and shook out the pill, then popped it into her mouth and washed it down with some diet pop.

Megan took another celery stick and dipped it into her feta cheese dip. "Well, I guess if it's working for you, but I think you should proceed with caution."

"Don't worry. I'm not taking any more than the bottle says to," Angela assured her, finishing her pop.

Megan shrugged. "I wouldn't trust any diet product that labeled itself a quick fix. I don't think there is such a thing."

"Me, either," Kizzy agreed as she set out pulled pork and cabbage salad. "That type of thing's been around since I was your age, and this just sounds like good, old-fashioned speed to me."

Angela frowned. "It can't be speed. It's herbal."

"Just because it's herbal doesn't mean it's good," Megan said. "Marijuana is an herb."

Angela shrugged. "Well, this isn't marijuana, so I'll be fine."

And she was fine until she woke up at one A.M. with the sweats and a racing heart.

"Oh, my God. I'm having a heart attack!"

Eleven

"Brad, Brad, wake up!" Frantic, Angela shook her husband hard enough to rattle every tooth out of his head.

"Wha?" He raised his head from the pillow and tried to focus on her.

"I'm having a heart attack," she wailed.

He shot up. "What?"

"My heart's pounding like it's going to come out of my chest. Oh, God, Brad. Who's going to raise my babies?"

He bolted out of bed. "I'll call 911." He rushed out of the room and Angela sat there in bed, willing her heart to stop this frenzied beating. She was too young to die.

He returned, phone to his ear. "What are your symptoms?"

"My heart's racing so fast and I can't make it stop."

"Her heart's racing," Brad reported. "Dizziness?" he asked her.

Dizzy? Did she feel dizzy? She fell back down, her head landing on the pillow with the thud. Yes, she decided. She felt dizzy.

"Yes," Brad said. "Sweating?" he asked her.

"Yes," she cried. "I feel all shaky."

"She feels shaky," Brad reported. He sounded as shaky as she felt. "How fast can you get here?"

Maybe not soon enough, maybe she'd die right here in Brad's arms. She felt chilled now. And shaky. And scared. *Oh, God!*

He rattled off their address, then sat down on the bed and hugged her. "They'll be here in just a few minutes. You're going to be all right."

Maybe she only had a few minutes left. "Brad, if I die I don't want the girls to grow up without a mother. You have to remarry." *But not Rachel. Dear God, please don't let him marry Rachel. Never mind that. Please don't let me die!*

It felt like forever before the aid car arrived, its flashing light splashing the dark night with red. *Red. Blood. Oooh.*

"I'll let them in," Brad said, and dashed out of the bedroom.

And then he was back and the bedroom was filled with para-medics and equipment, and a stranger was asking her all kinds of questions and fishing around in her ratty old sleep tee, sticking disks connected to wires all over her boobs. She felt like the Bride of Frankenstein, about to get zapped to life.

She didn't care. *Just let me live.*

It was the longest night of her life, and the most embarrassing. After testing her on his fancy machine and grilling her with all kinds of questions, the paramedic pulled the Dr. Frankenstein stuff off her, leaving sticky goop on her boobs, and gave her the good news that she was going to live. "But you should still set up an appointment with your doctor," he said. "Get checked out. And meanwhile you might want to lay off the diet pills and caffeine. That was probably what caused the problem."

"She will," Brad said, and gave her a stern look as he escorted the paramedics out of the bedroom.

"No more of those pills, Ang," he said when he came back. "I want you to promise me."

"But they were working so good." How sad. She'd finally found something that worked and it turned out not to be good for her.

"Yeah, they were working good at trying to kill you. No more. I mean it."

She nodded and slipped down under the covers. Quick Fixx would go in the garbage first thing in the morning. She wanted to lose weight, but she didn't want to wind up as a skinny corpse. Back to losing weight the hard way, she thought with a sigh.

"It may be hard, but it's still the best way," Kizzy told her the next time the Bikinis met.

"You're right. And you were right about the pills," Angela told Megan. "I asked my doctor about them and she said anything that speeds up your metabolism like that isn't good."

"I rest my case," said Megan. "I'm just glad you didn't do serious damage to yourself."

"Me, too," said Angela. "It wouldn't do any good to get hot if I didn't live to see it."

"You're going to get there," Kizzy told her. "We all are."

"I'll drink to that," quipped Erin, raising her glass of Diet Coke.

"Me, too," said Angela, and grabbed for a water bottle. "Just not with anything that has caffeine."

The Bikinis had been working on their new bodies for a month and making progress, but now Valentine's Day, diet death day, was breathing down their necks. And the e-mails were flying.

From Angela: I WANT CHOCOLATE. This sucks.

From Erin: Okay, confession time. I already bought one of those mini-Valentine candy boxes and ate the whole thing.

From Kizzy: I forgive you, my child. Now get back on the wagon with the rest of us!!!

From Erin: The worst day is going to be the day after VD, when all that chocolate goes on sale. I'll need a twenty-four-hour armed guard. Who am I kidding? I need a twenty-four-hour armed guard every day. Things are going great with Adam. So why am I cheating like this?!!

From Kizzy: You can still eat, just try and find things that aren't so bad for you. Pistachios are great.

From Erin: Nuts. Yuck.

From Megan: Remember, nothing tastes as good as thin feels.

From Angela: Except chocolate. DIETING SUCKS!!!!!

From Kizzy: Don't worry. I'm serving something this week to make all your taste buds happy. And it will be almost guilt-free.

From Angela: Is it chocolate?

From Kizzy: LOL. Yes.

From Erin: Guilt-free chocolate. I'LL DRINK TO THAT!

From Kizzy: ALMOST guilt-free.

From Angela: Almost is close enuff 4 me.

Megan read the exchanges and smiled. Now that she'd cut that stuff out of her diet she was finding she didn't have the cravings for it like she used to. She'd lost another two pounds—and a ton of negative feelings. That was the best.

Pamela had actually thanked her for the card. "But I'm still going to make partner before you," she'd warned.

"The verdict's not in yet," Megan had replied.

Another e-mail popped up in her mailbox. This one from Angela: "If Brad gets me chocolates I'm going to throw them at him. It will be too much, too late."

Brad Baker seemed like a nice enough guy, but you never knew. Poor Angela—if Brad was cheating on her, Megan would make sure she got the best divorce lawyer available.

Angela threw one of Brad's shirts into the washing machine. No hint of perfume on it. No lipstick—as Megan would say, no evidence. Maybe they hadn't done it yet. They were still brushing hands when they passed paperwork back and forth, enjoying an accidental boob graze here and there. She thought of Brad pulling an accidental boob graze on Rachel the puttana and her jaw clenched.

And then an even worse thought came into her mind. Maybe

the reason she wasn't finding any evidence was because they were staying late at the office and going at it bare naked on top of Brad's desk. Anyway, even if she didn't have *that* kind of evidence, she had other proof.

"I know he's cheating on me," she said into her phone headset. "I found the cell phone bill. He's made a ton of after-hours calls to Rachel's cell."

"You know for sure it's Rachel?" asked Erin.

"Oh, yes," Angela said grimly. "Believe me. I checked."

"I still can't believe it," Erin said. "He could be calling her about business."

"The kind of business that gets done while somebody's on her back." Oooh, she'd kill him dead.

"Maybe you should follow him," Erin suggested. Angela heard a muffled voice in the background. "We need to get on that right away," Erin said to the mystery person. Then to Angela, "Okay, I'm back."

"I shouldn't be calling you at work," Angela said. "I'm sorry."

"Don't be. We're there for each other. Remember?"

"Yeah. Thanks. And thanks for listening."

"No problem. I still don't think Brad would ever cheat on you, though. Really."

That was what Angela's mother had said, too. Mom had not been at all understanding. She'd informed Angela her husband was NOT cheating on her and concluded with the advice that Angela not do anything foolish, but instead concentrate on making her husband happy on Valentine's Day. And they said mothers were supposed to give you good advice. Ha!

"I never thought he would cheat, either, not until he started acting so guilty." Angela slammed the lid down on the washer.

"Innocent until proven guilty, that's what Megan would say," Erin advised.

"I know Brad. Something's going on," Angela insisted.

"Geez, I hope you're wrong. As far as I can see you guys have got a perfect marriage. Don't go bursting my bubble." Erin lowered her voice. "Here comes Gregory. I've got to go."

"And so do I," decided Angela. It was time to do something.

She arranged an after-preschool play date for Gabriella, then took Mandy over to her mother's. She didn't tell Mom what she was up to. Mom would have just given her a lecture about trusting her husband. Maybe Mom had forgotten about Grandpa Grigoni cheating on Grandma, but Angela remembered the story of how Grandma clocked the woman with her purse right in the middle of a busy restaurant. Sometimes a woman had to take action.

On the way into the city Angela called Brad on her cell phone. "Were you busy?"

"No, just about to go into a meeting. What's up?"

"Nothing. I just wanted to tell you that dinner might be a little late. I have to run some errands this afternoon."

"Okay."

"I guess you've got a full day, too," she said, fishing. She wasn't quite sure what she was fishing for, but she knew she'd recognize it once she caught it.

"Yeah, I do. I've got to go, Ang. I'll see you tonight."

"Okay." She rang off, and tossed the phone on the car's passenger seat.

She drummed her nails thoughtfully on the steering wheel. What did she know so far? Brad was still at the office. He hadn't gone out to lunch. If he was having an affair with Rachel they'd probably find a way to do lunch, among other things. She'd stake out the loan center and wait. When they came out, she'd follow them.

She parked across the street and down a half block from his building and drummed her fingernails, watching as people came in and out of the big, gray building and cars sloshed by on the rainy street. After an hour and a half she had a problem. Brad could be coming out any minute and she had to go to the bathroom. This never happened to detectives in movies. She told her bladder to be patient.

But her bladder wasn't listening. When it had to go, it had to go.

She got out of the car and ran across the street. There was a bathroom off the main lobby, far enough away from Brad's office that she could get in and out without him seeing her.

But wait. Marion the receptionist would see her. And she'd tell Brad.

Now Angela really had to go. What was she going to do? Inspired, she put her purse up to the side of her face, like a criminal on trial trying to avoid the cameras, and slipped into First National's loan center.

She was halfway down the hall when a female voice called, "May I help you?"

Marion! The jig was up.

Thinking fast, Angela dropped her voice a notch and said, "I was hoping I could use your bathroom. My car had a flat tire," she added, just to add some urgency.

"Right down the hall," said Marion. Her tone of voice made it sound like she thought Angela was completely whacked. Hopefully Marion wouldn't call security.

Angela hurried into the bathroom and did her business. Then, she opened the bathroom door a crack and peered out to make sure the coast was clear. She didn't see anything, but coming from down the hall she heard voices—a couple of men's voices, a woman's voice. One of the men's voices laughed. Brad! She'd know that laugh anywhere. That meant the female voice had to belong to Rachel.

The voices got closer and she drew back inside the bathroom. They were on their way to lunch, probably walking to the steak house down on the corner. She'd let them get out the door and then she'd follow them.

The voices were right by the bathroom now. *Give them time to get by.* She'd count to ten, slowly. *One, two . . .*

The door opened, and she turned away and pretended to be looking for something in her purse. A woman walked past her to a bathroom stall and she got a look at who it was in the mirror. Rachel!

Rachel went into a stall, and Angela slipped into the one next to it. She stayed there until she heard Rachel leave her stall and wash her hands. She forced herself to remain hidden until she heard Rachel exit the bathroom, then she bolted out of the stall and ran to the door.

She cracked it open and looked out. She didn't see anyone. The coast was clear. *Okay, go!* She hurried down the hall, keeping her purse to the side of her face. She was halfway to the door when she heard Brad's voice again. She whirled around and raced back to the bathroom.

Safely inside, she leaned against the door and tried to calm her breathing. That had been a close one.

Suddenly the door moved and she jumped away.

"Miss, are you all right?" Marion poked her head around the door. At the sight of Angela her eyes popped open wide. "Angela?"

Angela could feel her cheeks sizzling. "Oh. Hi, Marion."

"Are you all right?" Marion asked.

"Um, yeah. I was going to surprise Brad."

"He just left for lunch. If you hurry you can catch him."

"Okay," said Angela. "And Marion?"

Marion looked at her expectantly, maybe hoping for an explanation of her weird behavior.

"Don't tell Brad I was here. Okay? Then it wouldn't be a surprise."

"Okay," Marion said slowly.

"Thanks," Angela said, and left, trying to act like she hadn't a care in the world.

She got outside the building just in time to see Brad walking down the street with two other men. And Rachel.

Well, at least they weren't going to lunch, just the two of them. Hope seeped into her heart. Maybe Brad hadn't gone over the edge yet. Maybe she could still keep him safe at home.

But then the two men got into a car parked at the curb and drove off down the street and Rachel and Brad kept walking. *Oh, Brad. How could you?*

"I've got to lose weight faster," Angela said as the Bikinis dished up from their latest diet smorgasbord on Kizzy's counter.

"If you lose too fast you won't keep it off," said Megan, spooning some of Erin's Mexican veggie soup into a bowl.

"If I lose too slow I won't keep my husband," said Angela, making Kizzy frown disapprovingly. "I gained back half of what I lost on the diet pills," she added miserably.

"If it's any consolation, I'm not doing well, either," said Erin with a sigh.

"Maybe we need some kind of reward to help us stay motivated," Kizzy said. "A trophy or something that we can pass around. You know, whoever does the best in one week gets to take it home with her for that week."

"That's a great idea," Erin said. "What should we call it?"

"The Skinny Minnie Award," suggested Kizzy.

"The No-fat Nobel," cracked Megan.

Erin snapped her fingers and pointed to Megan. "The No-belly."

"The No-belly award. I like it," said Kizzy.

"There's a trophy shop not far from my office. I'll go there and find us something tomorrow on my lunch hour," Erin volunteered. "You know," she added thoughtfully. "Most athletes win a trophy and get some money, too. What if we each kicked in twenty-five dollars and the person who lost the most weight by bikini season got the pool as a reward?"

"Ooh, I like that," Angela said, perking up. "A hundred dollars would buy a new bikini and then some." She could already see herself in that bikini, strutting past Brad. Then out of the bikini as Brad made mad, passionate love to her.

"A new dress," said Kizzy.

"And shoes," added Angela, getting up. A bikini and high heels, just like Miss America wore—she would be *magnifica*. She grabbed her purse and fished out a twenty and a five and slapped them on the table. "Okay, ladies. Ante up."

They did, and put the money in an envelope marked "No-belly Prize Winner."

"And now, for dessert," Kizzy announced and disappeared into the kitchen.

She returned to the table with a cut-glass bowl full of a de-cadent-looking chocolate pudding dessert.

"That looks sinful," said Angela.

"It's almost guilt-free," said Kizzy. "I'm calling it Chocolate Rum Heaven."

"Chocolate pudding with rum. Where's the guilt-free part?" Megan asked.

"The guilt-free part is that it's sugar-free pudding, whipped cream—you can have that if you're Atkinsing it, right?—with no sugar added, and rum extract. No booze."

"Well, that sucks," said Erin.

"And how many calories are sticking out of the topping?" Megan asked, pointing to the bits of chocolate.

Kizzy shrugged. "Not many. I only used one dark chocolate bar."

"Well, it works for me," Angela said. "I'll get the dessert bowls."

"This is good," Erin said as they dug in.

Angela licked her spoon and closed her eyes. "Almost as good as sex."

"But not better," Kizzy added. "Nothing is better than sex. Choco-late is the world's best drug, but there are some things it will never replace."

Megan sighed.

Poor Megan, thought Angela. It was no fun to be alone. She remembered her mother's advice to concentrate on making her husband happy. Did she want to end up alone, trying to fill her days and her heart with chocolate recipes? She knew the answer to that. Mom was right. She needed to fight for her man.

So that night, she went home and fought like crazy. "Baby," Brad finally groaned, "I don't know what's gotten into you, but I like it."

She smiled as he pulled her close to him under the covers. *You think that was something, you just wait.*

As soon as the girls were fed Saturday morning, she went to the mall and made a beeline for Victoria's Secret and bought the sexiest nightgown they had, and a new bra and panties. It was not a cheap investment, but this was war, and war was never cheap. She stuffed the receipt into her wallet, then went to Nordstrom's perfume counter and bought more artillery. Back home she put away her purchases, then she went online and did some research, tapping the desk in excitement as she read. Ha! she thought with a grin as she found what she was looking for. This could be fun. If the Bikinis liked DDR, they'd love this. And maybe, just maybe, she could book a party before Valentine's Day next week. The night before would be great. She could put the girls to bed early and get Brad to go out with his brother or over to his parents for the evening.

She made the call and the answer was yes. Yes! This was going to be a Valentine's Day to remember. Now, back to the Web to send out an E-vite.

"Hey, baberino, what's for lunch?"

She nearly jumped out of her skin. Brad was already coming into their home office. She stood up to block the computer. "Oh, lunchtime already?"

"Twelve-thirty." He looked over her shoulder. "What are you up to?"

"Nothing. Just planning a party."

He gave her a teasing grin. "Yeah? For who? How do I know you're not having an affair?"

She frowned at him. "That is not funny."

"Sorry. So what are you doing? How come you're being so secretive?"

"Because it's a surprise. For Valentine's Day?"

He raised both eyebrows. "Oh, yeah?"

"Yeah. So, can you go open up a can of tomato soup? I'll be right out as soon as I finish with the surprise."

He was smiling now. "Okay. Although how you're going to top last night, I don't know."

Now she was smiling, too. "Oh, you'd be surprised." *Ha! Take that, hottie homewrecker. You'll never get him. Not now.*

Twelve

Kizzy read the E-vite from Angela with a frown. "Is she out of her mind?"

Lionel peered over her shoulder at the computer screen. "That sounds good to me."

"No men invited."

"Damn. You're going, though, right?"

She looked up at him. "What, I'm not good enough already?"

"Of course you are. I'd like to see you in action doing this, Kizzy girl."

She took a deep breath. "I swear, Lion, the things I do for you," she said, and typed, "It looks like I'm coming."

Megan stared at Angela's E-vite. She would have to be completely bombed out of her mind to do this. "This can take the place of diet club," Angela had written, "since we're not meeting Friday 'cause of Valentine's Day."

Valentine's Day, day of love, hearts and flowers, candy, couples, mortification, loneliness, resentment, grumpy behavior, eating too much, hating skinny women, resenting men with no taste who chased skinny women. No, wait. That was the old Megan. The new Megan loved Valentine's Day, loved hearts and flowers and candy—oh, wait, scratch the candy—loved hearts and flowers, and parties. So why not go to Angela's? It would give her something fun to look forward to. Well, sort of, if she could consider making a fool of herself fun. But these were women who liked and appreciated her. No one would laugh at her. And she didn't have to participate if she didn't want to. She could just come be a body, a getting-lighter-all-the-time body.

"I'll come be a watcher," she replied. There. Now she had something fun to look forward to, at least on the day before Valentine's Day.

But what about the day itself? She didn't want to be bummed on Valentine's Day. She sat at her desk a moment, chewing the corner of her lip. Okay, she was working on getting a new body, and she was changing the inside Megan, as well. What would the new and improved Megan like to do? She looked around her windowless office. The new and improved Megan would like to fill her life, and this pathetic shark tank, with beauty. She looked up the phone number for Changing Seasons, then placed an order.

"How would you like that to read?" asked Hope.

"To my new woman, from your number one admirer," Megan said with a smile.

"And who would you like that sent to?" asked Hope.

"Megan Wales, the First Orca Trust Tower, forty-first floor."

"Okay. And how would you like to pay for that?"

"MasterCard."

"And the name on the card?"

This was embarrassing. "Ummm. Megan Wales." Megan's cheeks suddenly felt sunburned.

There was a moment's silence on the other end of the line.

Megan's sunburn got hotter.

Then Hope surprised her. "You go, girl."

And she did. After finishing up on the phone, she took an early lunch break and went for a brisk walk to that little card shop, where she bought white and pink crepe paper, a box of kid Valentine cards, and a big, lacey heart filled with sugar-free chocolates. This was going to be a great Valentine's Day.

Normally Kizzy would be excited to go to a party, but she drove to Angela's house under a cloud of skepticism. This was dumb. She wasn't twenty anymore, and she was so big she'd probably break the pole. Why had she said she'd come, anyway?

She got to Angela's to find that the rest of the Bikinis had already arrived. And Angela's living room had been transformed. She had the lights turned down and votive candles sat everywhere—on the coffee table, on the end tables, on the bookshelves. Their instructor had set up a table laden with props: pink boas, feather-trimmed masks, and tiaras. The furniture had been pushed to the corners of the living room and there, in the middle of the room stood the pole. It seemed to taunt her. *I'm going to break your big ass, girl.*

Angela rushed up to her and hugged her. "Isn't this exciting? We are going to be so sexy by the time we're done."

"Or sore," Kizzy said, eyeing the two inches of steel with suspicion. She saw bottled water and Pellegrino already in evidence. Kizzy wasn't a big drinker, but right now she'd have given anything for a glass of white wine and damn the calories. Sadly, it didn't appear to be on the menu.

"Can I get you some bottled water or Pellegrino?" Angela offered. "Or we've got Diet Seven-Up."

"Water," said Kizzy. And anesthetic, she thought as Angela hurried off to fetch her a bottle. She crossed the room to join Erin and Megan, who were on the floor stretching with their instructor, and made sure to give the threatening rod of steel a wide berth.

Their instructor jumped up from the floor and glided over to greet Kizzy. She had a toned dancer's body and long, blond hair. Any dancer worth her salt should have long hair, Kizzy thought, fingering her short locks.

"Hi, I'm Jilly," the woman said. "And you must be Kizzy?"

Kizzy nodded.

"We're just doing a little stretching so our muscles will get warmed up," Jilly explained. "Would you like to join us?"

"Why not?" Kizzy said, and joined the others on the floor. "I suppose it's too late to go home."

"Absolutely," said Erin. "And when you find out how much Angela forked out for this you won't dare."

Kizzy stared at her. "She paid for this torture?"

"We're going to kick in," Megan added.

"Oh, no you're not," Angela told her. She gave Kizzy her bottle of water. "My idea, I'm paying. Well, for part of it," she amended. "My mom's paying for half."

"Your mom?" Kizzy echoed. She knew her eyes were bugging out. If she'd told her mother she was planning something like this, her mother would have descended on her with an entire army of church ladies.

Angela made a face. "She thinks it will be good for my self-esteem."

"It's worth every penny," Jilly assured her. "Sometimes we women lose that connection to our sexuality. This can give you new confidence."

"I don't need confidence in that area," Kizzy assured her. "What I need is confidence that that pole of yours will hold me."

Jilly smiled at her. "It will hold you fine, trust me. Okay, ladies, now let's stand and stretch our arms." She hopped up, linked her hands and reached for the ceiling in one fluid motion. All she needed, thought Kizzy, was the tutu.

The others followed her through the rest of the stretches, and Megan muttered, "This reminds me of my old gym class. When does the fun start?"

"Right now," Jilly said. "Before we begin with the lessons, let's form a friendship circle around the pole. Bring your drinks."

They grabbed their bottled drinks and gathered around.

"Now, let's toast to our inner goddess," said their instructor.

"Let's just toast to not breaking anything," Kizzy suggested, and the others giggled.

"To not breaking anything," Angela echoed. "And to driving our men crazy."

"To becoming someone new," Megan added softly.

"And you will feel like someone new when we're done," Jilly said. "I promise."

"Well, then, let's do it," said Angela.

And so they started learning how to slide up and down and around that stupid pole. As the oldest and their fearless leader, Kizzy was made to go first. She felt like a complete idiot, even with the Bikinis hooting and clapping, and telling her she was doing great.

"Okay, that's enough," she decided after a halfhearted effort. She was a pretty good dancer but a lousy actress, and it was impossible for her to get it on with a pole. The cheesy blues CD Jilly had brought didn't help. "I think I'm allergic to feathers," she added, removing her boa.

Erin, who weighed the least of all of them, looked gorgeous with her blond hair flying, and the way she was moving promised a great wedding night. And Angela got so into the whole thing, Erin told her she could moonlight as a stripper. And then there was Megan, serious, cerebral Megan. With moves like that, singleness was wasted on her.

As Megan had feared, pole dancing was not for sissies. She was already finding new muscles that had been hiding from her for years. But she was finding something else, too. As the rest of the Bikinis called encouraging words to her and rooted for her, she became freer and freer. She spun around the pole like a human tornado, her pink boa caressing her skin, her hair whipping out behind her, and suddenly she wasn't Megan the big girl anymore. She was someone new, someone free and sexy and desirable.

"My goodness," Angela told her when she finally sat down after her turn at the grand finale performance, "you were amazing."

Amazing. Megan smiled. Tonight she was pole-dancing. Tomorrow she was going to be getting flowers and handing out Valentine cards. Life was good.

"That was fun," she said to Angela later as she was leaving, and pressed a fifty-dollar bill into her palm.

"No, this is my treat," Angela insisted, trying to hand it back.

"I want to help. And, believe me, it was worth every penny."

"Are you sure?" asked Angela.

"Absolutely." She didn't know whether or not her future held a man, but for sure, it held a pole. She was going to take classes and get really good at this.

Or not. She woke up so sore the next morning she could hardly move. She rolled herself to the edge of the bed and let herself fall over the edge, taking the blankets with her and landing with an oomph. She caterpillared her way free, forced her legs out to the side, and did a stretch. Ohhhh. The electric chair had to be less painful than this.

No pain, no gain. She stretched again, every muscle in her body crying.

Okay, off to the shower. Warm water would help. So would about half a bottle of Advil.

The Advil had kicked in by the time she got to the office, and remembering how good she felt boosted her mood. She was early this morning, so she was able to deliver many of her valentines in secret. The last one—a big card featuring Tweety bird—she taped to Tanner's office door. Then she went into her own cage and admired her handiwork from the afternoon before. Pink and white crepe paper streamers looped from corner to corner, and the big heart sat on her desk. It looked like a party.

She was just trying a candy when Tanner arrived. He looked around and scowled. "Are you bored? Do you need more work?"

"Just celebrating love."

He held up the valentine. "I see. And what is this celebrating?"

It was an innocuous card and she'd only signed her name, although she'd been tempted to write, "To Simon Legree from his number one slave." She shrugged. "I gave one to everyone." She held out the candy box. "Chocolate? They're sugar free."

He grimaced. "That's disgusting."

She wasn't sure whether he was disgusted by her generosity or the fact that she was offering him sugar-free chocolate. She was about to ask when her phone rang and her extension lit up.

It was James the receptionist. "You've got flowers."

"Flowers? For me?"

Tanner shook his head, still frowning. "Well, go get them. Hopefully, they're from a potential new client."

Clients, rainmakers. Suddenly the day wasn't quite so wonderful.

Thirteen

$\mathcal{M}$egan stopped by Femme Fit on her way home from work. The gym was practically a ghost town, with only a couple of women making the rounds on the exercise-machine circuit. Of course, it would be. Most women were home getting ready to celebrate a romantic evening with their significant others.

Raine Goldman, the owner, had decked the place out in honor of the holiday, hanging purple and red heart-shaped foil doilies in the window. A vase of red roses sat on the reception desk, and behind them stood Raine herself, wearing pink warm-ups and only a hint of a smile.

Megan walked up to the desk to deliver the small box of sugar-free chocolates she'd bought for the woman who had been so supportive when she first began this scary fitness journey. Megan didn't know if Raine had anyone in her life or not. She was a nice enough looking woman, with a flair for makeup and a great colorist somewhere who helped her keep her age something of a mystery. Megan guessed she was in her late forties, but who knew? Most women these days didn't look their age. No wedding band, but she could have a boyfriend. As many times as Megan had come to the gym, the subject of men had never come up. Maybe Raine was depressed because it was Valentine's Day and she was alone.

"I brought you something," Megan said, offering Raine a heart-shaped box of chocolates. "Sugar free."

Raine smiled. Sadly. "Oh, Megan, that was so sweet of you. Thanks. I wish everyone was like you," she added.

If her mouth fell any lower it would pull off the whole bottom half of her face. "Are you okay?" Megan asked. Of course she wasn't okay, but Megan hoped by asking she would encourage Raine to get whatever was bugging her off her chest.

"Just having a bad day is all."

"Bad day? You look like you just got sued for everything you own and then some," Megan observed.

Raine's face went white. "Oh, my God. Don't even say that," she said in a whisper.

And then Megan knew. "Is someone suing you?"

"Angie," Raine called to her assistant, "can you come man the desk?" Then she grabbed Megan by the arm and towed her back to her office. Megan was barely seated when Raine burst out, "What can I do if someone is ruining my reputation?"

"You have legal recourse," Megan said. "Maybe you should give me some specifics."

Raine bit her lip. "There is someone who has been telling customers that my equipment isn't safe."

"Is this someone from another gym?" Megan asked.

"No. She was a member here. For about two weeks," Raine added in disgust. "She was out of shape. We advised her to go slow. She claims she hurt her back on our equipment, and that no one taught her how to use it properly, but that's not true. We show everyone how to use the equipment, and besides, she wrote on her medical history form that she's had chronic back troubles."

Suddenly Megan knew exactly whom Raine was talking about. She'd only seen the woman once, and once had been enough for

Megan. The woman had been a real downer for the others, who were trying to make the most of their misery by joking and chatting as they made the rounds. Not this babe. She'd moaned and complained her way through the whole workout. And one of the things she'd complained about had been her back. She'd looked like a nuisance lawsuit waiting to happen.

"You have insurance, right?" Megan asked.

"Yes, but I think she's after more than free physical therapy. She told someone the other day she was going to sue me," Raine said. Her mouth trembled. "I was just about to start franchising. She'll ruin me."

"No she won't. Have your lawyer send her a letter telling her to cease and desist slandering you or you'll be forced to take legal action. That should make her go away."

"I don't have a lawyer on retainer," Raine said, sounding panicked.

It was like a gift from Cupid, a little gray cloud right here in front of her. "As a business person, you should. And meanwhile I'd be happy to write this woman a letter on our Weisman, Waters, and Green stationery. That should put the fear of God in her."

"Would you? That would be great."

"Not a problem," Megan said, standing. "Just get me her name and address and I'll take care of it for you. But you really should think about what I said. It's a good idea to have a lawyer on retainer, especially as your business grows."

Raine looked at her eagerly. "Would you be my lawyer? Do you handle this sort of thing?"

"As a matter of fact, I do. And I'd be happy to be your lawyer," Megan said.

She was grinning like a woman who had just won a landmark case when she left. Yes! She had just brought in her first client. Granted, it was a small business, but hey, small businesses needed love, too. Maybe becoming a rainmaker wasn't so much about working a room as being interested in people and what happened to them. That, she was finding, was something she could do.

She got in her little gray Saturn and punched on the radio. Gwen Stefani was singing "Sweet." That was a good word to describe how this day had ended. No big romance, no tangled sheets, but Megan had just taken a bite of a sweet future, and that was a big enough buzz for her.

Kizzy had promised to serve Lionel all his favorite food for Valentine's Day. She'd stopped on the way home and picked up a bucket of fried chicken and some Ben & Jerry's ice cream. Then she'd made garlic mashed potatoes, cornbread, and a big tossed salad. They were going to have a Valentine feast tonight.

But Lionel came home with little appetite, not even for the sugar-free chocolates he'd brought her.

"What's wrong, Lion?" she asked, reaching across the table and laying a hand on his arm.

He shoved away his plate. "I guess I'm not very hungry."

"I can see that. But you've been waiting all week for this meal. What's going on?"

"You remember Joe Moran?"

"From work? The big man with the beard?"

Lionel nodded. "He had a stroke today."

"Oh, no. Have you heard anything? Is he going to be okay?"

"I don't know. He was diabetic."

"Stroke sometimes comes with the territory if you don't watch it. Poor man." Kizzy was borderline, herself. She pushed her plate away, too.

"He said once that the doctor had been after him to lose weight, that if he didn't things were just going to get worse."

Kizzy looked at Lionel's gut and felt a shadow pass over her. What would happen to Lionel if he kept on snacking for two?

"On the way home I heard something on the radio," he continued morosely.

Had someone famous died? "What?"

"Did you know that some doctor has found a link between prostate cancer and obesity?"

Lionel wasn't obese. He was just . . . on his way. The shadow got bigger. "Does that worry you?"

He frowned. "Hell, yeah."

"Maybe you need to make some changes so you won't get obese," Kizzy said, trying to keep her voice gentle.

He pushed away from the table and marched off.

Well, this was a romantic Valentine's Day. "Lion," Kizzy called, running after him.

He didn't say anything, just kept marching to the garage. She followed him and watched gape-mouthed as he made a raid on his junk-food stash. He flipped open the toolbox, yanked out the candy bars, and hurled them into the garbage. Next went the Pringles. She watched in amazement as he pulled junk food from places she never would have dreamed of looking.

"Go, Lion," she said, and applauded him.

When he was done he marched back over to her and stood, legs apart, hands on his hips, like a gladiator claiming victory. "I don't need that shit."

"Oh, Lion, that's the best valentine you've ever given me!" She threw her arms around him and kissed him. "You're my hero."

Brad had offered to take Angela out to dinner, but she'd turned him down, telling him it was too hard to get a babysitter on Valentine's Day. "Anyway, tonight you get the surprise I was planning."

She'd taken the girls to the park that afternoon and worn them out on the play equipment. Then she'd fed them early and gotten them in their jammies. Now it was seven o'clock and they were tucked away in bed sound asleep, and it was showtime.

She set the tray with Brad's and her dinner on the hope chest at the foot of the bed, then stepped back to survey the room. It looked good. There was the steak and baked potatoes with fresh asparagus, Brad's fave. Asti Spumante, her fave, sat chilling in the ice bucket on her side of the bed, and she had the little plate of chocolate-covered strawberries and a can of whipped cream ready and waiting on her nightstand. The bedroom looked very sexy, if she did say so herself. She'd draped red and white silk scarves everywhere, put red light bulbs in the bedside lamps, and scattered rose petals all the way from the door to the bed. The flowers Brad had brought home for her sat in a vase on the dresser. The CD player was all set up and ready to go. She'd already tried her routine, so she knew the bedpost would hold her. She grabbed her rose spray perfume and gave the room one final spritz. There. She smiled and cinched her bathrobe belt more tightly around her costume. Time to get her audience.

She went downstairs to the living room, where Brad had been confined ever since he'd gotten home from work. "You can come upstairs now."

"What are you up to?" he asked with a smile.

"Come see," she said coyly, and took his hand and led him up the stairs. Oh, this was going to be good. She'd like to see Rachel the puttana try and compete with this. She threw open the bedroom door. "Dinner is ready. Are you?"

He looked around, his mouth hanging open. "Wow, Ang."

She took his suit jacket and slipped him out of it, then draped the jacket over her slipper chair. The shirt and pants and shoes followed. She barely had to nudge him to get him on the bed. Then she played geisha and removed his socks. "Now, how about something to eat?"

"Sure," he said, grinning.

She passed him his plate and he sat on the bed, feet stretched out in front of him and dug in. She watched him eat, feeling very pleased with herself. This had been a great idea. They hadn't eaten a meal in bed since their honeymoon. She uncorked the champagne and poured them both glasses.

"This is great, baberino," Brad said. "Much better than going out."

"I thought so," she said smugly and took a sip of champagne. *Bene.* She took another sip.

"Aren't you going to eat?" he asked.

"Oh, yeah." She retrieved her plate and hopped onto the bed next to him. And took another sip of champagne. "How's your steak?"

"Just the way I like it," he said. He nodded at her bathrobe. "What've you got on under there?"

She gave him a Mona Lisa smile. "You'll see. Have some more champagne." She freshened his glass. And, well, well, hers was almost empty. She drank the last of it and freshened her glass, too. *Wooh!*

"You know, we should put the girls to bed early more often," Brad said.

"Yes, we should," she agreed and had some more champagne. She took a bite of potato and closed her eyes, savoring the treat. Sour cream, butter—she was going to have an orgasm right now. She took another bite and washed it down with champagne. Okay, one more bite of potato, then she should probably quit. Well, make that two. The skin was the best part. You couldn't not eat the skin. Oh. Where'd the potato go? Inside of her, every little bit, and all those calories were now swimming to her tummy as fast as they could. Who cared? It was Valentine's Day. *Salute!* She finished off the contents of her glass.

"Are you going to finish that steak?" Brad asked, pointing to the meat on her plate.

It wasn't good to eat too much before a performance. She'd read that somewhere. She held out her plate. "No. You can have it. I'll just have a little more champagne," she decided and hauled the bottle out of the ice bucket. It sloshed a little going into her glass. *Oops.*

She posed seductively next to him, knees curled up, one arm draped over the bed pillows, and rubbed her lips with her glass.

"I'll finish this later," Brad decided, and set his plate on the floor. He took hers, too.

Now it was just the two of them, the champagne, and the bed. "Close your eyes," she cooed as soon as he'd sat back up.

He smiled and closed them. She set down her glass and plucked a chocolate-covered strawberry from the plate. "Okay, open your mouth."

He obliged and she inserted the top half of the strawberry. He bit down and juices flowed over the corners of his mouth. "Whoa."

He started to open his eyes. "Keep your eyes closed," she instructed. Then she leaned over and licked the juice from the corners of his lips, making him moan. "More?"

"More," he repeated.

She giggled and put in the rest of the strawberry, then repeated the licking process. "Stick out your tongue." He did and she sprayed a dollop of whipped cream on it. Then, when his tongue was barely in his mouth, she kissed him, giving the whipped cream a stir. "That's for starters," she whispered when she was done. "I have a whole can."

"Am I in heaven?" he asked.

Oh, this was fun! "Keep those eyes closed." She chugged some more champagne, then slid off the bed, tilting to the side as she went. *Oops, stay upright here.* Her head was buzzing now. Maybe she shouldn't have had that last glass. Oh, well. It was Valentine's Day. *La bella vita* and all that.

She went to the CD player and started the music, then turned around to face her audience of one. "Okay, open your eyes."

Ravel's *Boléro* (which Kizzy had loaned her, assuring her that it would be perfect for this) began to serenade them—just the flute and a soft, pulsing rhythm. Angela untied the sash and opened her bathrobe, giving Brad his first glimpse of her Victoria's Secret purchase. Why hadn't she stuck to her diet better? She could have looked so much hotter. *Never mind that now. Stay in the second.*

Brad was obviously in the second. He was all eyes.

She let the robe slip halfway down her arms. Then she began the slow little dance step toward the bed that she'd practiced earlier. And all the while the drums thrummed. Bum! Bum, bum, bum, bum bum. Bum! Bum, bum, bum, bum, bum. *Whoops. Watch those rose petals. They're slippery.*

Brad moved to come catch her. She held up an arm. "I'm okay." *My head feels like a balloon, but I'm okay.* She let the bathrobe fall all the way off and snaked her way to the edge of the bed, her movements slow. The music was getting louder now. Two instruments danced together, repeating the melody. She picked up the champagne and poured herself some more. Then she planted one leg on the edge of the bed in her best porn star pose (did porn stars pose?) and quaffed the champagne. *I see London, I see France. Where are Angela's underpants? Hahahahaha.*

Brad was really grinning now. Oh, this was good.

More instruments had joined the party and the drums were getting louder. Or was that the blood pumping in her head? She moved to climb onto the bed and fell forward on her nose. Ouch! That hadn't happened when she practiced this. Brad helped her up, bringing their bodies close, and she pushed him away with a wicked grin, and backed up. *Wait a minute. Let's stop and look where we're going. We could back right off the bed.* Okay, there was the bedpost. *Time to unleash your inner temptress. You have the power. No woman is going to be able to take your man from you.*

The music was loud now and she was definitely in the second. The horns had joined the wind instruments and the drums were beating, beating, beating, pumping, pumping, pumping.

"Oh, baby." Brad was practically panting.

Yes, yes, yes. She had him in her power. The music got wild. The cymbals crashed. She leaned away from the pole for her grand finale and . . . whoa, who was tipping the bed!

With a yelp she went over the edge.

"Ang!" Brad was beside her before she could say "bed spin." "Baby, are you okay?"

"The room is spinning. Oh, Brad."

"Here." He hauled her onto the bed and laid her out. "There. Better?"

She closed her eyes. "I think so." Well, actually no, but she didn't want to ruin the mood.

"Good," he murmured, and kissed her, sliding a hand up her thigh.

"I didn't get to do my big finale," she protested. "We haven't gotten to the whipped cream."

"Later," he whispered. "Right now all I want is you."

All I want is you. Music to her ears. She wrapped her arms around him. "Here I am," she murmured. And belched. *Oops. Not very sexy.*

Brad never noticed.

Fourteen

Adam had planned a perfect night. First dinner, then they were going to the big Valentine's bash at the Last Resort, where there would be dancing. Tonight's cover charge included a Mardi Gras–style mask. Erin always wanted to go to Mardi Gras. This seemed like a good warm-up.

Adam had already gotten her a single red rose—very romantic—and the DVD of *While You Were Sleeping,* her and her mom's favorite classic chick flick, and now they were dining in style at Two Turtledoves, the swankiest restaurant in Heart Lake.

And she was looking at the menu, trying not to have a guilt attack. Had Adam known how expensive this place was? She peered at him over the menu. "I don't think we can even afford the appetizers."

"Yes we can," he assured her. "I budgeted for it. Order what you want."

Here was a shocker. He almost had a heart attack over every wedding expense but he could take her to the fanciest restaurant in town for Valentine's Day and not blink an eye.

Maybe that's because it was his idea. Maybe it's not just about the money. Maybe he likes being in control.

Erin frowned. Dan Rockwell was becoming way too frequent a visitor in her head.

Now, now, said her inner mother, *Adam is trying to do something nice for you, so quit questioning his motives and appreciate it.*

Dan Rockwell was the one who'd put that thought in her mind. Her inner mother should get after him. Erin looked again at the menu. She had never been faced with such expensive choices in her life. The guys she'd dated in the past took her to places where she only had to choose between burgers and nachos supreme.

Well, okay, Adam had said to order what she wanted. And she wanted lobster. She'd only had it once when her mom made it for her eighteenth birthday, but she'd never forgotten how wonderful it tasted.

"I think I'll have the Australian lobster," she said.

"Good choice," said Adam. Had his face just lost color? It was hard to tell in the candlelight. "How about a first course?"

Oh, she couldn't.

"Let's split one," he suggested. "Want the calamari?"

"Okay."

Their waiter slipped silently to the table and Brad ordered: the calamari, her Australian lobster, and chicken risotto, the cheapest thing on the menu. Probably not what he wanted at all.

She knew it. He was in sticker shock. She braced for his answer when the waiter asked what they would like to drink. Water, of course.

But no, he actually ordered wine. Okay, maybe he had wanted the chicken risotto.

The waiter took the menus and slipped away and she let her gaze drift out the restaurant window. This side of the lake wasn't as developed as the rest of it and firs, pines, and alders still hugged much of the shoreline. Farther down she could see house lights twinkling, reflected on the water's surface. The lake was calm tonight, and looking out at it made her think of old movies and romance novels. This would be a great place to raise kids.

She turned and smiled at Adam. "It's beautiful, isn't it? I'd love to live out here. Maybe Aunt Mellie would sell us the house. The commute's not that bad. Working and partying in the city, chilling out at the lake—what a perfect life."

"Live here? Babe, once I'm done with med school we can go anywhere."

Erin blinked in surprise. "I thought you applied to intern at Virginia Mason."

He shrugged. "That's not the only place."

"I know." He'd also applied at Providence and Harborview.

"My dad is pulling some strings. Fingers crossed, babe. I could end up at New York Presbyterian."

"New York?" she said faintly. "But that's on the other side of the country. What about family and friends? You never told me you applied to intern in New York. I thought we'd be living in Seattle."

"But think about the swanky parties you can plan in NYC," he said. "Are you telling me you'd pick this place over New York? Except for the Last Resort and Brewsters' they roll up the streets at nine."

"We could live in Seattle, in your apartment."

"Seattle can't compare to New York. And here? You've got plans for your life. You don't want to be a small-town girl."

He was right of course. A big city was the perfect host for an event planner. "Good point," she conceded.

She thought of her conversation with her aunt. There was something about living in a place where you had a history, of being near those you loved. But there was also much to be said for striking out and making your mark in the world.

She could strike out as far as New York, especially if she was doing it with Adam. He looked absolutely delicious tonight in that black turtleneck. His blue eyes appeared translucent in the candlelight. "I can live anywhere. Who cares where you live as long as you're with the person you love?"

He reached across the table and took her hand. "That's my girl. You'll love it there. Trust me."

The waiter returned with their wine and Adam sampled it and gave the nod to pour. This would be their future, dining in lovely, expensive restaurants at tables covered with white linen tablecloths and fine crystal and silver. Once Adam was a doctor, once she had launched her business, they'd both be successful, happy, and financially secure. She'd never have to worry about being sick because her doctor husband would take care of her. They'd both live to a ripe, old age. And their life would be perfect.

He raised his glass and smiled at her. "To us."

She mirrored the action. "To us."

"And speaking of us." She pulled the little gift bag she'd carried into the restaurant from under her seat. "Happy Valentine's Day."

"What have we got here?" he asked, smiling.

"Open it and see."

He did and pulled out a can of Almond Roca. "My favorite. Thanks, babe."

"There's more."

He fished inside the tissue paper and brought out a five-by-seven-inch pewter frame holding a picture of them taken on New Year's Eve, the night they got engaged. They were at his friend Dave's, snuggled together on the couch, holding champagne glasses and grinning like it was Christmas morning.

He was looking at it like he wasn't sure what it was.

"I thought you could put it on your desk," she said.

"Absolutely. Thank you."

The waiter arrived with their calamari and Adam shoved the presents back in the bag. "This looks good," he said, eyeing the food.

For a moment Erin found herself disappointed. She'd expected just a little more enthusiasm.

That's not very realistic, her inner mother whispered. True. A woman couldn't expect a man to gush over things the way her girlfriends did. Maybe she should have bought him something at Car Toys. He'd have probably gushed over that.

He did thank you, pointed out her inner mother.

True.

The dinner was perfect. Lobster was just as wonderful as she'd remembered, and the wine gave her a happy buzz. And now for the finishing touch: dessert. Erin had been salivating over the chocolate lava cake she'd seen a woman enjoying one table over.

She smiled up at the waiter, who stood poised to take her order. "Dessert? Absolutely."

"What about your diet?" Adam asked.

Her taste buds suddenly went dry. "My diet?" It was Valentine's Day. Who dieted on Valentine's Day?

"You want to split something?" Adam offered. He turned to the waiter. "She's dieting."

Erin's cheeks sizzled. Adam might as well have pinned a big, scarlet *D* on her chest.

Like she was going to order anything now? "I'll pass," she said. She could have sworn the waiter nodded approvingly.

"I guess we'll take the check then," said Adam.

The waiter left and she scowled at her fiancé. "That was totally tasteless."

"What?"

"You didn't have to say right in front of the waiter that I'm on a diet."

"But you are. Aren't you?"

"That is beside the point. And it's totally uncool to mention it when it's Valentine's Day."

"I didn't mean to be uncool. I was just trying to be supportive."

"Please don't be supportive like that ever again. That was completely humiliating."

"Sorry," he said.

She sighed. "Oh, well. You saved my diet from death by chocolate, so I guess I'll have to forgive you."

It was just as well she hadn't had dessert, she decided when she got a peek at the check. Adam had already paid enough.

She offered to take care of the tip and he let her. "The dinner was great," she told him as they slipped out of their seats. "Thanks." She hugged his arm and they started to leave, but she suddenly realized something was missing. "Your present!"

"Oh, yeah. Don't want to forget that," he said.

But he had. It wasn't as glam as dinner and dancing, but she'd put a lot of thought into his present. "You did like it, didn't you?" she asked as they walked out the door.

"Of course I did," he said, and hugged her to him. "I love Almond Roca."

"And?" she prompted, giving him a playful nudge.

He grinned. "And you."

Okay, good enough.

Their next stop was the Last Resort. The little club had opened in Heart Lake only a few months ago, but it was already the place to be on a weekend. It was decorated to look like a lounge from the late fifties, and every time Erin entered it she expected to run into Ingrid Bergman or Audrey Hepburn. Small tables with candle lamps dotted the floor with soft spots of light. Each of those tables held an old, chunky ashtray, usually filled with cocktail munchies. Black-and-white signed pictures of visiting B celebrities like former Sonics basketball coaches and the professor from *Gilligan's Island* marched along the far wall. One corner of the room held a small stage for a dance band or a DJ, although it was usually set up for karaoke singing or a comic or an MC on nights when trivia was the thing. The dance floor wasn't huge, but it could pack in a lot of people on a Saturday night. A big tropical fish tank divided the waiting area from the lounge, which was already a herd of people— most under the age of thirty. Tonight a DJ was set up and already spinning tunes, and some of the herd were shimmying around the floor. Many wore Valentine finery, others were costumed like French maids, pirates, or superheroes. Everyone wore their Mardi Gras masks. Erin suddenly thought of the masked-ball scene in *The Phantom of the Opera* and felt a tingle go down her back.

The bar was packed, too, she noticed as she and Adam donned their masks and made their way past it to the last unoccupied table in a far corner. It was mostly singles hoping to hook up with someone before the night was over. On Valentine's Day? Fat chance. Being by yourself on Valentine's Day was so not fun, so why would any sane person come out in public and announce it?

"This place is a mob scene," Adam said in disgust as they settled at their table. He ran a hand up Erin's arm. "Let's go back to the house and forget this."

"This is going to be fun," Erin insisted.

He cocked his head. He was wearing a tragedy mask, and the gesture looked oddly gothic. "Yeah?"

"You look scary," she informed him.

"Well, you look beautiful," he said.

She felt beautiful in her hot red dress, with her red sequined mask, beautiful and mysterious. It was a great way to feel on such a romantic day.

Their cocktail waitress came up.

"What do you want, babe?" Adam asked.

"Girl Gone Wild," Erin decided.

"Scotch, rocks," Adam told the waitress and she hurried off. "Going wild sounds good," he told Erin.

"Then let's get on the dance floor," she suggested, standing up.

Of course, it was too noisy to hear, but she was sure he'd just sighed. She knew he wanted to go home and collect his Valentine reward, but he could just wait a while. She took his hand and started boogying her way to the dance floor, Adam lumbering along behind like a captive bear on parade.

They barely had room to move, but she managed. The DJ was playing Sierra, who was singing about acting like a boy, and the music thrummed through Erin's veins. And, now that he was out on the floor, Adam was getting into the dancing, too. He was such a great dancer, graceful, gorgeous, and strong, and she loved it when he got physical, which he was doing right now, whipping her up against him and then spinning her till she couldn't stand up straight. Oh, yeah. This was fun. They stayed on the dance floor for four more songs. By the time they were done, Erin was hot and dying of thirst. And back at their table, her drink was waiting.

Adam saluted her with his glass.

She smiled at him and drank up. Moments like this, when he was being romantic and sweet, were when she remembered why they were an us. Adam was the most perfect man on the planet.

"So, what do you say we go home?"

"Just a little longer," she begged. "We just got here."

He slouched back against his chair and consoled himself with another sip of his Scotch.

He had done a lot to make sure she had a great evening. She supposed they didn't have to stay here all night. But. "One more dance," she said, offering a compromise.

"Okay," he agreed. "I know that really means three, so let me hit the john first."

She rewarded him with a smile. Okay, three more dances. That was a very good compromise.

He left and she sat watching the revelers and sipping her drink. Whoa, this stuff was well named. It packed a punch. But it suited her mood. A dark club, a Mardi Gras mask, a new, red dress—it was all a recipe for magic. Maybe she could persuade Adam to stay a little longer. So far the night had been wonderful, but she was sure if they stayed longer they'd go beyond wonderful and find the magic.

She felt a hand on her shoulder and jumped. Adam didn't usually sneak up on her like that. She looked up and saw that it wasn't Adam standing in back of her. It was Zorro.

He didn't say a word, just took her hand and tugged her from her seat. Here was the magic.

But it came with the wrong man. "I'm with someone," Erin protested.

"Yeah, me," said Zorro, and towed her out to the dance floor.

It was a slow dance. Adam would be pissed. And he'd kill Zorro.

Bob Seger and Martina McBride sang "Chances Are" as Zorro drew Erin up against him and started them swaying. The body contact sent a zing from her bra to her . . . "Dan!" She pulled back.

"No. Zorro," he corrected her in a phony Spanish accent.

She frowned at him. "What are you doing here? Why aren't you at work?"

"I've got Fridays off now, for good behavior."

"Well, this is not good behavior," she informed him. "My fiancé will be here any minute."

"So?"

"So he won't like me dancing with you."

"What, he won't let you dance with an old friend?"

"An old nuisance," Erin corrected.

Dan grinned. It was ridiculous how sexy a strip of black cloth could make a man look. "Aw, come on. You know you love me." He sobered. "But do you know you love him?"

She jerked out of Dan's arms. "Of course I do."

"Okay, okay." He pulled her back to him. "I just want to see you happy. If this is the guy who's gonna do it, then great."

"Thank you," Erin said stiffly.

And just when she thought they had this all settled, Dan added, "So tell me why he's the right one."

"You know, my own brother hasn't given me this kind of third degree."

"Your bro's a dipshit. Anyway, he's in California. He deputized me."

Erin gave a scornful snort. "Right."

"He did. You can ask him. So, tell me, why will this guy make you happy?"

"Because." Now, there was an impressive answer. It was that Girl Gone Wild. It was fuddling her brain. She couldn't think.

But she could feel. She was very conscious of their bodies

brushing against each other, of Dan's hand warm against her lower back. Ooh, and she was feeling things other places, too.

This is not good, fretted her inner mother.

"Because?" Dan prompted.

Because? What were they talking about? Oh, yes, Adam. "Because he'll always be there for me." There. That should explain everything.

"A lot of guys could fill that bill."

"He was there for me when my mom died." Adam had been a strong shoulder to cry on, her shelter in the storm, her rock, and she could never forget that.

"Some of us were out of the country when your mom died."

That time had been a horrible blur, but Erin suddenly remembered the card she'd received from Dan, the one with the military return address. She had it tucked away in a floral hatbox, along with all the other letters and condolence cards she'd received. "Wish I could be there with you," he'd written. "Hope you have a big wake in your mom's honor. She was an awesome lady."

Adam had never known her mother.

But he'd known grief, and he'd helped Erin through hers. He'd help her through her whole life. "Adam is perfect for me. He's handsome, he's fun, and he's very together. We'll make a good team."

"You forgot a couple of things."

"Like what?"

"Kind. Generous."

"He's kind. And as for generous, he just spent a fortune on me tonight."

"It's Valentine's Day. What guy doesn't spend a fortune on the biggest get-lucky day of the year?"

"You're disgusting," Erin informed him.

"Not disgusting. Truthful."

She looked over Dan's shoulder and saw Adam approaching. He'd lost the Mardi Gras mask, making it easy to see that he was mad. She put some space between her and Dan.

It was a little too late. When Adam reached them he was look-ing like he'd just gotten a taste of something sour. "Erin?"

"Adam." She shouldn't be sounding so flustered. She hadn't done anything to be ashamed of. She may have felt a few things, but . . . "This is our old family friend," she began.

"Zorro?" Adam interrupted in mocking tones. He took Erin's arm and pulled her away.

"Dan Rockwell," Erin finished.

"I guess congratulations are in order," Dan said easily, ignoring Adam's adversarial behavior.

"Yeah. We're getting married." Adam may as well have added, "Want to make something out of it?" He turned to Erin. "Come on, let's go home."

"I thought we were going to dance some more," she protested.

"I'm all danced out," he said. "Let's go."

"Well, nice seein' ya," Dan said to Erin. Then he leaned over and whispered in her ear, "Here's something else you forgot to put on that short list of McDoodoo's good points: unselfish. I wonder why." Then with a swirl of his cape he turned and melted into the dark.

Fifteen

"What the hell did he just say to you?" Adam demanded.

"That you're one lucky guy," Erin snapped, and marched off the dance floor.

"I don't know why you're acting so pissed," Adam said once they were in the car. "I'm the one who came back from the john to find my woman dirty dancing with some moron in a Zorro costume."

"He's an old friend. I was just being polite."

"I saw how close you were dancing. Pretty damned polite."

"I've known him since I was kid," Erin explained. "He's like a brother."

Adam frowned, facing straight ahead. "A girl dances that close with her brother and they call it incest."

"Are you going to ruin our Valentine's Day?" Erin demanded.

"Me!"

"You're the one who's fighting."

He shook his head and kept his gaze on the road.

They drove the rest of the way home in silence.

He stopped the car in front of her house and she turned in her seat. "Adam, I don't want to fight, especially not after the beautiful night we had together." All this squabbling, all these prewedding jitters—maybe they should just go to Vegas.

But she didn't want to go to Vegas. She didn't want to cheat herself out of something she'd been dreaming about for a long time.

Even if that dream turned into a nightmare? They couldn't keep going on like this. She couldn't keep going on like this.

Adam let out a long breath and turned to her. "I don't want to, either. I'm sorry." He reached out and fingered a lock of her hair. "I just saw him with you and lost it. I don't want to lose you. I know we're both under a lot of pressure right now. Once I'm done with school, once you've finished planning the wedding, it will be better."

Of course it would. She bit her lip and nodded. "But Adam, just because we're under a lot of pressure, we shouldn't take it out on each other."

"You're right." He smiled at her and slipped his hand around her neck, nudging her toward him. "Come here."

She came and he made it worth her while. This was the Adam she loved, the strong, in-control, but tender Adam. "Want to come in?" she whispered.

"You bet."

Once inside the house she lit candles and poured them champagne, and he stretched her out among the sofa cushions and kissed her crazy. And life was perfect again.

Until Saturday morning, when it was just her and her Valentine memories. She went to the kitchen counter to feed her fish and saw the DVD Adam had given her, still lying where she'd left it the night before, and something dark nibbled at her happy morning afterglow. She picked up the DVD and looked at the cover. There was Sandra Bullock in the arms of Bill Pullman. Sandra Bullock had thought she wanted the man with the big lips and the unibrow, but he'd turned out to be the wrong man.

See any resemblance? whispered a man in a Zorro costume.

She slammed the DVD back on the counter, facedown. No, none whatsoever! That was just a movie, nothing to do with real life. And anyone with a brain could have told Sandra Bullock that Mr. Unibrow was a dweeb. A woman didn't just pick a man because he looked nice in a suit. She picked a man who loved her, who would be good to her, who had the same goals. Erin had done that and she and Adam were going to be happy together, very happy.

And if she ever spoke to Dan Rockwell again, she'd tell him. She'd also tell him to quit messing with her mind. What did he know about anything anyway?

Suddenly, she felt an almost overwhelming need for a doughnut.

You paid a lot of money for that wedding dress.

Who was this? It sounded suspiciously like Adam. Oh, no. No more voices. It was already way too crowded in her head. She didn't need to add an inner Adam. She already heard enough from him as it was.

Eggs. She'd have eggs for breakfast. Eggs were great. She loved eggs. And she was going to fit into her wedding dress. "Don't anybody worry."

The voices all kept quiet.

Kizzy left Lionel sleeping and got up early Saturday, determined to go for a walk around the lake before going in to work in the shop. She pulled on some sweats, then slipped out to the kitchen where she boiled herself an egg. That, along with a piece of whole wheat toast and half a grapefruit, made up her breakfast. Very satisfying.

She wished she could say the same for being up early on a Saturday morning. But Oprah got up with the birds every day and exercised. If Oprah, who was the world's busiest woman, could squeeze in morning exercise, then Kizzy guessed she could, too.

She had just loaded her dishes in the dishwasher when Lionel walked into the kitchen wearing his old University of Washington

Huskies sweatshirt and his tattered gray sweatpants. "What are you doing up so early?" she asked him.

"I'm going walking with you and Gus," he said, pathing the dog's head.

If she'd had a hearing aid she'd have checked to see if it was working. "Really?"

"Really."

"Lion, you are a changed man."

"I am."

She put a hand on her hip and shook her head at him, smiling. "Well, what do you know? He can be taught."

"We'll see who's teaching who when we start that lap around the lake." He gave her butt a playful smack. "Come on, Kizzy girl, let's get this fitness train out of the station."

"How was everyone's Valentine's Day?" Kizzy asked the next time the Bikinis met at her house.

"I cheated on Valentine's Day. I had champagne and chocolate-covered strawberries," Angela confessed. "And Brad," she added with a self-satisfied smile.

"I take it your debut as a pole dancer went well," Kizzy said.

Angela surveyed her new, hot-pink nails. "Brad is not going anywhere now."

"He never was," said Erin.

"How was your Valentine's Day?" Kizzy asked her.

"It was great."

Erin's lips were smiling, and her voice almost matched them, but not quite. There was an insistence about the way she talked that a woman in love didn't need. Something was not right, and if you asked Kizzy something hadn't been right for a long time. "So, tell us about it."

"Adam took me to the Two Turtledoves for dinner. And he brought me a single red rose."

"Wow," breathed Angela.

"And a DVD. And then he took me to the Last Resort."

"I heard they were having a big Valentine thing," Angela said. "How was it? Who all was there?"

"Most of Heart Lake," Erin said.

"Did a lot of people wear costumes?" Megan wanted to know.

"Oh, yeah."

"I was half tempted to go," Megan admitted. "Were there any singles there?"

"A few. Dan Rockwell was there."

There it was, the something that Kizzy had been looking for, hiding behind an attempt to act casual. "Your brother's old friend?"

"He was there dressed as Zorro. Pathetic," Erin added, and almost succeeded in looking disgusted.

"I think Zorro is sexy," Angela said dreamily.

"You're thinking of Antonio Banderas," Erin informed her.

"So," Angela said, nudging Erin, "did you make Adam jealous and dance with Zorro?"

Erin rolled her eyes, but Kizzy noticed that she didn't answer yes or no. And her cheeks were suddenly looking sunburned.

"Isn't that the guy who checks over at Safeway?" asked Megan. "The one you almost ran over at the gym?"

Erin nodded and the blush spread.

"He is hot," Megan said.

Erin shrugged. "He's okay."

Kizzy waited for Erin to offer to introduce him to Megan. She didn't. Very interesting. "So, how are the wedding plans coming?" she asked.

"Fine," Erin said brightly. "It's going to be a beautiful wedding."

But, Kizzy wondered, was it going to be to the right man?

"I'm just glad I have a couple more months before I have to make my maid of honor dress," said Angela.

"You're married. That makes you the matron of honor," Megan informed her.

Angela made a face. "Matron, yuck. That sounds old."

"Well, you are," teased Erin. "The big three-oh is right around the corner."

Angela made a face. "Are you trying to drive me to chocolate?"

Erin gave her a bottled water from Kizzy's counter. "Here, have this instead. And remember, it could be worse." She turned to Kizzy. "How was your big love day?"

Kizzy couldn't help smiling. "Speaking of old?"

Now Erin's face turned crimson. "Nobody thinks of you as old."

Kizzy shrugged. "Well, compared to you babies, I'm ancient. But, let me tell you, I like where I am. Fifty is great."

"Fifty is the new thirty," said Angela. "So," she added with a grin, "did you and Lionel go at it like you were thirty?"

Kizzy pointed a finger at her. "Don't you go thinking we couldn't," and the others giggled. "But we did encounter a slight problem."

"You should have pole-danced for him," said Angela.

Kizzy couldn't help smiling. "Poor Lionel. He wouldn't have cared even if Beyoncé had pole-danced for him. He threw away his junk food stash and wound up eating half the sugar-free chocolates he got me. Let me tell you, by the time those got done doing a number on his insides, he was one miserable man."

"Not very romantic," Angela observed. "Poor Kizzy."

"Actually, I'm happy with the way things turned out. Lionel's finally on board with us eating right and getting fit, and to me that is about the sexiest thing on earth. And I lost three pounds this week."

"All right." Erin made a fist and bumped knuckles with her. "You're our hero. How are you doing, Megan?"

Megan smiled. "Great. I ate sugar free. And I got something for Valentine's Day, something really cool."

Kizzy looked at her in surprise. Had Megan found romance?

"Okay, so spill," commanded Erin. "We want details."

"You met a man," guessed Angela.

"Better than that. I got a client."

The others burst into excited congratulations.

"Who, and where'd you find him?" Angela asked.

"It's a her, and I found her at the gym," Megan said, beaming. "She owns it, and she needs nuisance-suit protection, which I am going to give her."

"I bet you write a mean cease-and-desist letter," said Erin.

Megan smiled. "As a matter of fact I do."

"This should get you in good at the firm," Erin predicted.

"A toast," said Angela, raising her bottle of water. "To Megan making partner."

The others echoed the sentiment and Megan smiled. "Life is good," she said.

Was it good for Erin? Kizzy had hoped for an opportunity to talk to her a little more about her Valentine encounter with Dan Rockwell, but the women moved on from the subject of Valentine's Day to diets and jobs, and no opportunity presented itself which was frustrating, because Kizzy was really getting concerned now. Erin didn't have a mom to advise her. Every woman needed an older, wiser woman in her corner to offer advice. Who was doing that for Erin? Hopefully, her aunt was. Kizzy wondered if Erin had told her aunt about her encounter with Zorro.

"Okay," said Megan, when they'd finished her lemon parfaits. "It's time for the No-belly award. Who did the best this week?"

"I'm not even in the running," said Erin with a frown.

"Me, either," said Angela, licking her spoon. "But I'll do better next week."

So it was up to Kizzy and Megan to compare weight loss numbers. And Megan came in the winner.

"Way to go," Erin told her. "You're making us all look like slackers. So, drum roll, please, while I go get the trophy."

She disappeared into the hallway while the other women drummed a tattoo on Kizzy's dining room table with their fingers. Then she bounded back into the dining room, holding a golden lady body builder trophy and crying, "Ta-da! And now, let me present this symbol of achievement to this week's keeper of the No-belly. Way to go, Megan," she finished, and they all applauded.

"Speaking of no bellies, I have something for us," Angela said. "Come on."

They followed her into the living room where she produced a *Dancing With the Stars* workout DVD.

"Oh, you got it!" cried Erin.

"I've heard this is hard," Megan said, looking suspiciously at it.

"No balking from you, Twinkle Toes, not after the way you danced at the pole-dancing party," Kizzy said to her.

"This will really make us hot," Angela promised.

After stumbling around trying to follow the fast steps of the professional dancers, everyone was literally hot in a matter of minutes. "Okay, just shoot me now," Kizzy said, and flopped on the couch.

"Water," croaked Angela.

That sounded like a great idea to everyone, and soon they were enjoying one last drink before breaking up for the night. This would be as good a time as any to try an amateur shrink session, Kizzy decided. But how to start? She supposed the wedding was a good ploy.

"You never did tell us the latest on the wedding plans," she said to Erin. "Anything new?"

"I've got the flowers picked out," Erin said.

She'd chosen the flowers for her wedding since they last met and she hadn't even brought up the subject?

"You did! Why didn't you tell us?" Angela accused.

"We got busy talking about Valentine's Day and I forgot," said Erin.

A woman didn't forget to talk about picking out the flowers for her wedding. This was not a good sign. "Tell us now," Kizzy urged.

"Well, I'm going to use Changing Seasons. Hope Walker, the woman who owns it, is a genius. They're going to be gorgeous."

"And you're getting everything you want?" Kizzy asked, trying not to sound like she was playing romantic detective.

"Pretty much."

"How does Adam like what you picked?" Angela asked.

Erin shrugged. "We didn't go into too many details. He's not that into flowers."

He wasn't that into much of anything, if you asked Kizzy. "Having your flowers picked, that really makes it all feel real, doesn't it?"

"It will feel more real when I can zip up my wedding dress," Erin said.

"Are you getting close?" asked Angela.

"Closer," Erin replied vaguely.

"Maybe you should postpone the wedding." There, it was out. Now maybe they could talk about this.

"There's no need for that," Erin said, her voice sharp. "If worse comes to worst, my aunt will alter the dress for me." She checked her watch. "I'd better go. Adam's probably already at the house."

The others decided to leave, too, and collected their leftovers. Erin and Megan left, but Angela lingered by the door. "Do you think Erin's worried about something more than her wedding dress?" she asked Kizzy.

"You see it, too?"

"Maybe it's just me, but when Brad and I got married I wanted to talk about everything with my friends. I mean, who doesn't want to talk about her wedding flowers? That's like a sign or something, isn't it?"

"I think so," Kizzy said. "How well do you know Adam?"

"Not real well. He seems like a nice guy," she added. Dubiously.

"But?" prompted Kizzy.

Angela shrugged. "I don't know. It's hard to put your finger on."

"Try."

"Well, he's kind of controlling. We went out with them a couple of times, but the guys didn't hit it off."

There was a red flag. Brad got along with everyone. "Why?" Kizzy asked.

"Adam had this way of deciding what everybody wanted to do

and what restaurant we should all go to that bugged Brad." She shrugged. "He just likes to have his way. I guess when it comes down to it, most guys are like that."

"Not to his extent," said Kizzy. She shook her head. "I'd sure hate to see our girl end up with the wrong man. It's no fun."

"Were you ever with the wrong man?" Angela asked her.

Kizzy nodded slowly, remembering the loser she'd been with when she was young and just too dumb to look beyond a great body and a smooth line.

"What happened?"

"I caught him in bed with my best friend."

Angela grimaced. "What did you do?"

"I let her have him," Kizzy said with a grim smile. "That way they both got what they deserved."

"Men," Angela said in disgust.

"Thank God they're not all like that. Lionel's the sweetest man on the planet. I'd like to see Erin end up with someone great, too."

"So, what are we going to do?" Angela asked.

"I don't know," Kizzy said with a sigh.

"Well, at least we still have four months left to think of something. Anything can happen in four months."

"Let's hope something does," said Kizzy. Erin deserved to be happy.

"You know what they say," Angela said in parting. "The path to true love is a long and winding road. Or something like that."

"Something like that," Kizzy agreed. Love was never easy, but it should at least feel right.

Feelings. Of course, that was the problem. Erin hadn't been feeling when she picked this man. She'd gone through a lot emotionally, first with her mom's illness, then her death, and it had left the poor girl numb. She picked Mr. Wonderful not because she was crazy wild about him, but because he was solid. He was a wheelchair for her crippled heart, a way for her to get someplace where she could be happy.

How on earth could she get Erin to see that?

Maybe she couldn't. Maybe this called for more wisdom, more power, more influence than she had. She did the only thing she could think of, she sent up a prayer. *Lord, this girl needs to be cured of her blindness. Now!*

Sixteen

Saturday morning the gray clouds parted their skirts to show the blue sky hiding behind. It was now or never.

Megan stepped out of the front door of her condo in her north Seattle suburb into the sharp February air wearing sweats and the oversized tee that made her look like a baby whale. There was nothing attractive about the sweatshirt she'd zipped over it, either. She couldn't believe she was going out in public dressed like this. But if she wanted to start running, she had to show her fat butt sometime. She got in her Saturn and drove to the nearby high school track and parked her car. Then she sat for a few minutes studying her opponent: that big, long track.

A middle-aged woman in a pink sweat suit was already on it, walking briskly and swinging her arms. The last thing Erin wanted was an audience. Oh, boy.

That woman is too busy fighting her own fat to watch you battle yours, she told herself firmly. *Right.*

She took a deep breath, then opened the car door and got out. She'd be lucky if she could make it halfway around that track. She should wait to do this until she'd lost more weight. Otherwise she was going to look like a fool, a big, fat fool.

"Oh, no you don't," she told herself. "No more excuses. Ever." She pressed her lips firmly together and locked her purse in the trunk, then put the keys in her sweatpants pocket and marched to the track. She'd start walking to get warmed up; then she'd run a little way and see what happened.

The walking went fine, and the sun, warm on her shoulders, felt like an encouraging hand. She smiled and picked up her pace a little. She'd been walking on her lunch breaks. The only difference between this track and her downtown route was the absence of stores and office buildings. She could do this. Okay, time to pick up the pace. She started to jog. All right! She was doing it. She flashed on a mental image of herself in shorts, her hair caught up in a ponytail and swinging behind her. With every step she was moving closer to being fit. Every step was exciting. This was exciting!

Okay, this was also work. She could feel her heart pumping. She was starting to sweat in spite of the crisp temperature. She kept her feet moving. *Don't give up yet.* But her heart was going to explode. Her lungs were burning. She slowed down. Her legs felt shaky, so she let herself grind to a stop, putting her hands on her thighs and bending over for a deep breath. She hadn't even jogged a quarter of the way around the track. She was a slug.

The other woman on the track walked past her and called, "Don't give up. You're doing great."

Megan straightened and took a deep breath. She *was* doing great. Winning cases were built slowly, over time. So were great bodies.

One of her stepfather's favorite complaints came back to kick her in the butt and get her moving. "The kid is a tub. If you don't do something she's going to have problems all her life."

Do something. She set her jaw and started walking again. *You can do this.*

She walked around the track twice and managed to get in another little spurt of jogging, too. It wasn't much, but it was a beginning, a good beginning. *You're going to succeed. One day you'll be wearing cute, little shorts and running like you're lighter than air.*

She was smiling like she'd just won a landmark case when she finally walked off the track.

Then she saw the snazzy silver Jaguar parked next to her car and the fit-looking man in the black running shorts and black T-shirt striding toward her and her smile faded. Oh, no. Wasn't it bad enough that he tortured her all during the week? Did he have to come to the same track, as well? Why wasn't he on a treadmill at some pricey gym?

"Megan," he greeted her. "I almost didn't recognize you in your civilian clothes."

She looked down at her baby whale costume, now dotted with perspiration. "These aren't my civilian clothes. And if I'd known I was going to run into anyone I knew," *especially my boss,* "I'd have stayed home."

"Then you'd have missed out on that runner's high."

"I haven't found a runner's high yet," she informed him. "Just a walker's high."

He smiled. Tanner Hyde actually smiled—not a sardonic smile, but the genuine article. She saw it so rarely, she almost felt like she'd spotted some endangered species. So, that was how he'd gotten those two ex-wives.

"I saw you doing some running," he said.

"How long have you been watching me?" Her tone of voice wasn't exactly respectful, but today he wasn't her boss. Today he was just a man with a lack of manners.

"Long enough to be impressed by your persistence. I'm glad to see you working on getting fit. A fit body will match that fit mind of yours damned well. Enjoy the sunshine." He coupled another of those disconcerting smiles with a curt nod, and then jogged off toward the track.

She frowned as she watched him bound lightly away. Show-off. And when had she asked him for a condescending pep talk, anyway? She fumed her way to her car. The man was her nemesis. Why couldn't she have gotten to work under someone nice at Weisman, Waters, and Green, like Bethany Hawke?

She retrieved her purse then plopped her sweaty self in behind the driver's seat. She flipped down her visor and looked in the mirror. Her face was crab red and sweaty. *Cute, Megan. Really cute.* Oh, well. She hadn't come here to impress anyone—certainly not Tanner Hyde.

She started her car and made her slow progress over the parking lot speed bumps. She made the mistake of looking in the direction of the track one last time and Tanner waved at her. She gave him a polite wave, then hurried over the last speed bump and out of the parking lot.

She was halfway home when she decided that she was being unfair to Tanner, that she was being hypersensitive, as she always was about her weight or anything related to it. Yes, he was a slave-driving shark, but he was the best and he was encouraging her. This was a good thing. Life was good. And she had run a little bit. Tomorrow she'd run farther.

Kizzy, Lionel, and the dog returned from their Saturday morning walk around the lake to find Larry the mailman stuffing envelopes into their neighbor's mailbox.

"I see you got a new walking partner, Kizzy," Larry greeted them.

Lionel patted his middle. "You bet. This is gonna shrink. In a couple of months you won't even recognize me."

"Go for it," Larry said, handing Kizzy their mail. "Looks like you got some real mail," he added, nodding to the small envelope in her hand. "These days it seems like all I deliver is junk mail and bills."

"I'll have to have Lionel start sending me more love letters so we can make your job more interesting," Kizzy teased.

"Good idea," said Larry, and whipped his mail jeep on down the street to the next row of boxes.

"So, what is that?" Lionel asked, leaning over her shoulder. "An invitation?"

She opened it and read, then shook her head and smiled. "Well, that answers a lot of questions."

"Except for how much you're going to spend on a new outfit for this," Lionel teased.

She ran a hand along his chin. "Don't worry, Lion. I won't spend a lot. Yet," she added. "But in another twenty pounds, watch out."

Erin parked her car in front of Changing Seasons Floral and answered her cell phone.

"You miss me?" Adam greeted her.

She turned off the car, and grabbed her purse, switching the phone to her other ear. "Yes. I wish you didn't have to be at the hospital today."

"Come June this will all be over," he assured her.

And then he'd be interning, and she knew what that meant. She watched *Grey's Anatomy.* He'd be working long hours. And she'd be alone. "I wish you could come with me and see the flowers I'm picking."

"That's more your thing. I think you can handle it. Just don't go crazy. I know you wanted to make me dinner tonight, but let's do it tomorrow. By the time I get home and finish studying I'm going to be fried."

She'd been planning to grill salmon, his favorite. Well, it could keep another day. "Sure," she said, resigned to an evening alone. She supposed this would be her life once they were married: her making plans, then having to remake them every time Adam had to get to the hospital for an emergency.

But those things don't matter when you love someone, she

reminded herself. "Okay, I'm there now, so I've got to go," she said, and got out of the car.

"Have fun. I'll catch up with you tomorrow."

Fun, yes, this was going to be fun. For a second there, she'd almost forgotten.

She walked into the shop and inhaled deeply. Those hyacinths were still going strong. Valentine goodies were now fifty percent off, and the shop was decorated for spring, with ceramic bunnies and decorative egg wreaths everywhere.

A girl with maroon hair and a pierced eyebrow was manning the counter. She smiled at Erin. "Hi."

"I'm here to see Hope," Erin said. "I want to finalize the order for the flowers for my wedding." Just saying the words was enough to make her excited. Who wouldn't be excited when she was about to be happily married to Dr. McDreamy?

"She's in the back room, doing an arrangement. I'll get her."

The clerk vanished behind maroon curtains that made Erin think of theaters. Plays. Actors. Pretend. She wandered over to the refrigerator case and checked out the arrangements.

"Hi," said a voice at her elbow.

She turned and saw Hope smiling at her. Today she was wearing a pastel green top. No wonder Erin hadn't seen her coming. With her quiet manner and that top she blended in with her surroundings like a chameleon.

"Hi. I'm ready to finalize the order for the flowers for my wedding," Erin said.

"Great." Hope led her over to the same little table where they'd sat before.

"I need to cut a few things, though," Erin said, spreading the sheet out in front of her.

"Actually, you don't." Hope grinned as she booted up her laptop. "I have a surprise for you. Someone has paid for your flowers—a wedding present."

"Really?" Aunt Mellie, of course. "Oh, that's awesome! Who was it?"

Hope cleared her voice. "Actually, the person wanted to remain anonymous."

Aunt Mellie wouldn't care if she knew. So, who then? Adam! "I know who it is," Erin said and flipped open her cell phone to call Adam. "My fiancé did this to surprise me." He just made that comment about not going crazy to throw her off.

"This wasn't your fiancé," Hope said. "It was someone else. An old friend of the family."

Old friend of the family. "Dan Rockwell," Erin growled as she snapped her cell shut.

Seventeen

Erin stormed out of the flower shop, determined to let Dan have it, but once she was in her car she realized she didn't know where, exactly, to find him. She had no idea where he was living.

Since it was Saturday he was probably at the gym.

No, he wasn't. He wasn't at work, either.

"Why don't you try him at his place he's fixing up," suggested Fred, the produce guy.

"Great, thanks," Erin said. "Um. Where is it?"

"Corner of Lake Drive and Pine—long driveway."

"Thanks," she said, and hurried to her car. Lake Drive and Pine— that was the less developed side of the lake. It was lovely over there, with lots of trees to remind people what Heart Lake had been like before word got out about it. In between the trees the lakefront was sparsely dotted with little vacation cabins, a contrast to the south end, which had been rapidly taken over by big homes and lawns.

She finally found Dan's place at the end of a long driveway flanked by fir and alder trees and huckleberry bushes and salal. It was small, probably only two bedrooms, snugged in by old, out-of-control rhodies. But it had a stone chimney and, as she walked around to the front, she saw it had a long front porch, perfect for relaxing on a warm summer night. One side of the house was dotted with moss and the whole place needed paint. Once it was fixed up, though, it would be a charmer. Inside, she could hear a hammer banging and Bryan Adams singing about loving a woman.

"Hello," she called. "Anybody home?" Well, that was stupid. It wasn't ghosts swinging that hammer. "Hello?"

No one answered her, and now she could figure out why. Because Bryan Adams wasn't the only one singing. Between the pounding and his duet with Bryan, Dan wouldn't have heard if a bomb went off on his front porch.

She went inside, picking her way around debris and piles of lumber. The house had pretty much been gutted, but the big river-rock fireplace on one side of the room was intact. She took in all the windows framing a sunlit view of the placid lake and could see them strung with little fish-shaped party lights. This would make a perfect house for entertaining.

And there was Dan, on the far end of the room, working on what looked like a frame for a new window. A packed tool belt pulled dusty jeans low on his narrow hips. He had his shirt off, baring a well-muscled back. There was something so sexy about a man in jeans and no shirt.

You're engaged. Remember? her inner mother reminded her. *Don't forget you're here for a specific reason.*

Right.

She walked up practically behind him. "Hello."

He gave a start and dropped his hammer, then whirled around. "Erin. What are you doing here?"

"I came to talk to you about the flowers."

His cheeks turned russet. Then his brows came together. "Who told you?"

"Never mind who told me. I'm just here to say thanks, but I can't accept."

"Why?"

"Because. It wouldn't be right."

He grimaced. "You know, if your mom was here right now she'd really let you have it. Are you going to go around to everyone who gives you a wedding present and tell him to knock it off? If you are, send the goods my way. I could use a new toaster."

"Well, now you'll have enough money to buy one."

He scowled at her. "You need the damned flowers. Take them."

"I will not," she snapped. "How do you think that would make Adam feel if he knew some other man had chipped in for the decorations at his wedding reception?"

Dan rubbed the back of his neck. "Look. I just wanted to help you get what you really wanted. I think that's what your mom would have done. But, hey, if you don't want the fancy stuff I'll go buy you a toaster." He turned his back on her and picked up his hammer.

She suddenly felt as small as that hammer. "I don't mean to be ungrateful," she said, "but I just don't feel comfortable with you do-ing that."

He said nothing, just took a nail and banged it into the frame.

"I'm sorry," she added. The words were right, but they came out wrong, making her sound bratty and defensive.

"You should be." He turned around to face her, shoving the hammer into his tool belt like a gunslinger. "You've got a real snotty side to you, Erin. You always have had."

That was totally unfair. "Oh, like you never brought it out. You did your fair share to make me feel like a fool when I was young."

"You punished me pretty good once you got older and grew claws," he retorted. "But we're grown-ups now. I'm trying to act like one."

She felt her cheeks burn. "It's not that I don't appreciate the gesture."

He didn't say anything, just stood there, looking at her, his face like granite.

She nudged his foot with her toe. "My mother would have told you to get the toaster."

"You know what I think?" he asked.

"That I'm a snot." He was right. She was.

"I think deep down"—Dan tapped on her chest, sending a jolt running along every nerve ending in the vicinity—"you know something's not right, and it's eating at you, and that's making you pissy. It's like you've got chronic PMS."

"Well, thank you, Dr. Dan, for your diagnosis. I'm a snot with permanent PMS."

He gave her a half grin. "You're not a total snot. Remember how you used to always make M&M cookies every time I came over?"

Her cheeks got hot again. "Brett liked them."

"So did I. You knew it. And remember that time Brett and I broke into old man Mosier's place and drank all his beer? You knew, didn't you? But you never ratted us out."

"I didn't want Brett to get in trouble."

"You could have ratted me out." He smiled. "You're only a snot when your back is up."

"You're one of the few people who gets my back up."

Dan grinned. "What can I say? It's a gift."

She shook her head at him and turned, walking back to the door.

"Speaking of gifts, change your mind and accept mine," he called after her.

She stood in the doorway, looking out at the lake, shimmering in the early afternoon sunlight. In the middle a fish jumped, making a splash and sending out quiet ripples. "I think if I had a place like this I'd never want to leave."

She heard the sound of Dan's work boots as he walked up behind her. "Too bad it won't stay this way forever. Everything changes eventually—places, people."

"People do change," she agreed. "You can't go back." And that was a good thing. Going forward was where a woman found her true happiness.

"You're right," Dan agreed. "You have to go forward. But there's nothing wrong with looking back and remembering."

Yes there was. And lately, just looking at Dan made her feel like she was in some stupid remake of *Back to the Future,* trying to rewrite her way to a sappy new ending. As much as she wanted to think of him as a goofball, he'd grown into a very attractive man.

"Take the flowers," he said softly. "Please."

Erin sighed. "Okay."

And now it would be best to leave.

"Thank you," Erin said. Then she bolted for the door before she could be tempted to make herself at home on that porch in the morning sunshine.

It had been another grueling week of toil at Wise Ass and Greed, and Megan was fried. Even so, she wished she had some interesting plans for the weekend. Other than taking a spin around the track on Saturday afternoon (when Tanner would not be around to see her sweat), she had nothing going. Pretty depressing. She consoled herself with a promise of checking out some of the online options for meeting men once she'd lost some more weight. Right now she wasn't ready to be posting a picture of herself on the Internet for all the world to see.

She sighed as she shoved papers into her briefcase. All those TV legal shows made a lawyer's life look so glamorous. What a joke.

Someone knocked on her door, probably Tanner with some fun project to eat up the entire weekend. Oh, well. What did she care, really? She had no weekend to eat. "Come in," she growled.

Pamela Thornton stuck her head around the door. "My, aren't we bitchy? Is Tanner picking on you again?" Megan opened her mouth to shoot back a smart retort, but Pamela didn't give her time. "Randall and I are going to go wash away our bad memories of the week with grapefruit martinis. Want to join us?"

Pamela wanted her to go out with them? What did they need her for, ballast in case they encountered a strong wind?

"Well, let's go," Pamela said impatiently as if it was all decided. "People are dying of thirst."

And so she went. And drinks slid smoothly into dinner. And by the end of dinner she realized that friends came in all sizes, and sometimes a girl was wise to try on one that looked too small. Looks could be deceiving.

It was now the beginning of March, and the daffodils were about to bloom. Angela had finally joined Weight Watchers online and lost six pounds. She wouldn't be hot by her birthday, which was only a few days away, but at least she was on her way. And she intended to keep going, too. She'd already asked her mother to go easy on the fattening food when they went to her parents' for her birthday dinner on Sunday. She'd liked to have gone someplace a little more special for her thirtieth—no offense, Mom—but, oh well. Rachel was history, she was sure of it, and she had her dolce vita back. That was what mattered.

But on Friday things changed. While Brad was showering for work Angela went looking in his wallet for a spare dollar to give Gabriella for popcorn at preschool and found not only the needed dollar but a receipt from Victoria's Secret. Of course, it was a birthday present for her, so she didn't say anything. She played dumb and sent him off to work with a big kiss.

And then she began the hunt for her birthday present. Brad was a terrible present hider. In all the years they'd been married, he'd never been able to keep anything from her. She went to the closet and opened his carry-on suitcase, his favorite hiding place, for a peek at the prezzie. Empty. Okay, that meant it was stuffed in his second-favorite hiding place, the filing cabinet in their home office. Nothing but files. She scooted out to the garbage and wheeled his big tool chest away from the wall. Only wall. Hmmm. He'd done a good job of hiding her present this year. Where was it?

Nowhere in the house, she concluded after a thorough search. Maybe he had it stashed at the office. Maybe someone was keeping it for him.

Maybe someone was wearing it for him.

Where had that come from? That was ridiculous. Everything was fine now and Brad wasn't cheating on her. But he always kept her present somewhere in the house. That was part of the birthday tradition. He'd hide it and she'd find it.

So he did something different this year, she reasoned. There's no need to panic. She went back into the house—not panicking—and tore the hall closet apart. Nothing. Nothing, nothing, nothing! Something was wrong here. Her woman's intuition was going off like a three-alarm fire.

Brad called that afternoon and announced that he had to work late. And then she knew. She knew! First the receipt for the invisible present and now this.

She tried to talk herself down from the ledge. So he had to work late. That didn't mean anything. Brad was happy with her again. They were happy. "Who else is working late?"

"Just me," he said.

Brad never lied, he was always reminding her about that. But there was something in his voice that told her he was now. That meant it was just him and Rachel.

She ground her teeth. "Okay," she said tightly.

"I'm sorry, Ang, I really am. Something came up."

She just bet it did. She should have kept her mouth shut, but she couldn't resist saying, "And Rachel isn't working late, too?"

"Oh, Ang, come on," Brad said, sounding irritated. "Of course she's not."

"I was just wondering. Go ahead, work as late as you want," she told him, trying to sound like she didn't want to run down to his office and put him through the paper shredder.

Wait a minute. Maybe she did want to run down to his big office in the city and pay him a surprise visit. If he was with Rachel she could put them both in the paper shredder.

"I'll be home as soon as I can," he promised.

"Okay. Bye." She hung up and looked at the clock. It was now a little after four. If she booked it, she could get there before the after-hours party even started. She looked to where the girls were playing dolls in the living room. She couldn't take them with her. That would scar her babies for life.

Kizzy. She never stayed late at her kitchen shop on Friday.

Kizzy answered her phone on the second ring.

"I've got an emergency. Could you watch the girls for an hour?" Angela begged.

"Oh, my God. What's wrong?" Kizzy gasped.

"I'll have to tell you later," Angela said, not wanting to get delayed by explanations and, knowing Kizzy, counseling sessions. It was too late for counseling now. She was Oprah bound.

"Angela, what's wrong?" Kizzy asked again once Angela was on her doorstep.

Angela plopped Mandy in her arms. "Be good for Aunt Kizzy," she told Gabriella. To Kizzy she said, "I don't have time. I have to get there before five."

Otherwise, it would be awfully hard to follow Brad and Rachel to whatever seedy hotel they were going to. Who was she kidding? They weren't going to any seedy hotel. They were probably going someplace really expensive.

She roared down the freeway, zipping in and out of lanes of traffic, using every Italian curse word she could think of and when those ran out she switched to good, old American ones.

She'd deprived herself of pasta and cookies and chocolate, had sex like bunnies with that man, even learned how to pole-dance—and for what? So she could whet his appetite for Rachel.

"Move it," she yelled at a pokey Cadillac in front of her. Of course, no one was in a hurry when your life was falling apart. She swerved into the slow lane and sailed past the Caddy, then whipped back into the fast lane. This was not good driving. She had to slow down or she was going to kill someone. Or at least get a ticket. Unless the cop was a woman. A woman would understand.

She lightened her foot on the gas and forced herself to take deep breaths, but that didn't help. It only made her feel like she was going to pass out. Maybe she would. She'd pass out and crash into a cement wall and die behind the wheel and Brad and Rachel would raise the girls together. That possibility started her crying. *Oh, Brad, we were so happy. What have you done?*

Maybe she should forget Brad and ask herself what she'd done. Had she taken him for granted, taken their good life for granted? Had she just set herself on happy homemaker autopilot and cruised through these last few years? Yes, she had to admit that until recently, she had done just that. And now look what happened.

She got to First National's loan center at ten minutes to five and parked on the corner where she could have a good view of the parking garage. Then she turned off the car and waited. When Brad and Rachel came out, she'd follow them.

But what if they didn't come out? What if they waited until everyone else had gone and then went into his office and went at it on his desktop? The image that came to mind blurred her eyes with fresh tears. *How could you do this to the woman who stuck with you through thick and thin?* Okay, more thick than thin lately, but that was beside the point. She'd wait until twenty after five, then if Brad hadn't come out, she'd go in there and catch him in the act.

The thought of catching her husband naked with another woman broke her heart. It was raining now. Hordes of fat drops beat on the windshield, and she had to turn on her wipers. Even with the windshield wipers going she could barely see for her own tears.

At ten after five the office started emptying. There went Gary, there went Marion the receptionist who was supposed to have been retiring. There went. Oh! There went Brad's car, shooting out of the parking garage. She started her engine, but forced herself to wait until another car was between them, like any good private eye would do.

They were halfway down the block when she realized that the car between them was Rachel's red PT Cruiser. It was all Angela could do not to ram it. As they threaded their way through the downtown streets, she tried rehearsing what she'd say. *I've given you the best years of my life and this is how you thank me?* That was what women said in movies. In real life it didn't seem like enough. Sadly, it was all she could think of.

Their sick little convoy got on the freeway, northbound. Where was Brad taking this woman, anyway? Angela let out an angry shriek when they took the Heart Lake exit. What was this? He was having an affair right in their own front yard? Brad was a monster!

Her husband and his mistress parked their cars in front of Brewsters' Brews microbrewery and restaurant. As they got out of their cars Angela scrambled out of hers and ran across the street. Brad had just opened his car trunk and was handing off a pink carry-on suitcase when Rachel saw Angela approaching and nudged him.

He saw her and suddenly looked like a little boy who had just gotten caught raiding the cookie jar. Well, that would teach him to pick a cookie jar so close to home! "Ang," he stammered.

"You lied to me," she cried.

"I'll just take this inside," Rachel said to Brad, and scurried away like the cockroach she was.

Angela stepped up to Brad and gave him an angry poke in the chest. "You, you, you." *Poke, poke, poke.* "You bastardo," she sobbed. "I want a divorce!"

"What?" Brad was looking at her like she'd just gone nuts.

"Oh, stop pretending already. I caught you red-handed with that, that home wrecker."

He threw up his hands. "Okay, I give up." He reached into the trunk and pulled out some sort of plastic banner and unfurled it. "Surprise," he snapped.

She tipped her head and read, "Happy Thirtieth . . . Angela?"

"You have just officially crashed your surprise party," Brad informed her, looking at her as if she was Gabriella, caught coloring on the wall.

"Birthday?"

He reached in and pulled out a roll of pink crepe paper streamer and then a white one. "I've been trying to plan a surprise party for you. That night you came home and caught me on the phone we were choosing the restaurant. You caught us, all right. You caught us dropping off the decorations for the party tomorrow."

"You're not? She's not? Oh, Brad!" Angela threw herself against Brad with such force she almost knocked him over. The rain was drenching them. She didn't care. She wrapped her arms around him and squeezed as tightly as she could. He was still hers. Thank God. She looked up at his frowning face. It was the most beautiful sight she'd ever seen. "I was so worried. I've been such an idiot."

"Yeah, you have." He took her hands and pried them off him. "I told you over and over again that I wasn't cheating on you, that I wasn't lying to you, but you wouldn't believe me."

She hung her head. "But you were acting so suspicious, and I got fat," she said in a small voice.

He gave a snort of disgust. "My God, Ang, what kind of a shallow prick do you think I am?"

"I didn't think," she realized.

"Oh, you thought all right," he said bitterly. "You thought you couldn't trust me even though I've never given you a reason not to. Well, here's something new to think about: what man in his right mind wants to be with a woman who doesn't trust him?" He slammed the trunk shut and stamped to the driver's side of his car.

"Brad! What are you doing?" She rushed after him and grabbed his arm.

He threw it off and got in the car, shutting the door in her face.

"Where are you going?" she cried.

He didn't answer. Instead he started the car and squealed away from the curb, drenching her pants in a rooster tail of water in the process.

She barely noticed. "Brad!" she shrieked after him. He didn't stop. The rain was coming down hard now. Cold droplets slipped under her coat collar like icy fingers. "Brad," she whimpered. What, oh, what had she done?

Eighteen

She trudged back to her car and fell inside, laid her head on the steering wheel and wailed. All this time she'd been afraid of losing Brad. Now maybe she really had.

Still crying, she finally forced herself to start her car and turn toward home, praying all the way that by the time she'd stopped at Kizzy's and collected the girls Brad would have beaten her there.

Once in front of Kizzy's house, she sat in the car and tried to pull herself together. She caught a glimpse of her reflection in the rearview mirror and nearly started crying again. Her eyes were all bloodshot, her makeup was a mess, and her wet hair was plastered to her skull. She looked like she should be in a horror movie. As far as she was concerned, she was.

Outside the rain was still sluicing down her windows. The sky was leaden and angry, and under it the lake looked depressing and gray, its surface pockmarked by the barrage of raindrops shelling it.

She covered her face, wishing she could rewind time. If only she'd trusted her husband. If only she hadn't jumped to the conclusion that he was as unhappy with her overweight condition as she was. She'd thought less of herself, so she'd assumed he did, too. How dumb! She'd been so quick to suspect another woman of taking her husband. Now she'd driven him away, maybe for good, and the only woman she had to blame was her own insecure self.

A tap on the passenger side window of the car made her jump, and she let out a startled yelp. She looked to see Kizzy's concerned face. And then Kizzy was climbing into the car. "I saw you from the window. Is everything okay?"

"Nothing is okay," Angela cried. "Brad, Brad . . ."

Angela gathered her into her ample arms. "Oh, now honey, don't go crying. Your husband loves you."

"Not anymore," Angela stammered between sobs.

Kizzy sighed. "All right. I shouldn't be telling you this, I'm going to blow the surprise."

"I know about the surprise," Angela howled.

"Well, then. Why do you think he doesn't love you?"

"Because we had a fight and he drove away and didn't even tell me where he's going." She turned desperate eyes to Kizzy. "He's really, really mad. And he said, he said . . ." Again she couldn't go on, couldn't say those terrible words Brad had said to her.

Kizzy stroked her wet hair. "It will be all right," she crooned. "You'll see. Come on, now. Pull yourself together. You don't want your girls to see you like this, do you?"

The girls. She had to be strong for the girls. She made a determined sniff.

"That's better. Now, blow your nose and dry your eyes." Kizzy pulled a tissue out of her sweater pocket and handed it to her. "This will all be history by your party tomorrow. You'll probably get home and find Brad there waiting for you. The girls are fed. You can put them to bed early and then you two can curl up on the couch and make up. Okay?"

Angela forced herself to nod her head even though deep down she knew Kizzy was wrong. Brad couldn't even stand the sight of her right now. Maybe he'd never be able to stand the sight of her again.

She forced herself to smile for the girls as if her heart wasn't in shreds. She gritted her teeth to keep from bursting into wails when they returned to an empty house.

"Where's Daddy?" asked Gabriella.

He could be anywhere—his parents' house, his brother's. "He had to work late, honey," Angela lied, trying to keep her voice steady.

Gabriella's lower lip went out. "I don't want Daddy to work late. I want him to come home and read me a story."

I just want him to come home. "I know, *bambina,*" Angela said, laying a hand on her daughter's head. "Mommy will read you a story tonight."

And wouldn't you know? The story Gabriella wanted to hear was Cinderella. Angela felt like her head was a fire hydrant about to burst. Any second tears were going to splash everywhere. "And they lived happily ever after," she finished and almost choked. She and Brad had been doing that until she had to go and spoil it all.

"I want another story," Gabriella pleaded.

"'Nother story," Mandy echoed.

"No, we need to get to bed," Angela said firmly.

The thought of going to bed by herself just about did her in. She wiped away the tears leaking from the corner of her eyes.

"Mommy, are you crying?" asked Gabriella.

"That nice story made me cry," Angela lied. "Come on, now, let's go brush our teeth."

She held it together until she got the girls settled, then she scurried to the bedroom, buried her head under a pillow, and had a good cry. She stayed in bed alone, sobbing, until she gave herself a headache. Then she got up and went in search of aspirin. While she was up, she called Brad's cell. Of course, he only gave her his voice mail.

"Brad, please," she begged. "I'm so sorry. Please forgive me. Please come home. I promise I'll never mistrust you again. Ever, as long as I live."

But he didn't come home. And he didn't call her back. And on her thirtieth birthday she woke up alone.

Kizzy called her shortly after ten. "How are you doing?"

Having to answer started a fresh flow of tears. "Brad never came home," she said in a wobbly voice. "I called his cell and he never called back."

"Uhn, uhn," said Kizzy, and Angela couldn't tell if that disgusted tone of voice was for Brad or her or both of them.

"I don't know what to do," Angela confessed. "You've got a lot of experience. Tell me. What should I do?"

"Send him an e-card," suggested Kizzy. "Then work on getting pretty for your party."

A surprise party without her husband there? That would be the ultimate humiliation. "I can't go."

"Yes you can."

"Not without Brad."

"Angela, honey, your life will go on with or without Brad. You have a lot of people who love you coming to this party. And I suspect, in the end, one of them will be your husband."

"He's so mad at me." And she couldn't blame him.

"We all do things to disappoint each other. Brad will come around. And if he hasn't come around by seven, Lionel and I will be by to pick you up."

"Thanks," Angela murmured and hung up.

She so didn't want to go to that party. What did she have to celebrate? Hitting thirty as a failure. Maybe she would get pneumonia or the flu or something before seven tonight. Maybe she'd call in sick, tell Kizzy she was throwing up, had a fever, her feet had fallen off, she'd had a heart attack.

Except the heart attack had happened yesterday. She couldn't believe she was still alive today.

She called Brad's cell phone again and still got no closer to him than his voice mail.

"Brad, are you ever going to talk to me again?" she asked sadly. "I guess I can't blame you. I was such a stupido to think that just because I didn't like me that you wouldn't, either. Except now you don't like me. And I hate me. I wish it was yesterday and I wish I'd never come into the city. I wish you could forgive me." She hung up with a sob.

When she still hadn't heard from Brad by five-thirty she knew her life was over. And that was all the reason she needed to give Kizzy for not going to the party. There was no sense going to a birthday party when you were a corpse. She would stay home tonight, turning her house into a fort, hiding inside these four walls, protecting her dead self from gawkers and kindly mourners who might think they could somehow bring her back to life when her life was over.

She was making dinner—pizza, who cared about losing weight now?—when the doorbell rang.

From the living room, she heard Gabriella cry, "Daddy!"

Angela knew her daughter would be on her way to open the door. But she wouldn't find Brad there since he had a key and wouldn't have used the doorbell. And it wasn't the babysitter, either. Angela had already called her and canceled. So, whoever that left at the front door, it was someone she didn't want to see.

She hurried from the kitchen and across the living room, hoping to stop Gabriella from opening the gate to Fort Baker, but it was too late. Kizzy and Erin and Megan were already walking into the entryway, Lionel trailing behind.

"It's time to get dressed," Kizzy informed her.

"I can help you with your makeup," Erin offered.

"I brought Visine," added Megan, holding up a small bottle. "Good thing, too," she muttered. "You look like a vampire."

Angela shook her head. "I'm not going."

"We're having pizza," Gabriella added.

Erin picked her up and gave her a kiss. "That will be fun. Is Emily coming over to have pizza with you?"

Gabriella shook her head. "Mommy told Emily not to come. We're going to have a party."

Kizzy cocked an eyebrow. "Canceled the babysitter, did you?"

Angela crossed her arms over her chest. "I'm not going."

It was about to get ugly. "Let's go out and check on that pizza," Erin said to Gabriella, and carried her out of the room.

"I'll go help Erin with the girls," Megan said. "Here," she added, passing Angela the bottle of Visine. "Don't forget to use this."

"I don't want it. I'm not going."

"Yes you are," Kizzy informed Angela. "It won't do you any good to sit in here and mope."

"I can't go to a party and pretend everything is all right," Angela protested.

Kizzy put an arm around her. "Come on, honey, try. Brad is probably feeling pretty bad right now. I bet you'll walk in and find him there, waiting for you."

Angela shook her head violently. "He won't take my calls. I haven't talked to him all day."

"Sometimes it takes guys a while to cool off," put in Lionel.

"He hates me," Angela wailed.

"Naw," said Lionel gently. "He's just real pissed."

"Come on," Kizzy urged. "Call the babysitter back, then let's go upstairs and get you all pretty. If Brad isn't there, then you can say you're sick and we'll bring you right back home. How's that?"

Angela began to wring her hands. This was awful. She and Brad had never had a big fight like this. "I don't know what to do."

"I think you do what we all do when we're not sure," said Kizzy. "You put one foot in front of the other and just move forward the best you can."

It took an hour of persuading and primping, but finally Angela was able to set foot outside the house, ready to endure her birthday party alone. "But only for a few minutes," she reminded Kizzy. "If he's not there you have to bring me home."

"We will," Kizzy promised.

With every step toward Kizzy's car Angela kept an eye on the street, hoping to see Brad pull up, but he didn't.

They walked into the private party room at Brewsters' and found it filled with all Angela's friends, her parents, and even her grandparents, who had flown in from Florida, but no Brad. She immediately burst into tears, thus managing to convince the guests that she was completely surprised.

People hugged her and told her how great she looked. Many asked her if she'd lost weight. She wiped at her eyes, nodded, and tried to smile, but smiling hurt. Thinking about how she'd managed to ruin Brad's surprise and their life in one afternoon was really making her sick now. She had to get out of here. Where was Kizzy?

She searched the room. Oh, no. Here came Brad's parents. Did they know? They couldn't. They were smiling. They still didn't know what a rotten, untrusting person she was.

"Happy birthday, dear," said her mother-in-law.

She couldn't answer. Tears choked her throat. She looked longingly toward the door.

And that was when she saw him. He was wearing the same suit he'd worn yesterday, maybe even the same underwear. Poor Brad. He looked at her and the hard set to his jaw softened. Ignoring the greetings of the other guests, he was walking straight toward her.

"Brad!" she cried and flew to him.

She threw her arms around his neck and he wrapped his arms around her waist as the other guests cheered like this was all planned.

She looked up into his handsome face and begged, "Please say you forgive me."

"I didn't want to, but I love you too much not to," he said softly, and kissed her.

Now everyone was applauding. "You got her good, Brad!" someone called.

"Yeah, well, wait till she sees what else I've got up my sleeve," he said, and smiled at Angela.

"I don't need anything else," she told him, and hugged him again. "All I want is you."

There was no need to fake surprise when Brad presented her with her birthday present. He instructed her to open the pink carry-on suitcase, and inside she found two tickets to Italy and a nightgown from Victoria's Secret.

"We're going to Venice in April to celebrate your birthday and our tenth anniversary," he told her. He'd even arranged for her parents to take care of the girls. And then he raised his glass of champagne to her and said, "Happy birthday to my beautiful wife."

His beautiful wife—still thirty-four pounds overweight and he didn't see it. Love really was blind.

No, love was faithful, and that was even better.

Kizzy hugged her as the Bikinis gathered for a group shot, and Erin said, "You've got a great guy. It was all I could do not to smack you when you kept insisting he was having an affair."

"I should never have doubted him," Angela said. And, more important, she should never have doubted herself.

Much later that night, when she'd done her best to make up for how she'd hurt him, they lay in bed together, Angela's head on his chest, his arm wrapped around her. "I'm sorry I stayed away," he said. "I was just too mad to come home."

The very memory of how awful that had been was enough to start the tears again. She nodded and wiped at the corners of her eyes. "I don't blame you. I can't believe I could have thought such a dumb thing. I guess I figured I somehow didn't deserve you the way I looked."

"Aw, Ang, I'm no prize." He hugged her close to him. "Let's never fight like that again."

She nodded. "Okay. And if you decide you don't want to be with me, just tell me."

He kissed her forehead. "That's never going to happen, believe me. I'm not in love with your waist size. I'm in love with you. And I married you for better or worse."

"For fat or thin?" she prompted.

"Fat or thin, old or young, you'll always be beautiful to me," he murmured.

It was the most wonderful birthday present she'd ever gotten. She took his face between her hands and kissed him gratefully.

Nineteen

Megan had enjoyed her weekend. She'd mingled at Angela's party like an old pro and had even made an attempt at flirting with Angela's single brother-in-law. She'd gone to a matinee with Erin on Sunday and resisted the popcorn temptation, and afterward they'd gone out for drinks—diet pop at McDonald's. All in all, it had been a rewarding weekend. And this morning had been even more rewarding when she stepped on the scale and saw that she'd lost another three pounds. She'd left for work singing.

But now she was back in legal hell, plodding through a paper trail that was surely going to lead her to a nervous breakdown. Time was running out and, at the rate they were not building this case, poor Sandra Owens would be forever branded an urban cougar, a sexual predator who had taken advantage of a poor, young man trying to fight his way to the top and then got him fired. But the poor young man was a biotech crook who was trying to get Sandra out of the way by framing her with a phony memo where she allegedly admitted to having had an affair with him and stating that he had to go. The trial started next week and they still had nothing with which to nail the guy to the wall. Damn.

She glared at the Redwell expandable folder in her hand. Redwell. More like dry well. This was a hopeless, futile task, and any minute Tanner would be walking in here, demanding to know when she was going to give him something. Well, damn him and damn this rotten, smelly mess he'd dumped on her. *Damn, damn, damn!* She threw the file across the room and watched with vicious pleasure as it whacked against the wall and spilled its paper guts all over the floor.

The pleasure only lasted for a minute. All she'd done was make a mess for herself to pick up. She stalked over to the puddle of papers, bent down and picked up the Redwell, which she had now succeeded in ripping. And that was when she saw the little yellow sticky note with the crumpled receipt caught on it. She detached the receipt and examined it.

And almost let out a war whoop. Yes! This little bit of hidden evidence must have gotten caught in Mr. Scumbag's paperwork and accidentally passed on to his lawyer, who hadn't found it. Opposing counsel sure wouldn't be happy when they learned she had. Oh, this was beautiful. She gathered up the papers, dumped them on her desk, and then rushed to show Tanner.

Once behind his thick office door, she did a smug stroll to his desk and silently laid her offering on his ink blotter.

He looked up at her, an eyebrow arched. "What's this?"

"Merry Christmas," she replied.

He picked it up and read it. Then he laid it back down on his desktop and gave her one of his sardonic Tanner Hyde smiles. "Well, well. Congratulations. You just struck gold. But then I knew you would."

What kind of BS was this? "So you're psychic?" Megan retorted. "And here all this time I thought you were just a sadist."

"You think I've been driving you too hard?" He leaned back in his chair and regarded her over steepled fingers.

She raised her chin. "Are you looking for an honest answer or a brown nose answer?"

"I think you're incapable of giving me the latter so why don't you try for the former?"

"I think you give me tasks that are almost humanly impossible."

"You managed this one just fine, and I knew you would. You're an interesting woman, Megan, and I think you're only beginning to discover how much you're capable of. I'm going to enjoy watching you develop into a legal monster."

These were hardly words she'd expected to hear from Tanner. She smiled at him as urbanely as she could, murmured a thank-you, and then turned and walked out of the office. A legal monster—maybe he'd share that prediction tomorrow when the senior partners voted on the candidates waiting to join their august ranks. This would be one more feather in a cap that was now looking pretty damned good.

She was barely back in her office when Harrison Cutter, one of the partners, dropped in. "Megan, how are you doing? Nervous about making partner?"

Every associate at the firm was, but she certainly wasn't going to show a sign of weakness and admit that to Cutter. Why was he asking her this? Did she need to be worried?

"Should I be?" she countered.

"Oh, not necessarily." He shut the door behind him, then sauntered across the room and perched on a corner of her desk. It left her looking up at him. And there was plenty to look at. Harrison was a hefty man. He smiled at her, a smarmy, condescending smile. And then he brushed a hand over her arm, making her think of spiders. "I have influence. I'd be happy to help."

She sat back in her chair, effectively moving her arm out of reach. "That's very kind of you," she said cautiously.

"I can be a kind man, for a woman who is appreciative."

Megan suddenly felt like something slimy had just crawled up her leg. "Are you suggesting some kind of quid pro quo?"

"That is how the big, bad world works," he said lightly. "How about stopping by my place tonight and we could discuss your future at the firm?"

Not even dinner in the deal. What a rat!

"Not everyone appreciates a woman who is . . . heavy," he continued, "but I do. And I'm sure you appreciate a man who isn't so picky."

Yuck. Now she was talking to Denny Crane from *Boston Legal*. "And of course, fat girls are so easy because they're desperate?" she suggested through gritted teeth.

He pretended to look hurt. She was sure he was incapable of that particular feeling. The man probably didn't have a genuine bone in his body. "Why, I didn't say that."

"Yes you did." She stood. She was shaking now, with a barely controlled rage. She would have loved to slap him, but she settled for marching to her door and opening it. "I'm afraid I've got plans for tonight, and they don't include bribery."

"Megan, what a thing to say! I only want to see you succeed." He joined her at the door. "Tomorrow could be a big day for you. If you change your mind . . ."

"I won't."

He shrugged as if it didn't matter to him one way or another. "We have other young women at this firm equally as deserving as you."

And willing to sleep with Cutter? They could have him.

"Then I suggest you go find one," she said, and motioned to the hall.

"Suit yourself," he said amiably. "It's your career." Then he sauntered out the door.

She shut it after him, then returned to her desk on shaky legs and fell into her chair. Had that really happened? And if she didn't make partner, would she have Cutter to thank? Was this how these people wanted to run their firm?

Not all of them, she assured herself, remembering Tanner's encouraging words. She'd have one champion tomorrow when the partners met. Anyway, her work spoke for her. So did the fact that she'd brought in a client. She'd be fine.

Knowing that, she should have enjoyed her sudoku puzzle that evening, should have been able to concentrate on her murder mystery. But she couldn't. All she could think about was Cutter's insinuated proposition. And it was all insinuation, impossible to prove sexual harassment. It would be a case of he said–she said.

She went to bed, determined not to think about the disgusting encounter any more, but at two A.M. she was still awake and tossing. "This is ridiculous," she told herself. "You've got nothing to be worried about. You won't be chasing ambulances now." She'd worked hard for the firm for seven years, and now she'd proved herself a rainmaker and a discovery bulldog. How could they not want her?

She finally repeated her assurances enough to lull herself into a very short slumber. When the alarm went off at seven she awoke feeling like someone had poured ground glass in her eyes. Never mind, she told herself, you won't care once you get the good news.

The other candidates were all nervous. "I'm going to throw up," Pamela said as she paced Megan's office. "Why can't they hurry up and finish?"

"These are big decisions," Megan said with a calm she was far from feeling. It was now almost eleven A.M. and Pamela's near-panic was infectious. "Will you please stop pacing? You're giving me motion sickness."

"They're only picking three of us," Pamela said.

"So, I wonder who they'll pick besides you and me?"

Pamela barely managed a smile.

Megan's phone rang and she pressed her extension number and picked up the receiver with a trembling hand.

"The meeting is over," said James the receptionist.

"Thanks," she said and hung up. "They're done," she told Pamela.

The blood rushed from Pamela's face. "I'd better get back to my office," she said faintly.

Megan nodded. She watched Pamela slip out the door. She had nothing to worry about. She'd make partner, easily.

That left two positions, and five people. Megan pulled her bottled water out of her bottom desk drawer and took a steadying drink. This had to be what a defendant felt like when waiting for the jury's verdict. It was awful, hellacious.

Her phone rang again twenty minutes later. "They're ready for you in Tanner's office," James said. "Good luck."

"Thanks," she murmured. She stood, smoothed her skirt, took a deep breath, and then went to Tanner's office to meet her fate with her head held high.

There, among the leather and mahogany and book-lined walls, sat Tanner and Jonathan Green, the partner who handled the firm's business.

"Megan," Jonathan greeted her. "How are you?"

It would be very unprofessional to tell him that she thought she was about to wet her panty hose. She forced herself to smile and nod and say, "I'm fine, Mr. Green. Do you have some news for me?"

Both men looked at each other. And exchanged smiles. "As a matter of fact, we do," said Tanner. "Would you like to sit down?"

"No, thank you. I'd like to know what the partners decided about me."

Jonathan smiled. He looked like Gene Hackman, and every time she saw him she thought of the movie *The Firm*. "Megan, we had quite a discussion about you."

A discussion. She thought of Harrison Cutter, busily discussing her out of making partner.

"You have a fine mind," Jonathan said. "No one can argue that."

She hadn't made it. She'd misread their body language. She forced herself to remain ramrod straight, chin up.

"Such a mind is a wonderful asset to any law firm. You also are tenacious. The evidence you uncovered just yesterday proves that. Our only concern has been over whether or not you can bring in the kind of high-powered clients this firm represents."

But she had brought in a client. Hadn't Tanner told him? She looked to Tanner, who stared back at her and gave her the faintest of nods.

"We are aware you have already brought a client to this firm, and we appreciate that. In the future, we hope you'll aim even higher."

There was nothing wrong with the client she'd brought in. Raine Goldman was a nice woman. Granted, she didn't have a billion-dollar business, but she had legitimate needs all the same. Why discriminate against the little person?

Silly question. You couldn't bill the little person for a big bundle. Law was noble when you were a student or a public defender. When you got out in the real world, it was only about money. Megan frowned. Was that why she'd gone to law school, just to make money?

Jonathan cleared his throat, yanking her attention back to him. "So, we would like to offer you a partnership in the firm of Weisman, Waters, and Green."

They would? She'd made it. In spite of her piddly little client, in spite of Harrison Cutter's nasty insinuations, she'd made it. She'd proved she could be a rainmaker.

She managed a faint, "Oh," and fell onto the nearest chair.

"We're hoping you'll accept," said Jonathan.

Megan blinked. *Come on lips, work.* They failed her; her brain had failed her. In about one more second her heart might fail her.

"She accepts," Tanner said on her behalf, making Jonathan grin. "Megan, snap out of it."

She forced herself to blink. Then she rose from her chair and shook hands with both men. "Thank you. You won't regret it."

"I always knew we wouldn't," Tanner said.

"We hope you'll join us Saturday night at a special dinner at Canlis," added Jonathan.

Canlis was the swankiest restaurant in Seattle. "Yes, thank you," she managed.

She left Tanner's office on wobbly legs. Back in the safety of her own windowless office, she allowed herself to rejoice. "I made it! I made it! I made it!" She needed to call her mother. Then she needed to go shopping for a dress for Friday.

But first she needed to find Pamela. Buzzing with adrenaline, she made her way down the hall to Pamela's airy office. She threw the door open. "Let's go shop . . ." The sentence died unfinished. Oh, no.

Pamela raised a tearstained face from her hands. "I didn't make partner."

Megan rushed over and sat down on the corner of Pamela's desk. "That's impossible. How could you not?"

Pamela shook her head and stared at her desktop. "While I'm personable and hardworking, there were other personable, hardworking candidates who showed more promise," she said, her voice mimicking Green's. "In other words, I'm not smart enough."

"You were smart enough to get hired by a prestigious firm," Megan argued. "And can bring in the clients."

Pamela scowled. "Not enough."

"You brought in two clients in six months, and just last month you hooked Puget Cruises, for God's sake."

Pamela shook her head. "They changed their minds and went with another firm last week." Now her mouth puckered like she'd just tasted something sour.

"I don't understand. You had Nick Wallace eating out of your hand."

"He wanted to do more than eat out of my hand." Pamela covered her face and began to cry again. "I blew it. I could have had him and I blew it."

"You mean you could have had him if you slept with him. You shouldn't have to prostitute yourself for the firm."

Pamela didn't even hear her.

Megan leaned over and put a hand on her arm. "You have more than one chance to make partner."

Pamela sniffed and nodded. "I know. I just wanted it so bad. You know? And you, oh, I didn't ask. Did you?"

Megan bit her lower lip. Her good news tasted like ashes.

Pamela looked at her, wide-eyed. "You made partner?"

Megan sighed and nodded.

"Oh, that's great." Wearing a Miss America runner-up smile, Pamela jumped up and hugged her. "They're lucky to get you."

"Thanks," Megan murmured. Then she excused herself and went to her office to think.

She thought all afternoon. Then she thought all the way home on the bus. She was a partner now. She didn't have to take the bus. She'd have her own special parking spot in the First Orca Trust Tower.

Big deal.

Her mother called that night, anxious to hear the news.

"Yes, I made partner," Megan told her.

"Darling, that's wonderful! I'm so proud of you."

"I'm proud of me, too," Megan said.

Making partner at a prestigious firm, it was a huge accomplishment. And okay, so Pamela didn't make it. It was a shark-eat-shark world, but she'd still be okay. She'd find another big client, and by this time next year, she'd be a partner, too.

Megan had a salad and Perrier for dinner. She left the champagne she'd bought sitting in the fridge. She'd drink it later. She'd celebrate later, when she felt more like it, when her good fortune had really sunk in. That was the problem of course, she hadn't fully digested just how lucky she was. She took a hot bath, then fell into bed.

The next day everyone at the firm was full of congratulations. Ashley, Pamela's old buddy, had made partner and was strutting around like a peacock.

"What did you expect," whispered James the receptionist. "She's sleeping with Waters." Then he looked speculatively at Megan, as if trying to decide who she'd played.

"I'm sleeping with all of them," she said, making his jaw drop.

In her office, she found flowers waiting, along with a card from Tanner that read, "Always knew you could do it."

She and Tanner would be equals now. And she was going to have a new office, hopefully one with a window.

"I know you'll miss working so close to me," said a voice from the doorway.

She turned to see him smirking at her. "Oh, I definitely will. Thanks for the flowers."

"My pleasure."

"And thanks for pushing me through."

"You pushed yourself through."

She shrugged and turned back to survey the flowers.

"I haven't seen you on the track. Are you still running?"

"Yes, but under cover of darkness."

"Keep it up. It's a good stress reliever," he said. "Now hurry up and get out of here, will you? I want to move in someone new to torture."

He was about to leave. "Tanner," she said.

He stopped and looked over his shoulder.

"Do you ever wonder if you made the right decision going with a big firm?"

"No," he said. "I like big cases and big battles. And I'm not into tilting at windmills. A big firm is where the action is." He smiled, that same smile he'd showed her at the track. "You belong here. You're going to do great."

He started to walk away again. "Tanner."

He turned and raised an eyebrow.

"Is it true that Ashley is sleeping with Waters?"

Tanner frowned. "You're just moving into Olympus. It's a little soon to start questioning the gods."

"That wasn't an answer," she said as he shut the door. She sat down at her desk and picked up a pen and began absently tapping it on the desktop. Was she moving into the wrong neighborhood?

Twenty

Erin sat at her desk at Great Events, Inc., looking at her computer and envisioning her wedding reception. It would be fine, lovely. Not everything she'd once dreamed, but close enough. And she could live with that. The flowers would be fabulous, that was for sure. Hopefully, by June she'd be able to enjoy them with a clear conscience.

She still had to figure out what to do for music, though. A band was probably out of the question.

Band! Oh, no! Her heart thudding sickly, she frantically whipped around her computer mouse and opened the document marked "Entertainment." There it was, the list of bands from last year, bands she should have already sent contracts to weeks ago. Here Gregory had put her in charge of the Heart Lake Slugfest because of her hometown connection and now she was totally blowing it. It wouldn't matter that she'd already lined up a hot local radio personality to emcee the slug races or that she'd pulled in new sponsors for the vaudeville show if she didn't have any bands in the beer garden. No bands in the beer garden, less customers; less customers and all the restaurants participating would lose money, and then they wouldn't want to do it next year. And it would all be her fault. The beer garden would be a bomb and Gregory would kill her. How had this slipped past her? How? How? How?

The wedding, of course. It was consuming her. But that was no excuse. This was her job, her future, and she couldn't screw it up. If she didn't have music for the Slugfest her name would be slime here at Great Events.

Don't panic, she told herself. *You still have time. You already got a verbal yes. This is just a teeny technicality.* Oh, what power a teeny technicality had to make a girl sweat!

She grabbed her phone and called the cell phone for the leader of the first band on the list, all the while wishing she hadn't gotten rid of that stash of Cheetos in her bottom desk drawer.

"This is Shay," he said.

"Shay, hi. This is Erin from Great Events. How are you doing?"

"Fine. We're booked solid, man."

Fine for him, not for her. "Well, I hope you've still got the Slugfest on your calendar. I'm going to be e-mailing your contract today."

"Dude. I thought you were going to send those out in January."

"Something came up." *I got engaged and all my brains fell out.*

"Well, sorry. We just finished booking a tour in Canada. We'll be gone that whole month."

"Oh." *Crap.* "Can we get you for next year?"

"Sure. But you gotta send the contracts sooner."

"Oh, I will," Erin promised.

She went to the next band on the list. They'd broken up. "We didn't have a contract anyway," said the leader.

"But we had a verbal agreement," Erin protested. Surely Megan would say that could be just as binding as a written one.

"Sorry," he said.

The next band she called had broken up, too. Great, now she was down to one band.

And, lucky for her, Stupid Bitch was still together.

But not interested. "You never sent the contract. We took a gig in L.A." said the lead singer. And his tone of voice added, "Stupid Bitch."

What to do now? She didn't know any other local bands. Who did? Who could get her in touch with a band as of yesterday?

Desperation dug around in the back of her brain and came up with Dan Rockwell's name. He had said he knew a great band. Oh please, oh please, oh please, let him still know them. First wedding flowers, now a band. At this rate she was going to have to name her first child after him.

Erin looked up the number of the Heart Lake Safeway and called it. It was late afternoon on a weekday. He should be at work by now. *Please be there, please be there, please be there.*

Miracle of miracles, he was. She barely waited for him to say hello. "That band you know, are they booked in May?"

"So you decided to go with the band after all," Dan said. "Good idea. Except I thought you were getting married in June."

"It's not for my wedding," she told him. "Actually, it's a much bigger gig. I need a band to play in the beer garden during Slugfest. If they want the job it's theirs."

"Whoa, that is a sweet gig. But don't you want to hear them first?"

Like there was anyone left to choose? But he was right. She should go through the motions of giving this band, whoever they were, an audition. And if they sucked she could always kill herself.

"Okay," she said. "Do you know your friend's phone number?"

Dan rattled it off. "They practice on Fridays. I'll bet you could go over to Gary's this Friday and listen."

"Thanks," Erin breathed. "Thank you so much."

"You're welcome. See ya Friday," he added, and hung up.

Wait a minute. What was that about? She called the store again and asked for Dan. "What do you mean, see you Friday?"

"I said that?"

"Yes." And, grateful as she was, she had no intention of hanging out with Dan Rockwell on a Friday night. Adam wouldn't understand. Anyway, it seemed best not to encourage Dan in any way, shape, or form.

"Oh, well, I just meant if I happened to be there I'd see you."

"Don't you have to work?" Or something.

"I have Friday nights off. Remember?"

"I forgot," she said. She'd been trying to forget as much of their Valentine's Day close encounter as possible. Then she felt it necessary to add, "I won't be there long. I'm sure I'll be doing something with Adam later."

"Sounds like a waste of a Friday night to me."

"That shows how much you know," Erin said firmly. "Anyway, thanks." Maybe, if she was lucky, by Friday she'd have a band signed for Slugfest and she could live another day.

On Thursday night Megan took Pamela out for drinks after work and proposed partnership.

Pamela leaned back in her chair and looked down her nose at Megan. "Are you insane?"

"No, I don't think so."

"Why would you want to blow the chance of a lifetime?"

"I don't think I am. I think I can make a go of this. If," she added with a smile, "I have a rainmaker."

Pamela frowned and took a sip of her grapefruit martini. "In case you didn't notice, this cloud dried up. I guess Ashley had the right idea," she added bitterly, glowering at the contents of her glass.

"Ashley wouldn't know an idea if it served her a summons. And a potential client can slip off anyone's hook."

Pamela shook her head. "It sucks."

"And it could continue to suck for a long time. Did you ever stop to think about that? Do you really want to stay at Wise Ass and Greed, begging for crumbs?" Megan demanded.

"Do you really want to leave Wise Ass and Greed and starve?" countered Pamela.

"I don't think we will. Anyway, I don't like the way they go about picking their partners. I'd rather starve than align myself with that." She patted her middle. "Besides, I can afford to starve for a while."

Pamela just shook her head.

Megan leaned forward, pleading her case. "This could be a chance to really do something important with our lives. Do you remember why you wanted to go into law in the first place?"

"To make lots of money," Pamela said, and toasted Megan with her martini glass.

Megan fell back against her chair. "Okay. Stay. Who knows? Maybe if you beg, Green will toss you my leavings." She pulled some bills from her wallet and set them on the table. "Good luck. You're going to need it in that shark tank."

"The whole legal profession is a shark tank."

Megan stood up and gathered her purse and jacket. "If you change your mind, let me know."

Pamela looked up at her and smiled. "I won't, but I admire your guts. Good luck."

"I don't believe in luck," Megan said, and left the bar.

She went home and drafted her letter of resignation. The next day she typed it up and submitted it, then started cleaning out her big, cherrywood desk in her new, fancy office.

She was almost finished when Tanner entered. "What the hell do you think you're doing?"

She raised her chin. "I guess you heard."

"Yes, I heard," he snapped. His eyes were flashing. Talk about gods. Right now he looked like he could hurl thunderbolts from his fingertips. "What are you thinking? Or should I ask what you've been smoking?"

"No, you can ask what I'm thinking. And I'll tell you. I don't want to work in a big shark tank where I'm going to be poked and prodded to go trolling for big clients. I don't want to work at a firm where hopefuls have to put up with getting propositioned by the resident Denny Crane, and where a woman who just happened to sleep with the right 'god' gets to enter Olympus while a woman with more merit has to remain below with the mere mortals and try to figure out which one of you can raise her up next time."

Tanner had stood there, jaw clenched, while she delivered her speech. When she finished, he gave his sardonic smile and applauded her. "That was a well thought out summation. Have you thought out an equally excellent business plan or are you just going to ride off on your white horse and hope that God is on your side?"

Her chin went higher. "A little of both. I'm not stupid. I'll find a way to succeed."

He shook his head and let out an exasperated breath. "I do believe you will. Waters once told me I was backing a dark horse, but I knew you were special."

He walked toward her, obviously ready to shake hands and wish her well. She stuck out her hand.

He ignored it and snaked an arm around her waist, pulling her up to him. Then he kissed her, setting off three-alarm fires all through her body.

She pulled away, blinking. "What was that about?"

He shrugged. "You don't work here anymore. No danger of a sexual harassment suit. And I've wanted to do that for a long time."

Megan realized she was speechless. Hardly surprising. How could she know what to say when she didn't even know what to think? One of the biggest sharks in the tank had just kissed her and turned her toes into curling ribbon.

He smiled down at her. "Don't look so surprised. Didn't your mother ever tell you that brains are sexy?" he teased. He turned and sauntered out of her office, leaving her scrambling for a reply.

All she managed as the door closed was, "No, she didn't."

Twenty-one

Gary Idol—that had to be some kind of stage name—lived on the outskirts of Heart Lake on a partially cleared lot that housed a modular home, a carport complete with a Jeep and a rusty, old Mustang up on blocks, a spotty lawn that was more dirt than grass, and two sort of German shepherds. It had rained off and on all afternoon. Erin took in the wet soil and the muddy, excited dogs and hoped she'd make it to the house with her clothes intact.

She saw Dan's truck parked next to a couple of other cars in front of the house and swore. Didn't he have anything else to do?

She pulled her car in back of his truck and got out. The dogs rushed her, barking and wagging their tails. She managed to just prevent one from jumping on her, but it did succeed in sliding a muddy paw down her jeans. Maybe Gary Idol couldn't afford dog obedience school.

"Fender! Martin! Down!" called a voice from the porch.

The two dogs wheeled around and raced back to their owner, a guy in jeans and a sweatshirt with shaggy, dark hair. "Sorry," he said as Erin approached. "They got no manners."

"No problem," she lied. If it meant getting a band for Slugfest she'd let one of the animals take a chunk out of her butt.

"I'm Gary," said the guy. "Come on in. We're just getting set up."

She followed him and one of the dogs inside, into a small living room covered with ugly brown carpet. Or maybe the room just looked small due to the fact that it was crammed with enough musical equipment to fill a shop. Two cute, blond-haired guys sat on a leather couch, fiddling with guitars; the one with a cigarette dangling from his mouth smiled and nodded at her. The coffee table in front of them looked like a garage sale special and was littered with beer bottles, cigarette packs, and an ashtray. The room smelled like dog and secondhand smoke. *Yuck.* She could just imagine what she'd smell like when she left here.

A fourth band member stood with his back to her, tuning his bass. Wait a minute. She knew that back. He turned around and smiled at her.

"Since when do you play the bass?" she demanded.

"Since I was seventeen," said Dan.

"I never saw you," she accused.

"I was a closet player."

"He's damned good," said Gary. "Great at vocals, too."

Erin fell onto the leather footstool. The dog came to her, laid its head on her lap, and looked up at her. And then put a muddy paw on her other pant leg. Lovely.

"Martin, damn it," said Gary. He walked to the door and yanked it open. "Get your muddy dog butt outside right now." The dog tucked its tail between its legs and walked out the door and Gary said, "Sorry. He's still a puppy."

Erin forced herself to keep smiling and nodded.

Gary climbed onto his drum stool cowboy style and picked up his drumsticks, giving one a twirl. "Okay, you know Dan. And this is Jake and Larry. Jake sings lead and plays rhythm guitar. Larry plays lead."

Whatever all that meant. "What kind of songs do you play?" Erin asked. As if it mattered. At this point they could play nursery rhymes and she'd hire them.

"Oh, we're kind of a variety band. We play eighties, classic rock, some country, a little R and B, Santana, Marc Anthony."

"No rap," said Dan. "No hip-hop. We're too white."

"Wanna hear something?" asked Gary. Without waiting for an answer, he counted them off and the band jumped into playing "Message in a Bottle." Suddenly it sounded like the Police were right there in the room.

"You guys are great," she said when they'd finished.

"Want to hear something slow?" Gary offered.

She didn't need to hear anything more. They'd be perfect. But before she could say as much they launched into a Bryan Adams song. And then Dan started singing.

This time the choice was "When You Love Someone." He sang about loving someone so much he'd do anything, and the words crawled inside her ear and began waltzing around in her mind. He sang on, about sacrificing, risking it all and not thinking twice, and the words slipped down and twisted around her heart. This was like trying not to listen to the Lorelei. She stared at her knees and wondered when Dan Rockwell had become a host body for a rock star. And was it hot in here?

They finished the song and she jumped up from the footstool and fumbled the contract out of her purse. "You guys are great. You can play Friday and Saturday night and for the Sunday afternoon show, too. If you'll just sign this contract."

"Cool," Gary said, and happily scribbled his name. "You better make sure you get that Saturday and Sunday off, Rockwell."

"I will," Dan said easily.

"Dan says you need a band for your wedding," Gary said to Erin.

"Oh, well, we haven't—"

"We'll play it for you for free," Gary offered.

—*quite decided.* "Oh, I couldn't."

"Hey, the Slugfest will be great exposure for us. It's the least we could do. Right, guys?" They all said yes, but she noticed Gary was looking right at Dan.

All the words he'd sung were using her brain for a mosh pit. She couldn't think. She let instinct take over, and instinct said, run. "Well, thanks," she managed, and started for the door. "Everything you need to know is in the contract, but if you have any questions feel free to call me. Gary," she added. She didn't need Dan calling her.

"I'll walk you to your car," Dan said, slipping off his bass.

"That's okay. Don't bother." She opened the door and ducked out.

But she was barely onto the porch before he was beside her. "It's dark out there, and Martin's probably waiting to jump on you again."

Neither dog was anywhere to be seen. Dan was right about one thing, though. Once they got away from the porch light it was dark. No streetlights out here—just trees and sky and stars.

She cast around in her mind for something to say as they picked their way across the spotty grass. "You guys are really good." Cute. She sounded like a groupie.

"We're okay for a garage band," he said.

"You're a lot more than okay."

She was suddenly very aware of the yin and yang of them as they stood there in the darkness—his strong male lines, her softer ones, his low voice, her high voice, his hard muscles, her . . . mushy insides.

This was ridiculous. What was she doing? Those Bryan Adams lyrics had programmed her to start thinking like a thirteen-year-old.

She opened her car door, stumbled around it, and fell onto the driver's seat. "I'd better go."

"Yeah, I guess you'd better," Dan agreed. "McDoodoo is waiting."

"That's McDreamy," she corrected him. And he wasn't waiting for her. He was home with his head stuck in a medical book. She shut the door and started the car. And then, because her brain was mush, rolled down the window to talk some more. "You really saved me tonight. Thanks. I owe you big-time."

"No problem. And you don't owe me anything. I like helping you."

"Well, thanks again," she managed, then stuck the car in gear and got out of there.

And all the while someone's voice—Bryan Adams? Who knew anymore? Her head was getting so damned full of them!—kept crooning, "When you love someone," over and over again.

I do love someone, she told herself as she drove away, I love Adam. Of course she did. And Adam loved her.

And what would Adam say when he learned they'd gotten a band for the wedding reception for free and that it was Dan Rockwell's? She let out an angry breath. Dan Rockwell, closet bass player. Why hadn't he stayed in the closet where he belonged?

Suddenly, for no reason, Erin had a burning desire for Fritos.

Don't do it, cautioned her inner mother. *You'll never fit in your wedding dress at this rate.*

I'll get back on track tomorrow, Erin promised. Right now she needed to grind something between her teeth.

Megan looked around her at the dingy office space. It was small, the hardwood floor was worn and paint spattered, and the windowsill looked like it had been painted shut since *Roe* v. *Wade.* Dust motes danced on a weak sunbeam, taunting, *Ha, ha, ha, ha, ha—this is all you can afford.*

"You won't find a bargain like this in the city very often," said the property manager at her elbow.

There was a reason for that. Megan nodded. Could she fix this place up so it didn't look like Sam Spade's office? *Okay, use your imagination. Picture new paint, some nice rented art.*

She sighed inwardly. Even her imagination couldn't fix this place. She needed an office that would impress clients, not scare them away. "I'll have to think about it," she lied.

"Okay, but don't wait too long," cautioned the property manager. "Space like this is hard to find."

If space like that was hard to find, how would she ever find a really good office space? She left the building completely disheartened. Maybe Pamela had been right. Maybe she had been crazy to leave the shark tank. She should have at least waited until she had more than one client. At this rate she'd blow through her savings in six months. And then where would she be? Maybe it wasn't too late to go back.

Her cell phone rang, and she looked at the screen. Pamela. Maybe the sharks had given her Megan's partnership.

Pamela didn't bother with greetings. "Where are you?"

"I'm out looking for office space."

"Have you found one you like?"

"Not yet."

"Good, because I've found one for you." Pamela rattled off an address, commanded Megan to be there in ten minutes, and then hung up.

Like I'm going to be able to afford that part of town, Megan thought. But she went anyway. She hadn't talked to Pamela since that day in the bar and it would be nice to see her and catch up on what was going on over at the firm. And, speaking of the firm, why wasn't Pamela at work?

The building was slick—all steel and turquoise glass. The lobby was full of gigantic metal sculptures. Everything about it said money.

And money says success, Megan reminded herself. But on her limited budget she couldn't afford this much talking. What kind of sick joke was Pamela playing?

She rode the elevator up to the twenty-first floor and got off. Directly in front of her she saw a sprawling insurance office with an impressive reception area. She turned right and walked down the hall in search of 2106. And there it was, a big, open space with huge windows looking out over the city. And standing in the middle of the room was Pamela, wearing her lawyer pinstripe suit and looking like a navy blue Bic pen with blond hair.

"So, what do you think?" she asked.

Megan looked around in amazement. "It's great." But she'd never be able to afford it.

"I think the space will work quite well for us."

Us? "Am I missing something here?"

Pamela raised an eyebrow. "Your offer's still good, isn't it?"

She wouldn't have to go it alone after all? It was all she could do not to jump up and down and scream. She beamed. "Absolutely."

"Well, then." Pamela spun around, arms out. "Welcome to Thornton and Wales. I'm the rainmaker so I get top billing," she added. "Besides, it sounds better with my name first."

"It would," Megan teased. "But, are you sure?" This was too good to be true.

"Absolutely. We can go over the partnership agreement this afternoon if you want."

"I'll have to clear my busy calendar, but I think I can make time," Megan cracked. "What changed your mind?"

Pamela gave a little shrug. "You were right about the firm. It is a shark tank. I don't want to be there."

"Okay, who propositioned you, Cutter?"

"The disgusting lech," Pamela said with a frown. "As if."

"Poor Cutter," said Megan. "He can't seem to catch a break."

Pamela's eyes widened. "You, too?"

Megan nodded. "I'll say one thing for him," she added with a smile. "He's got good taste."

"Yes, he does," Pamela said with a grin.

"And so do you. This is a class act," Megan said. She walked over to the window and looked out. The sun was shining on a shimmering blue Puget Sound. She watched a ferry slide into Coleman Dock. This was a view to die for. Alone, she could never afford it. With Pamela, she could still never afford it. This had to be way out of the price range for a brand-new firm. "How much is the rent?"

Pamela was behind her now. "Rent is not an issue, at least not for the first year. We're getting a really good deal."

Megan frowned. "A deal on prime office space like this? How is that possible?"

Pamela linked an arm through Megan's and towed her out of the office. "Come on. We're going out to lunch where all will become clear."

Megan balked. "What are you getting us into?"

"Don't worry," Pamela said, moving her along again.

"Oh, I'm not," Megan said, "because if this stinks I'm not doing it."

"Believe me. The only thing this deal smells like is money."

When they walked into Ruth's Chris Steak House Megan knew Pamela had suckered some hapless male into becoming their sugar daddy. Steak was a man's kind of lunch. And this steak house was a rich man's kind of place. And then the maître d' led them to their table and she saw her sugar daddy assessing her with those eagle eyes of his and her legs felt suddenly weak. "Tanner."

He half stood and nodded a greeting. "You're looking good, Megan."

Speaking of looking good, she thought as he flashed that rare smile. He was wearing his favorite black suit today. That combined with his dark hair and complexion always made him look like legal counsel for the Prince of Darkness.

"What are you doing here?" she blurted. Which, of course, sounded beyond stupid.

"I'm helping you," he said simply.

The office space, of course. "But why? I didn't ask for your help." Now she sounded stupid and ungrateful. Pamela kicked her under the table, and she winced.

"No, you didn't. And that's why Pamela here is going to make a good partner for you. She has no problem asking for what she wants." To Pamela he said, "The partners were shortsighted in their decision, and they'll probably live to regret it, especially now that you've teamed up with this thing," he added, favoring Megan with one of his ironic smiles.

"We appreciate what you're doing," Pamela said, and kicked Megan again.

Megan glared at her, then said to Tanner, "I don't see how you can be involved with us when you're already a longstanding partner at Weisman, Waters, and Green. That's a conflict of interest."

He leaned back and slung an arm over his chair. "I'm not really involved. I happen to own a share in this building. I happen to have pulled some strings. That's all."

"And now we happen to have a great office space for a song," added Pamela. "Thank you, Tanner," she added. "We really appreciate it."

"One of you does," he said, favoring Megan with his trademark sardonic smile.

"I appreciate it, too," she said. "I really do. But why?"

"I told you that I like big cases and big battles, and that I'm not into tilting at windmills. But I never told you that I also like to watch a good fight. You two should provide me with endless entertainment. Now, shall we order drinks? I think champagne is in order."

Megan suddenly felt like she was standing on the roof of that fancy building that would be their new home and experiencing vertigo. What if they failed? And what if, now that he'd invested in her, Tanner never kissed her again?

Erin sat at her desk and ate her yogurt with very little relish. What was the point? She was doing terrible. She wished she hadn't stepped on her scale this morning. The needle hadn't even moved.

She shouldn't have been surprised, not after her relapse the other night. She should never have watched her DVD of *While You Were Sleeping*. She'd wound up running to the store partway into the movie and had come home with a humongous bag of Fritos, then proceeded to eat half of it in one sitting. Then, not wanting Adam to find the evidence, she'd brought the rest to work with her today and ate some more. At least she'd finally had the smarts to give the rest away. Fine time to find her willpower, after she'd slapped another pound on her middle. Dumb, dumb, dumb. At this rate she was never going to fit into her wedding dress. She was the only one of the Bikinis not having any success. The others were losing weight. She should be, too. And tomorrow they were all going out to eat at Brewsters' to celebrate St. Patrick's Day. Green beer, Brewsters' incredible JoJo's—there would be temptation everywhere.

But she'd be with her friends. They'd protect her from the JoJo's. And she would only have one beer. Then she'd have a salad tomorrow. She'd be fine. Everything would be fine. She only had twenty pounds to lose, for crying out loud. She had time. She'd be in her wedding dress by the middle of June, no problem.

She drummed her desktop, suddenly feeling a craving for something salty. She thought of the Fritos her coworker was consuming in the break room this very minute and tossed the last of her yogurt into her waste can. She was sure getting sick of yogurt.

The Maxwells and the Bakers arrived at Brewsters' at the same time, all of them wearing something green. The place was packed, with every table full. Mike, the owner, stood at the long bar framed by a big mirror and an array of bottles, working the taps and grinning. His wife, Samantha, as always, was seating people. Today she and all the wait staff wore green polo shirts over their slacks. She'd dyed the tips of her short brown hair green and green shamrock earrings dangled from her ears.

"Happy St. Patty's Day," she greeted the foursome. "You're all looking good."

Yes, they were, thought Kizzy, who had lost an impressive twenty-four pounds. Tonight she was wearing a green blouse she hadn't fit into in years and she'd never felt better. Lionel was making progress, too, although tonight she'd teased him that he looked like an unripe tomato with legs in that big, oversized green T-shirt.

Angela had lost some of her momentum now that she wasn't worried about her husband, but she was at least keeping off the fourteen pounds she'd shed.

"I love your hair," cried Angela, touching her fingers to the green fringe at the top of Samantha's head.

"Oh, I do that every year," Samantha said. "Life is short. You've got to enjoy it."

"I like the way you think," said Lionel. He rubbed his hands together. "I'm ready for that green beer."

"Then let's get you seated," said Samantha, and led them to a window table.

Megan was the next to arrive. So far she had lost the most of all of the Bikinis, approaching her diet and exercise program like she was preparing for a Supreme Court case. And it was paying off. She'd lost twenty-seven pounds since January and she was starting to look good. Tonight she wore a brown wool poncho thrown over stretch jeans and a low-cut green top. The poncho was slimming and her boots gave her height. Kizzy noticed that a couple of men at the bar were taking in the new and improving Megan with approving glances. It wouldn't be long before she had a man in her life, Kizzy was sure.

"Oh, good," she said, sliding into a seat. "I'm not the last one here. Freeway traffic is a mess tonight."

"It's a mess every night," Kizzy said, glad she lived and worked in Heart Lake. The commute from her kitchen shop to home took her a whopping seven minutes.

Erin and Adam were the last to arrive. Kizzy noticed that Erin was wearing a baggy sweater (green, of course) over her jeans. She knew that hide-the-flab ploy from personal experience. Poor Erin. She was having the hardest time of all of them to keep on track with her diet. It seemed like every time she lost a couple of pounds something would happen either at work or with Adam and then she'd be back binging on the chips again. Judging from the outfit, this had been a binge week.

"This was such a good idea," she said to Angela as they settled in. "After what Gregory put me through today I am so ready for a beer. But just one," she added.

Next to her, Adam flashed a smile that should have been on a billboard somewhere. No doubt about it, the boy was one of the most gorgeous things God ever made. But Kizzy wasn't convinced he was the man God made for Erin.

And she was even less convinced when, after dinner, he informed Erin they had to pass on coffee and some DDR at Lionel and Kizzy's.

"Oh," she said, sounding a little surprised.

"I'm afraid I've got to get back home and study," he explained to the others.

It must not have been something he'd explained to Erin. She looked chagrined. "Sorry, guys. I didn't know."

"How about a rain check?" Adam said to Kizzy.

"Sure."

He shot that Colgate smile at everyone and said, "Good to see you all. See you at the wedding?"

"Yeah, see you," Brad replied in a tone of voice that said he'd as soon not.

Adam took Erin's arm and, with one final flash of his pearly whites, steered her out of the restaurant.

"Is it just me or is that weird?" Megan said, watching them go.

Angela sighed. "I think it's normal for Adam."

"I mean, he just took over," Megan continued in disgust. "And I understand about having to study, but once you've made a commitment to do something with people . . . I mean, it was like he could barely wait to get away."

"In all fairness to Adam, we invited him for dinner and he came for dinner," Kizzy said. "And medical school is hard. I'm sure he did have to study."

"Law school's no picnic, either, but nobody studies twenty-four/seven. He only had to come by the house for an hour," Megan finished with a frown.

"The guy's a dickhead," Brad said. "Let's forget about him and go have our coffee."

The women got the message and dropped the subject. But back at the house, once they'd banished the men to the living room, they conferred in the kitchen under the guise of making coffee.

"Brad's right, you know," said Megan. "Adam is a dickhead."

"Okay, so he ditched us, but he's got some good qualities, I'm sure," Kizzy said. What a lie! She wasn't sure at all.

Megan shook her head. "The jury's still out on that."

"I still don't see why we couldn't have stopped by Kizzy's for a little bit," Erin said as she and Adam walked into her house.

"Because a little bit would have turned into all night. And I wasn't lying. I do have to hit the books later." He caught her and pulled her to him. "But first I wanted some time alone with you. You know, you should have moved in with me in January. Then we could have been together more."

"You'd have just been studying anyway," she said, still feeling a little pouty over the way he'd swooped her off.

"I could always find time for you, babe," he said. "Now, come on. Kiss me. I'm Irish."

She couldn't help smiling. "You are not."

"I am for tonight," he said, and kissed her.

Twenty-two

Angela returned from her trip to Italy with dreamy eyes and six extra pounds. "But it was worth every one," she informed the Bikinis as they gathered around Kizzy's kitchen island to sample each other's diet appetizers. "Venice is amazing. Brad is amazing. Do you know he'd been saving for this trip for two years?"

"That is impressive," said Kizzy.

"Going to Venice on your anniversary, that is too romantic," said Megan with a sigh.

"It was romantic. And fun, too. Brad is still my best friend."

"Friends with benefits. Sounds good to me," quipped Megan.

Erin smiled right along with the others, but behind her smile she felt a question lurking. Was Adam her best friend?

Best friends told each other everything, and there were some things she still hadn't told him. Like who paid for their flowers. And whose band was going to play for their wedding. She needed to tell him about the band, she decided, neatly sidestepping the issue of the flowers.

"We don't need to hire a DJ. I've got it covered," she told him as they settled in to watch a DVD on Saturday night.

"You do? You never told me. Who?"

"The local band I've hired to play at Slugfest. They offered to do our wedding as a thank-you."

Adam looked genuinely pleased. "No way."

She nodded. "Way."

"Good job, babe."

"Thanks," she murmured as he pulled her to him for a kiss.

You didn't tell him that the band belongs to Dan Rockwell, scolded her inner mother.

No, but what did it matter who played at the wedding as long as she and Adam were dancing happily together?

The Heart Lake Slugfest, named after the Northwest's famous pest, was in full swing or, as Erin's boss liked to say, full slime— Gregory considered himself a real wit. Her team had actually pulled it together, adding a rock-climbing wall and a bounce house for the kids and bringing together what Gregory had rhapsodized over as the best arts and crafts fair yet. In addition to Dan's band, one of the girls on Erin's team had found them another act, a rapper named B-Kool, who was serving as a warm-up for Dan's band. Erin thought a better name for the guy should have been B-Bad, but he was drawing a crowd so she didn't care. The street dance officially started at eight, but for the first hour it would be more like a street mill, while people patronized the food booths, talked, and listened to the music and parents twirled their kids in circles. Later in the evening, things would really get rocking.

Now she stood at the edge of the beer garden, smiling over a job well done. It seemed like all of Heart Lake and at least half of Seattle had turned out. And most of them were in the beer garden, which occupied one entire side of the Safeway parking lot, conveniently located so people could easily drink and join the street dancers. It was roped off by a low, white picket fence and decked out with little white twinkle lights and Chinese lanterns. People were enjoying themselves and it was getting rowdy. The revelers who got too rowdy would be escorted somewhere to dry out by one of the Heart Lake Police Department's finest, many of whom were picking up some overtime patrolling the event.

Erin sighed. She wished Adam would have come and kept her company. But of course, he had to study. "You don't need me there," he'd told her. "You can do parties in your sleep, and I really have to hit the books this weekend."

Of course, she'd understood.

"Looks like we've got a good crowd for our Slugfest debut," said a voice at her elbow.

She turned and saw Dan Rockwell standing next to her, hands shoved in his jeans back pockets, surveying the crowd. With the jeans and his black, tight-fitting T-shirt and his slightly shaggy brown hair, he looked like a rocker, a sexy rocker. A couple of women walked past them and one of them looked Dan up and down in a way that invited him to look back.

"I see you're already collecting fans," Erin observed.

"What can I say? When you're hot you're hot."

"You'd better be hot up on stage or they'll throw empty beer bottles at you," she teased.

"We will be." Dan looked around her. "Where's your man?"

"Studying."

Dan nodded thoughtfully. "He does a lot of that."

"It's part of being a medical student. It will be different once he's an intern."

"Yeah, then you'll really never see him."

"I'll see him," Erin said. She looked at her watch. "Isn't it about time for you to go on?"

"As a matter of fact, it is. Wish me luck?"

"Break a leg," she said, and turned her back on him.

It wasn't as easy to turn her back on his music, especially the love songs. There was something about them that made her feel so . . . lonely. Of course you're lonely, she told herself, Adam isn't here with you.

"Great band," Samantha told her when she stopped by the Brewsters' beer garden booth to see how they were doing.

Kizzy and Lionel were there, buying beer and pretzels. "Light beer," Kizzy was quick to explain.

"You may as well not drink beer at all if you're going to swill that stuff," Samantha sneered.

"It's better than nothing," Lionel said.

"This is great," Kizzy said, surveying the makeshift fairground with its arts and crafts booths, big kid toys, and the dance and refreshment area. Below the Safeway in the Heart Lake Park, kids were enjoying pony rides, while couples rented swan-shaped pedal boats for a romantic interlude on the lake. The air smelled like cotton candy and elephant ears. "And it's not even raining," she added. "Did you phone in a special request to the weatherman?"

"I went a little higher up than him," Erin said with a smile. She saw Angela and her family and waved at them.

Angela pointed Brad and the girls toward the pony rides, then came over to say hi. "This is great," she congratulated Erin. "The girls are having a blast."

"I think everyone is," Erin said happily. And next year she'd top it.

Except next year she probably wouldn't be here.

People party in New York, she reminded herself.

The band finished their first set, then stopped for a break, and the sound guys switched to preprogrammed music.

"Looks like the band's going to take us up on our free drink offer," said Samantha.

Even before she turned around, Erin knew she'd see Dan Rockwell. She'd gone years with never seeing him except at Christmas, and now every time she turned around there he was, getting under her skin like a giant tick.

"You guys are good," Mike greeted him.

"Ready for that free beer?" added Samantha.

"I could go for a brew," Dan said amiably. He smiled at Erin. "Great crowd."

She looked around, pleased. The pony rides were just closing down and parents were starting to lead tired children off to their cars, bright balloons bobbing along in their wake. Tweenies and teens darted in and out of the crowd and the beer garden was packed.

"Now it starts getting really good," Mike said with a grin. "The grown-ups will kick loose, drink a little more, dance a lot more."

"And drink a little more," Samantha added with a grin. "Ka-ching."

"Remember, if someone's had too much you're cutting them off," Erin reminded her.

Samantha looked offended. "Of course. We just want people to have fun. We don't want anyone to get killed." She shot a look at her husband. "And speaking of fun."

He held up a hand. "I know, I know. Don't worry. I'll dance with you before the night is over."

"Dancing," Dan said, setting down his drink. "There's a good idea. How about keeping the help happy?" he asked Erin, taking her hand.

Valentine's Day all over again? She didn't think so. "Oh, I don't—"

Samantha cut her off. "Go ahead. Unwind a little."

"I don't think Adam—"

"Is going to care if you dance one dance with an old friend," Dan finished for her. "Let's take a vote. All in favor of the boss having fun for three minutes say aye."

"Aye," everyone chorused.

"It's like Vegas," Samantha added. "What happens at Slugfest stays at Slugfest."

That was all the encouragement Dan needed. He towed Erin over to the middle of the street where the die-hard street dancers were now going at it to Wreckless Eric's "Whole Wide World."

"I shouldn't be dancing with you. I'm engaged," she said sternly as he put an arm around her and started them doing some kind of crazy swaying thing. She suddenly felt like a contestant on *Dancing With the Stars*. "I don't know how to dance like this. What are you doing?"

"Having fun."

"I'm glad someone is."

He shook his head at her. "Just relax and let go. I'll lead you."

She didn't want to relax and let go, and she didn't want Dan to lead her anywhere. She was just about to say so when he pulled her against him and spun them in a circle. *Zing.*

Then he pushed her away from him and twirled her back under his arm, wedging her up against his chest. *Zing, zing.*

"Okay, how about this move?" he said, and spun her in a whole new way.

Several people clapped and somewhere in back of them a woman howled.

"All right, big finale," Dan said. "Trust me."

"What are you . . . ?" She didn't have time to finish the sentence. In one smooth move, he flipped her completely over, making her feel like she was on some wild ride at the amusement park. The Dance-O-Tilt. Every endorphin in her brain stood up and cheered. So did the crowd they had now gathered.

The song came to an end and people applauded. "That was awesome," a kid with a face full of piercings told Dan.

"Do you rent him out?" joked a middle-aged woman.

"He's not for rent. He's free," Erin said. Okay, enough fun. It was time to go now, before she did any more zinging while she was on duty. "Thanks," she said to Dan, and started to walk away.

"That's all you're good for? One dance?"

"Got to get back to work. I am on duty, you know."

"Hey, I'm on duty, too, but that's not going to stop me from having some fun," he said.

"That woman is interested," Erin told him, nodding to where the middle-aged woman stood with her friends. "Actually, it looks like you've got a lot of interested customers," she added, taking in the group leer.

Dan made a face. "A little too old for me. I have standards, you know."

"So do I. You're lucky I lowered them for one dance."

"Once a cheerleader always a cheerleader," he taunted.

She almost retorted, "Once a dork, always a dork." But somehow, she couldn't get out the words. She told herself it was because that would be mean. "I need to go check in with the rest of my staff."

"Come on. One more dance won't hurt."

The next dance is bound to be a slow one, warned her inner mother. *That would not be a good idea.*

"One dance," he said softly, taking her arm and giving her little tug toward him.

Sure enough, her inner mother was right. It was a slow dance. But it was too late to leave now. She didn't want to make a scene.

So she let Dan draw her to him and slide an arm around her. It was just a dance.

"Where did you learn to dance like that?" she asked.

"I took lessons once with an old girlfriend."

The remark stirred up an odd mixture of curiosity and irritation in Erin.

He cocked his head and smiled. "Don't look so shocked. Some women like dorks."

Erin felt her cheeks warming. "I did call you that once, didn't I?"

"Or twice."

"Okay, I'm undorking you now. Congratulations."

"Thanks," he murmured, and drew her closer.

It was almost scary how well their bodies fit together.

They may fit together, but they don't belong together. You're engaged, her inner mother scolded.

We're just friends, she argued, and to prove it, she started making conversation. "So what happened to the old girlfriend?"

"We broke up."

Erin made a face. "I figured that much."

He shrugged. "She was nice and it was good. But when you're looking for the person you want to spend your life with, it has to be more than good. It has to be a perfect fit. Like with dance partners," he added softly, and snuggled her up against him.

Her body went into melt mode. Of course you're melting, she told herself, you love to dance.

"When the fit's not right," Dan continued, "it doesn't matter how great the person is. It won't work. You've both got to get each other, be able to move together, like one." He demonstrated, twirling them. "You've got to have that connection. Here." He tapped his chest and then hers, sending a jolt through her.

She tried to ignore it. "You're never going to find the perfect woman, you know."

He shook his head. "Now that was spoken like a chick."

Erin frowned. "What's that supposed to mean?"

"You know one of the differences between men and women, why men get paid more, for example?"

"Sexism?"

"Nope. Women settle. They never think to ask for more. They do that when it comes to men, too. It's why you'll see a woman with an ugly guy a lot more than you'll see a man with an ugly woman."

"That's not a matter of settling. That's just men being shallow," Erin argued.

He shook his head. "Nope. That's holding out for the best."

"Okay, so what's your idea of a perfect woman?"

"One who's got some fire in her, and some ambition, someone who likes to have a good time—someone who's strong and who can go through hard stuff and survive. Someone like you," he added softly.

The look in his eyes was enough to give Erin's inner mother a fit, but before she could protest he said, "Okay, no more talking. Close your eyes and feel the music. This is a perfect slow dance song."

It was. A guitar softly strummed as Dierks Bentley urged her to come a little closer and let go.

Dan slipped a leg between hers and swayed them gently. Now they were entwined, bodies touching intimately, and the music poured over Erin, warm and sweet like honey. She could feel herself going limp. Her eyelids fell shut.

"You look beautiful tonight," Dan murmured, his warm breath ruffling her hair.

Those were the words of one lover to another! *What are you doing?*

Erin's eyes popped open and she stepped away. "I can't be your perfect woman, Dan."

His lips compressed into a tight line. Then he said, "How do you know for sure that this other guy is really right for you? It's not too late to put on the brakes."

"I don't have to. I know what I'm doing. I want to marry Adam."

Dan took a deep breath and nodded. "If he's perfect for you, then you should." And before she could insist that he was, Dan turned and left her standing alone among the swaying lovers.

"Did you see what I saw?" Angela asked Kizzy.

Kizzy nodded slowly.

"There's the man she needs to be with," Angela said. "What are we going to do?"

Lionel chose that moment to insert himself into the conversation. "You're doing nothing."

Kizzy frowned at him. "I don't remember asking your opinion."

"Well, I'm going to give it to you anyway. You don't want to be poking your nose into someone's love life, Kizzy girl, unless you like getting it punched."

Kizzy shook her head at him. "Men may let their friends do stupid things, but women don't."

"That's called meddling, and it's never a good idea," Lionel said.

"Lion, she's with the wrong man!" Kizzy protested.

"Wait a minute," said Lionel. "Am I missing something here? You watched her for one dance and now you know for sure that she's with the wrong guy."

"Yes," said both women.

Lionel rolled his eyes and shook his head.

"And she knows it, too," Kizzy said. "She just hasn't admitted it to herself yet. That's why we need to help her, before it's too late."

"Well, when you learn how to get a woman who's determined to do something not to do it, then let me know. I'm all ears," Lionel said to her.

"No, you're all mouth," Kizzy said. Then added, "But I love you anyway."

"Are you sure?" he shot back. "What do your girlfriends think?"

The women ignored him. "What are we going to do?" worried Angela.

"I have no idea," said Kizzy.

"You have got to try and talk to her," Angela pressed. "You're our leader. If she's going to listen to anybody she'll listen to you."

Kizzy doubted Erin would listen even if Cupid himself whapped her on the head. The girl was that determined to marry the wrong man. She sighed. If she talked to Erin would it wind up being the last time Erin ever talked to her?

Twenty-three

So when are you going to talk to Erin?" Angela nagged as Kizzy rang up her purchases.

"Not yet," Kizzy said. "I'm waiting for the right time."

Angela grabbed some napkins proclaiming chocolate a girl's best friend from a display rack next to the counter. "Add these on, too. They're too cute to pass up." Just when Kizzy was beginning to hope that she had dropped the subject, Angela picked it up again. "If we don't do something soon she'll be married to the wrong man."

"This isn't as easy as you think."

Angela drummed her fingers on the countertop. "Maybe we should all talk to her. Then it wouldn't just be you."

Kizzy shook her head. "If we do that she's liable to think we're ganging up on her."

"We're not ganging up on her. We're helping her."

"I don't know," Kizzy said doubtfully.

"Well, I do. We can't afford to waste any more time. I think we should say something on Friday."

"At her bridal shower? That will be cute."

"She can keep the gifts. She just needs to see she should be using them with a different man. And we can't keep waiting. Time is running out."

"Okay, okay, I'll talk to her," Kizzy promised.

So, true to her word, she gave Erin a call at work and invited her over for dinner with the vague idea of bringing up the subject of marriage at some point during the evening.

"I probably won't even be hungry for dinner," Erin said miserably. "Not unless it's nachos or something else bad for me. My computer crashed and I didn't back up my file for the Black and White ball. I've lost months of work and I've already gone through half a bag of Doritos. I feel like my head is going to pop off."

"Oh, I'm so sorry," Kizzy said. This was hardly the time to talk about Erin's love life, not when her work life was swirling around in the toilet. But then she remembered Angela's plan to gang up on Erin and made herself push forward. "How about burning off some frustration with a walk around the lake after you get off work?" she suggested. "That way you could burn off the stress without eating."

And then she'd stress poor Erin out all over again. That would go over about as well as a church picnic with no potato salad and fried chicken. How was she going to manage this, anyway?

"That sounds great," said Erin. "I know I've got to find better ways to cope than sticking my head in the chip bag."

"Don't be too hard on yourself. There's a reason they call those goodies we love so much comfort food," Kizzy said. "We're trying to change lifelong habits. I don't think that happens overnight, maybe not even in a couple of months."

"It's been longer than a couple of months." Erin sighed. "I'm a mess."

"Then come on over to my place after you get home. We'll burn off some of that bad energy. And meanwhile I hope you can regain some of your lost files somehow."

"Someone from the Geek Squad is coming over this afternoon, but I'm not holding my breath."

Kizzy wasn't, either. In Erin's present mood she'd never get through to her.

But Erin's mood had improved vastly by the time she got to Kizzy's house. "Those guys are amazing. He actually recovered all my lost documents. It's a miracle," she finished, hugging herself and beaming. "Now our walk can be just for fun."

Just for fun. Oh, Lord. "Well, then," Kizzy said resolutely. "Let's go."

And so they started off at a good clip, which quickly left Kizzy winded. At times like this she remembered she was the old woman in the group. She grabbed Erin's sweatshirt. "Slow down, Road Runner."

"Oh, sorry," Erin said. "I guess I am walking a little fast. It's just that I'm so relieved I want to run and jump and go crazy. Life is good."

Okay, here was a tiny opening. It could be the only one she'd get. "I guess so. Everything smoothed out at work, and everything all set for the wedding?"

Erin nodded, smiling.

Push the opening a little wider. "And you and Adam have reached an agreement on all the wedding expenses? No more arguments?"

"Nope. It's going to be fine."

"Everything you hoped?"

"Close enough. A woman has to compromise. You know that."

"True," Kizzy nodded. *Great. Where to go from here?* "And when you know it's the right one you don't mind compromising."

"That's what it's all about," Erin agreed.

They were getting nowhere this way. Kizzy took a deep breath and kicked down the door. "And you're sure Adam is the right one?"

Erin's brows drew together. "I'm getting married in a month. Why would you ask that?"

Oh, Lord, this was awkward. "Oh, I don't know. You two were fighting so much for a while there, I guess I was a little worried about you."

"Well, you don't need to be. Adam is exactly what I need. He's sweet and stable, and life with him will be perfect."

"And he's the only one who turns your heat up," Kizzy added. If Erin agreed with that she'd be lying. To both of them.

"Of course he is."

"Because I always say it's never too late to change your mind."

Erin turned and looked hard at her. "Is there some point you're trying to make?"

"No, no. I just want you to be happy."

"Why wouldn't I be?"

"You're marrying someone who's pretty much your opposite."

"So? Opposites attract. Anyway, we're not all that opposite."

"You're spontaneous. You love parties. You love things messy. Does Adam?"

"Of course he loves parties. And okay, he is a little bit of a neat freak."

"And maybe a bit of a control freak?" Kizzy suggested.

Erin's cheeks turned pink. She was probably remembering how he'd hauled her away on St. Patty's Day. "He's not really a control freak. He just likes to keep on top of things. And there's nothing wrong with that. I don't want my life to be out of control. When my mom was sick . . ." Her sentence died, and she blinked furiously.

"I know," Kizzy said, patting her shoulder. "It was hard."

Erin took a swipe at a corner of her eye. "My life growing up was fun, but it was kind of crazy, too. I don't want to live the rest of my life like that. Adam is the most stable man on the planet. He was there for me when I needed him."

Kizzy nodded. Okay, she'd tried. "I understand. You have to make the choices that are best for you."

"Yes, I do. So what's with the third degree?" Erin asked with a puzzled frown. "I'm the one getting married. Why are you getting cold feet?"

"I just saw you dancing with that cute bass player at the Slugfest and—"

Erin cut her off. "Dan Rockwell," she said in disgust. "Why would I want Dan when I could have Adam? Adam is amazing. He's smart and handsome, goal-oriented. He's so perfect he could have been on *The Bachelor*."

"He's got the whole package," Kizzy said. "But is it the right package for you?"

"Of course it is. And I'm very happy," Erin added, punctuating her statement with a scowl.

"Good. I'm glad," Kizzy said. "That's what we all want for you."

"Well, then, you've got it," Erin said, and changed the subject.

Okay, thought Kizzy, so she's going to be happy even if it kills her. And she'd tried. She really had. Short of kidnapping Erin, there wasn't anything more she could do.

Erin did a great job of looking like a happy bride-to-be at the Bikinis' bridal shower for her on Friday night.

Maybe they'd been wrong, Kizzy thought. Maybe she and Angela had imagined what they saw that night at Slugfest.

"Did you talk to her?" Angela whispered.

Kizzy looked to the living room where Erin sat with Megan, noshing on chocolate-dipped strawberries. "Yes. She assured me she knows what she's doing."

"Well, she doesn't," Angela said and bit the head off a broccoli spear. "This is bad. *Malissimo*."

"I'm not her mother. I can't tell her what to do."

"I can," Angela said, and started for the living room.

Kizzy grabbed her jeans belt and yanked her to a stop. "No you can't, and you know it. We've got to let her make her own decision here. It's her life."

Angela shook her head. "This is all wrong. I can feel it."

"That may be, but unless she asks for our help our hands are tied."

"Come on, guys. Let's open the presents," Megan called.

"The best present we could give her is to have the groom kidnapped the day before the wedding," Angela muttered.

Kizzy sighed and raised her eyes heavenward. *Lord, we're still needing a miracle down here. This girl needs her eyes opened. And before the wedding would be good.*

Erin was more than ready for the big day now. The Bikinis had showered her with enough Victoria's Secret to put on a fashion show. Two weeks before the wedding her aunt had thrown a kitchen shower for her, and this week the gang at work gave her a Macy's gift card. She'd known exactly what to do with it. On the way home from work Friday she stopped by the mall and bought a high-end espresso maker.

"Look what I got," she said to Adam when he came over.

He frowned at it. "I thought we were making our purchase decisions together."

"I got this with a gift card that was a present to me. I thought it was something we'd both enjoy. You love my lattes and my old expresso maker is dying. And you know we save a fortune making them instead of buying them."

He held up both hands. "Okay, okay. Never mind. Just promise me when we're married you won't do this." He slid an arm around her shoulders.

It didn't make her feel all warm and fuzzy. "You know, you *are* a control freak."

"What?"

"I never realized it. I don't know why not, but I didn't. Are you going to try to micromanage me after we're married?"

"Micromanage you? Is that what I'm doing?"

"Yes, as a matter of fact, it is."

He heaved a long-suffering sigh. "Look, I don't want to fight," he said.

He never did. He just wanted to get his way and have that be the end of things. "You know things can't always be the way you want them, Adam," she snapped.

He pulled back and looked at her like she'd just had a psychotic break. "What is with you tonight?"

"Nothing. I was fine until you came over and started making me feel bad."

"Come on. I'm not trying to make you feel bad."

He had rolled his eyes. He had actually rolled his eyes, like she was the problem. "You know, you have just managed to suck all the happiness right out of me."

Now he looked hurt. "Oh, babe. Come on. You know that's not what I'm trying to do. Come here." He tucked a finger under her chin and kissed her.

She was too irritated to feel anything.

He looked at her like she was a naughty child. "Come on now. You don't want to be mad. Let's save that for the big stuff."

He was right, of course. "Okay. No more being mad," she said, and they kissed again.

There. Everything was fine.

We're going to be so happy, Erin told herself as she drove to the Heart Lake Lodge to go over all the final details with Bev. It was now three days until the big day. She had taken the week off to give herself some breathing room, maybe get some extra sleep. Oddly enough, though, she hadn't slept that well. She kept tossing and turning and dreaming strange dreams. In one she'd outgrown her wedding gown and it had popped open right before she said, "I do." In another, she was walking up the aisle while the groom stood with his back to her. He turned to take her hand and she saw it wasn't Adam. He looked like Dracula. He grabbed her with an evil chuckle and said, "I vant to suck your blood." She woke up just as he was sinking his fangs into her throat.

But this morning the silly dreams were just that. Her newly altered wedding gown was still fitting and Adam, after hearing about her dream, simply laughed and assured her he hadn't grown fangs overnight. The sun was shining, the sky was blue, and the weatherman had promised it would stay that way through the weekend—a perfect June wedding.

The Heart Lake grounds were lush with rhododendrons and azaleas, camellias and wild roses. Tall fir trees stood guard over the large timbered lodge and the smaller buildings, which were scattered about the grounds like children playing in the yard. The lodge itself had a huge reception room with a wall of glass looking out at the stone veranda, the sweeping lawns, and beyond, the lake itself.

It was going to be a lovely wedding, Erin told herself as she carried her box of Wal-Mart napkins into the lodge. That had been Adam's suggestion and it had been a good one. It had taken her a while to see that, but now she totally got it. Who cared if the napkins didn't have their names on them? She could re-use the leftovers for any occasion, and they were the perfect shade of green. They'd be wonderful.

"Are you all ready for the big day?" Bev greeted her.

"Of course. I had to let out my wedding gown, though. How pathetic is that?"

Bev waved that failure away with a flick of her hand. "You were too skinny anyway."

Erin smiled and shook her head. "You always know the right thing to say."

Bev led Erin into her office and they settled in with cups of tea. "So, I see you brought the napkins." Bev made a check on the piece of paper in front of her. "Sweet Somethings is delivering the cake Saturday morning."

"Good."

"Then Changing Seasons will be setting up the flowers at two."

"Great."

"And," Bev continued with a sly grin, "we'll have the salmon dinner buffet set up to serve one hundred and thirty."

Erin's heart stopped. Salmon dinner buffet? Where had that come from? "Bev, I didn't order the salmon dinner buffet. You know that." That would cost a fortune. Adam would kill her. "We're having fruit platters from Safeway, and appetizers that my aunt is making."

"Well, you still are. But you're getting this, too." Bev beamed. "Happy wedding."

Erin sat back in her chair, dumbfounded. "Bev, you can't afford that."

"You're right. It's not from me."

"Who, then?"

"Your brother."

"Brett? He can't afford that."

"Okay, Brett and someone who preferred to remain anonymous."

Anonymous, just like with the upgrade on the wedding flowers. "I don't want it," Erin snapped.

"What do you mean you don't want it?" Bev protested. "I don't understand."

"I just . . . don't want it."

"Erin, the salmon's already here. You may as well take it."

Erin pressed her hands to her forehead and groaned. "Why is he doing this to me?"

"I don't get you," said Bev. "Someone is nice enough to spring for this for a wedding present and you don't want it? I know brides who'd kill for a gift like this."

"It's . . . complicated."

"Can you please uncomplicate it and take the gift?"

"I'll let you know," Erin said.

She finished with Bev and then drove to the Safeway. Dan

wasn't in. "He doesn't come on until three," said Fred the produce guy. "Try him at the lake house."

Sure enough, she found Dan at his fixer-upper, painting away. No music this time, just him in a paint-spattered shirt and jeans working in silence, slowly turning the house into a masterpiece. He'd painted the outside now and it was a pale yellow. He was in the process of turning the window trim lime green. She wondered what color he'd painted the inside of the house.

With no music blasting he heard her coming. He set down his paintbrush and wiped his hands on a cloth as she parked her car. Then he stood there on the porch and waited for her, saying nothing, just looking at her.

"You did it again, didn't you?" she greeted him.

He shook his head, looking disgusted. "Brett and I went in together."

"And how much did Brett pay?"

"Isn't that kind of a rude question?"

"You paid for most of it, didn't you?"

"I paid half," he admitted.

"I don't want it."

"You're such an ingrate."

"I don't mean to be, but it's too much. What am I supposed to tell Adam?"

Dan shook his head. "You don't want me to tell you what to tell Adam."

"This is wrong, all wrong. You can't afford it," she informed him.

He gave her a smile that was almost a sneer and shook his head. "Because I happen to work at a grocery store? Come on, Erin. Don't be such a snob. Didn't your mom ever tell you it's not how much you make, it's how you use it? I have plenty of money."

"But it's not right. Let me pay you back. You already paid for the flowers."

"So? It's my money. If I want to use it to help my best buddy's

baby sister have a nice wedding I should be able to do that, right?"
He hitched up a leg and sat on the porch railing. "Your mom was
like a second mom to me. I think this would have made her happy."

"So that's the only reason you're doing this?" If so, then maybe
she could live with the guilt.

"I want you to be happy."

"That's all?"

He sat there, his lips clamped shut, jaw working. She could see
in his eyes what he wouldn't say. She recognized it because it was
the same thing she was feeling. She didn't say anything either,
though. What was the point? She'd made her choice, and it was a
wise one.

"You made your choice," he said at last, echoing her thoughts. "I
wish it had been a different one, but things don't always work out
the way you wish."

She dropped her gaze. "I'm sorry. I shouldn't have asked."

"Did you really need to?"

She bit her lip and shook her head. Her eyes were stinging now,
threatening tears. She blinked them back. It was too late for tears,
too late for her heart to wander off the reservation. She needed to
end this conversation, get out of here. "You've known me for years.
Why didn't you do anything, say anything?" Damn him!

"You shot me down so many times I guess I was gun-shy. You
went from being a beautiful girl to a beautiful woman. Beautiful
women can be intimidating. Then last year I got out of the army
and came home and heard you had a boyfriend. And then you were
engaged." His smile was bitter. "That's how life plays out sometimes. Anyway, this isn't about me. It's about you. I want to see you
happy."

He was miserable and all he cared about was seeing her happy.
Next he'd offer her the moon.

You have got to leave right now! screamed her inner mother.

"I shouldn't have come. I'm sorry. And I'm sorry I've been . . .
ungrateful. Thanks for being such a good friend."

He nodded.

That was all there was to say. "I'll see you at the wedding." She turned to go.

"No you won't."

That stopped her in her tracks. "But your band?"

"Is playing without me."

"But they need a bass player," she protested.

"They got a guy. Erin, I was glad to do what I could to give you the dream wedding you want, including the band. That's what a man does for a woman he . . . cares about. But I won't come watch you marry another man."

The tears were back again, insisting on escaping. Erin nodded, unable to look him in the eye. Now it really was time to leave. She started to walk away.

"Wait." She turned and he closed the gap between them. He smelled like sweat and paint. It should have been a turnoff. He put an arm around her shoulder, pulled her to him, and kissed the top of her head. "Be happy," he said, then released her and went back to his paint can.

She stumbled down the porch, nearly blinded by silly tears. This sudden need to cry was ridiculous. She was just emotional because Dan had stirred up a yearning for something she could never have: the past. That was all. She didn't really love him. She loved what he represented.

She got in her car and drove back down the road, telling herself it wasn't meant to be. Dan Rockwell had had years to do something. So had she. She was meant to be with the man she was with. She'd chosen well and they'd be happy and that was that. The tears retreated.

So, with her runaway-bride moment conquered, she sailed into the final wedding events. She picked up Brett and his wife Carly at the airport on Friday afternoon and they all trooped over to Aunt Mellie's to chill on the deck before the rehearsal.

It was a perfect day for a wedding, just the kind of day she'd dreamed about. The sun was beaming in a blue sky, and the lake was shimmering with sunlight diamonds.

"How's Adam doing? Have you had to stick his feet in hot water to thaw 'em yet?" teased Brett.

"You're so funny," Erin shot back.

"Why should he have cold feet? He's lucky to get Erin," her sister-in-law said, smiling at Erin. Carly was going to be one of her bridesmaids, along with Megan and Angela, the matron of honor.

Erin stuck out her tongue at her brother. "So there."

"Yeah, well. You don't know her like I do," Brett said, and gave Erin a playful nudge with his foot. "So I hear Dan's band is playing for the reception. Are they any good?"

"They're great," Erin said. "Except Dan won't be there."

Brett's brows knit. "Why not?"

Erin felt her cheeks sizzling. "I think he had to work."

Now Brett was frowning. "What kind of lame excuse is that? He couldn't get off for an old friend's wedding? Man, I'm gonna have to go drag his sorry butt to the church."

"Don't say anything," Erin begged. "It's already settled. He got another bass player to take his place."

Brett shook his head. "What a bum. But I guess helping with the eats gets him off the hook."

Erin nodded. She suddenly felt like crying again. *Oh, Mom, would you have been proud of me? Would you have approved of the choice I made?*

Aunt Mellie joined them now and sank into a lounge chair with her glass of iced tea. "It's so lovely out today. You couldn't ask for a better weekend weatherwise," she told Erin. "Happy the bride the sun shines on," she added, raising her glass in salute.

"Yeah, and happy the brother who finally gets his snotty little sister married off," cracked Brett, returning to form.

"Ha, ha," Erin retorted.

"Be nice," cautioned his wife. "You may want free medical advice from her husband someday."

Brett gave a snort, then added, "Seriously, I'm happy for you, sis. Adam's a great guy. You picked good."

"I think so," said Erin.

Oh, dear, fretted her inner mother. *I hope you know what you're doing.*

When it came to love, who knew anything? All a woman could do was make the wisest choice possible and hope it turned out okay.

Uncle Jake got home from work, quickly showered and changed, and then it was time to go to the lodge for the rehearsal. After that Adam's parents were taking the wedding party to the Family Inn, a quaint family restaurant at the edge of town.

They got to the lodge to find the others already there and waiting: the groom and his parents, the groomsmen and bridesmaids, and Kizzy, who was going to be singing at the wedding, with a slimmer Lionel as her escort. She had her arm linked through Lionel's, and Erin looked at them and thought, there's a picture of what a marriage can be. She hoped that would be Adam and her someday.

Adam came over and gave her a kiss. "How's my bride?"

"Fine," she murmured.

His parents stepped up beside him. "Hello, dear," said Mrs. Hawthorne, giving her a stiff peck on the cheek. She smelled like Chanel No. 5. Slim and well dressed, she looked like Lauren Hutton.

"Nice to see you again," Erin said. That sounded stupid. This was going to be her future mother. "Thank you again so much for the cake. That was really sweet of you."

"Our pleasure," said Mrs. Hawthorne.

She had the oddest way of looking pleased, Erin thought, observing her tight smile.

She ventured a look at Mr. Hawthorne. His smile at least was genial. He was as good-looking as his wife, an older version of Adam with graying hair and the tanned skin of a doctor who was able to spend a lot of time on the links in between patients.

"Well," said Uncle Jake in his booming voice, clapping his hands together. "It looks like we're all here. Shall we go through the motions?"

Good old Uncle Jake. After she became engaged he got licensed to marry and conduct funerals. Active in his church for years, Uncle Jake had joked that with as much as he did for the church he might as well have a piece of paper that made him official, but Erin knew he'd really done this just so he could officiate at her wedding. Her uncle marrying her and her brother giving her away—what more could she ask for? Suddenly, she wanted to cry.

Aunt Mellie gave her a hug and a kiss on the cheek. "Your mother would have been so proud."

They trooped into the little building directly across from the main lodge, which had been turned into a wedding chapel. Erin tried to imagine it full of people and flowers and music the following day and couldn't. She tried to see herself up at the altar. All she could see was old-fashioned wooden pews and old wood floors, stained-glass windows filtering in colored light. It will be beautiful tomorrow, she told herself.

"Are you okay?" Kizzy had whispered at one point during the rehearsal dinner.

"Me? Yes, I'm fine."

She told that to Adam, too, who asked her the same thing later that night. "It's been a long time coming. Now that it's here it almost seems surreal."

"It will all be real tomorrow," he whispered, and kissed her gently.

It will all be real tomorrow.

That night she tossed and turned and wrestled with her pillow. The Sandman finally escorted her into Dreamland some time before dawn and then smacked her in the face with a bad dream. In it she was getting married in army fatigues in the middle of a combat zone. Their minister was a drill sergeant, who kept shouting at her, "This is not a drill, soldier!" And then the ground under her feet began to shake and the candelabras started swaying, flicking melted wax on everyone. "Earthquake!" screamed her aunt.

She sat up in bed in a cold sweat, panting. Okay, it was only a dream. She shouldn't have eaten so many pickles at dinner.

Eating. She suddenly felt a need for . . . something. She looked at the bedside clock. Eight A.M. She had time. She showered and slipped into jeans and a top and drove to the Safeway.

A mocha, that was what she needed. She bought a Grande at the Starbucks kiosk and then wandered the store, sipping it. Maybe she'd get some pastries to take over to Aunt Mellie's where everyone was congregating for brunch.

She slipped down the frozen food aisle past a couple around Kizzy and Lionel's age, lingering in front of a selection of frozen desserts. Something in the man's tone of voice as he talked to his wife made her stop to eavesdrop.

"For God's sake, Martha, are we going to be here all morning?"

"I was just thinking a pound cake would be nice," said the woman.

"Oh, come on. You don't need that."

Erin jumped away as if she'd been scalded. *You don't need that.* Where had she heard those words before? As if she didn't know.

But Adam would never talk to her like that. That wouldn't be them in thirty years.

She fled the store for the safety of Aunt Mellie's house. *Nerves, it's just nerves.*

Twenty-four

The day became a blur: breakfast with the wedding party and family at her aunt's, then the afternoon hair appointment and makeup session with her bridesmaids, then off to the lodge to take pictures before the ceremony.

Adam was gorgeous, attentive, and romantic. "You look beautiful," he whispered. "I'm the luckiest man in Heart Lake."

The butterflies in her tummy began to settle down.

And then, on their way to the gazebo for some bride and groom shots, they walked past the bank of glass windows and he looked in at the reception area. "All that for appetizers?" he wondered.

Erin followed his gaze to the tables dressed up in fine linen and sparkling with crystal and silver. In the center of each table, beta fish swam inside tall glass vases sprouting exotic Japanese grasses and flowers. Short glass candleholders with votive candles surrounded them, waiting to be lit.

Erin's pulse quickened and her stomach clenched. "Actually, it's going to be a little more than appetizers."

"What do you mean?"

"We're having the salmon buffet."

"What?"

"Don't worry. It was a gift."

"A gift? Awesome. Who gave us that?"

"My brother." No lie. Brett had paid for half.

"No shit? I thought he was broke."

"Well, he went halves with someone." Her cheeks were getting warmer by the minute. Her face had to be turning red. Hopefully, Adam wouldn't notice.

He looked at her suspiciously. "Who?"

"Just an old family friend," she said breezily.

"Does this friend have a name?"

"Dan Rockwell," she said quickly. She lifted her skirts and picked up her pace.

"Dan Rockwell, why does that name sound familiar?"

They were at the gazebo now. The photographer Adam had wanted to use was already there, fiddling with his camera as if he was trying to figure out how to work it.

He looked up at them and grinned. "So, how about you two go on in there and we'll take a couple of shots."

"Wait a minute," Adam said to Erin, his brows lowering, "isn't that the guy who was dancing with you on Valentine's Day?"

"Yes." Now Erin's whole face felt hot. Why was she blushing? She had nothing to be embarrassed about.

"That's a damned expensive gift. Why is he doing that?"

"I just told you. He's an old friend of the family."

"And why didn't you tell me about this before now?" Adam demanded.

"I only found out a couple of days ago."

"You could have told me a couple of days ago."

Yes, she could have, and now she wished she had. "Adam, I'm sorry." Why, oh, why hadn't she told him? The answer to that was simple. They'd have fought about it, like they were about to now.

"I don't like some guy giving you such an expensive present," Adam continued, frowning.

"Well, it's a little late to say 'no, thanks.'"

"You could have when you first found out."

"The salmon was already in."

"And it was what you wanted all along anyway, wasn't it?"

"What is that supposed to mean?" As if she didn't know. She could tell by his snotty tone of voice exactly what he meant.

Adam shook his head. "Never mind. It doesn't matter now. I don't want you seeing this Dan clown after we're married. And no more presents."

"So, how about you two hold hands?" suggested the photographer.

They grabbed each other's hands.

"That's pretty ungracious," said Erin.

"How would you feel if some old girlfriend decided to pay for our wedding dinner?" Adam demanded, scowling.

"Grateful," Erin snapped.

"And how about a smile?" added the photographer.

"Adam, it's too late to do anything about it at this point. Can we forget who paid for the salmon and remember why we're here? Please?"

"Still looking for that smile," coaxed the photographer.

"That will be hard to do when it's time to eat. I just think you should have told me," Adam reiterated. "That's all."

"I think I'll just go take some candid pictures. You guys let me know when you're ready," said the photographer, slipping away.

Adam was pouting now. "I don't like it."

Erin threw up her hands. "This is ridiculous. This is supposed to be the happiest day of our lives and we're arguing over a salmon dinner. That someone else paid for. What's wrong with that picture, Adam?"

He plopped down onto the little wooden bench that ringed the gazebo and scowled up at her. "You tell me."

"All right, I will. It's you."

"I'm not the one with old girlfriends hanging around," he retorted.

"He's not an old boyfriend. I told you, he's an old friend of the family. He and my brother were best friends."

"Did he buy a salmon supper for your brother?"

Erin sat down next to him and laid a hand on his arm. "You're the one I'm marrying. Doesn't that mean anything to you?"

"Of course it does," he said, his words clipped.

"Then please, let's not fight." She took his hand in hers. "I want this day to be memorable, don't you?"

He looked out at the lake, calm and shimmering blue, and nodded. "It just bugs me that this guy—"

She put her fingers to his lips and stopped him. "Adam, people who care about us have done a lot of nice things to make this day special for us. Aunt Mellie and my sister-in-law spent a whole day making appetizers, your parents gave us our wedding cake. Let's just take all those nice gifts and say 'thank you,' okay?"

He frowned and nodded. "You're right. I'm being an asshole." He gave her a quick kiss. "Come on, let's go find the photographer."

Erin bounced up, nearly crying with relief.

"But just remember. After we're married that guy is history."

Everything was fine after that. They smiled for the photographer, they stood at the edge of the lake and looked lovingly into each other's eyes. They kissed. Then they made their way back to the chapel to wait in their respective corners with their attendants for the big moment. They passed by the glass-encased reception room and saw the china and crystal twinkling in the early evening sunlight. Somewhere off in the distance a woman laughed. Inside, Erin saw movement and realized it was Dan's band setting up their equipment.

Kizzy's words blew through her mind like a hurricane. *It's never too late to change your mind.*

She turned her head away, looking instead at Adam, smiling at Adam, gripping Adam's arm. She didn't need to change her mind.

He covered her hand with his, whispered, "I love you," and kissed her.

It was perfect. Perfect!

She walked into the ladies' lounge off the foyer at the back of the chapel and the door shut after her.

Her bridesmaids stopped chatting and smiled at her. They looked perfect in their sage-green evening skirts and chocolate-brown tops. Perfect. Oh, God.

"There you are!" Angela cried happily. "You look beautiful."

Erin turned to look at herself in the full-length mirror on the wall. Her aunt had let out the dress, but you'd never know by looking at it. It still looked beautiful: taffeta eyelet with lace detail, a pale green ribbon around the waist, and a trumpet skirt with a sweep train. The floral comb in her hair and her green tourmaline earrings made her look like a woodland fairy queen. The woman in the mirror looked perfect.

The woman looking at her suddenly couldn't breathe.

Angela, who had been standing next to her, smiling, suddenly looked as panicked as Erin felt. "Erin, what's wrong?"

"I can't breathe," she panted, grabbing at her chest.

Megan was up to her in two quick strides. "You're just having a panic attack. Here, sit down."

"Get a doctor," Erin gasped.

"Get Adam," Megan ordered.

"Not him!"

"She has to breathe into a bag," said Angela. She grabbed a handbag from a nearby chair and rushed over to Erin, opening it as she went. "Here, breathe into my purse."

Erin couldn't even hold the purse. It slipped from her hands. "I can't breathe, I can't breathe." She was going to die, right here in the chapel bathroom.

"You can," Megan said firmly. "Look at me. Take a slow breath." To Angela she said, "Get Kizzy. Now."

With a whimper, Angela fled the room. Carly knelt in front of Erin, taking a hand and chafing it.

"You're going to be fine," said Megan. "Take another breath."

Erin shook her head wildly. "I can't do this."

"Yes you can. Breathe slowly."

"I can't marry Adam." There. She'd said it. It was out. The weight that had been pressing harder and harder on her was suddenly off her chest.

Megan sat back on her heels. "Well, it's about time."

Erin thought of the guests, of the wedding cake her non-future in-laws had bought, of the salmon buffet and the guests arriving. And Adam. What was Adam going to say? "I can't breathe!"

Now Kizzy was in the room. "What's going on?"

"She's finally come to her senses," Megan said, and Erin burst into tears.

"I don't want to marry Adam," she cried.

"We know," Kizzy said comfortingly.

"What am I going to do?"

"Just say no," advised Angela.

"My wedding," Erin lamented.

"Is screwed," Megan said, and Kizzy glared at her. "But better a screwed wedding than a screwed life," she quickly added.

Kizzy took both Erin's hands. "I know you thought you were making a smart choice, but a woman's got to choose with her head and her heart. Your heart's been numb for a long time."

"Well, it's not now. It hurts," Erin sobbed.

Kizzy sat on the arm of the chair and hugged her. "I know. Go ahead and cry."

And so she did. She cried over the way she'd deceived both herself and Adam into thinking they'd be great together, for the way she'd used him like a security blanket. She cried over how stupid she'd been, pretending that planning a perfect wedding would translate into a perfect relationship. There was only one man who could give her that.

She was still crying when Aunt Mellie entered the room. "Ready to start down the . . . Oh, dear."

"It's all right," Kizzy assured her.

"Yes," added Angela. "It's really worse than it looks."

Aunt Mellie knelt in front of Erin. "What is it, sweetie?"

"It's an earthquake," Erin whimpered. "I can't marry Adam."

Aunt Mellie nodded. "You're right. You can't."

Erin wiped her eyes and said in a shaky voice, "I have to talk to him."

"Do you want me to go with you?" offered her aunt.

She shook her head.

"Okay. We'll be right here," said Aunt Mellie.

"What just happened?" asked Carly, looking from one woman to the other as soon as Erin was gone.

"A mess," said Angela.

"It would have been a bigger mess if she'd married the wrong man," said Kizzy.

"Especially with the right one here in town under her nose," added Angela.

"The right one?" asked Aunt Mellie.

"You never noticed anything between her and Dan Rockwell?" Angela asked her.

"They've known each other for years," Aunt Mellie said dismissively. Then her eyes widened. "When did this happen?"

"Not soon enough," said Megan.

"Wait a minute," Angela said thoughtfully. She started out of the room.

"Where are you going?" Megan called.

"To get a groom."

"Wait for me. I'm coming, too," said Kizzy, and hurried after her.

Twenty-five

You're going to kill us," Kizzy protested, bracing her hands on Angela's dashboard.

"Oh, I am not. I was the queen of drag racing when I was in high school."

"If you don't slow down you're going to wind up the queen of the dead," said Kizzy. "I didn't go to all this trouble to get healthy to get killed in a car accident."

"We'll be fine," Angela assured her, and sailed through an intersection as the light turned red.

"Lord," Kizzy whimpered. "I don't know what we think we're doing," she added. "They don't even have a wedding license. This is insane."

They screeched into the Safeway parking lot, and hopped out. Angela lifted her skirt and began to run, Kizzy hot on her heels. "I hope Erin appreciates what we're doing for her," Angela called over her shoulder. "I'm going to break an ankle running in these heels."

"Never mind your ankle. You almost broke my neck driving like a crazy woman," Kizzy panted.

It was Hawaiian Days, and the checkstand area was awash with tropical greenery, the checkers all wearing Hawaiian print shirts. They found Dan at his checkstand, gaudy in a red one, a fake grass skirt over his jeans, ringing up an old man with a sour expression. Dan's expression wasn't real happy, either.

Angela inserted herself in front of the man. "Dan, you've got to come to the lodge right now."

"Excuse me, young woman, but you need to go to the end of the line." The man pointed to a can of chili and said to Dan, "That's on sale, you know."

"I know, Mr. Borden. It'll show up when we finish ringing you up."

"Never mind the chili," Angela cried. "Erin needs a groom!"

Dan scanned another can of chili. "She's got a groom."

"She's not going to marry him."

Dan stopped his scanning and stared at her.

"People are waiting here," said Mr. Borden.

Angela frowned at him. "Can't you see we've got a romantic emergency?" To Dan she said, "What's the matter with you anyway? How could you even think of working when the woman you want is about to marry someone else?"

Dan frowned. "Because she loves him. Not that it's any of your business," he added.

Angela gestured to her clothes. "Look how I'm dressed. I'm the matron of honor. This is my business."

Kizzy moved her aside. "You are handling this all wrong." She put her hands on her hips and went into full lecture mode. "Dan, we know you two both love each other. We've known it since we saw you dancing at Slugfest. You know it, too. This would be a good time to seize the opportunity and admit it."

"Never mind that. Ring up my groceries," commanded Mr. Borden, shaking a finger at the food piled up on the conveyer belt.

"Shame on you," said the old woman waiting in back of him. "Can't you see this is important? Don't you remember what it was like to be in love?"

"Yeah," put in Angela.

"Bah," spat the man.

"She's about to dump the groom," said Angela. "She's got the dress, the party guests, the food, and the band. She needs a wedding. Are you going to man up or not?"

The pianist was playing softly, ad-libbing since she had now gone through her entire repertoire of prewedding music. The guests were visiting and checking their watches. Gregory, Erin's boss, elbowed his wife and nodded toward the back of the chapel.

She turned and saw the bride marching to the opposite side. Husband and wife exchanged looks. "Odd," whispered the wife.

Now there went the bride's brother, who was supposed to be giving her away, running after her.

"Very odd," agreed Gregory.

Other guests had seen it, too. They began to whisper. "Is everything all right? What's going on?"

At the front of the church, the mother of the groom heard the swell of murmuring and looked back over her shoulder, saw nothing, and wondered what was delaying the ceremony. Why hadn't her son and the groomsmen come out yet? Had something gone amiss? It wouldn't surprise her if something had, poorly planned as this had been. And that last-minute change in the menu—it was shocking and ridiculous. This girl was a mistake. She would drain poor Adam, financially and emotionally. But Adam was a grown man and he had made his choice. Still. She sneaked a look at her watch. Twenty minutes late. She tried not to get her hopes up.

Erin was about to tap on the groom's dressing room door when her brother came up behind her and hissed, "What are you doing? We should have already been walking down the aisle."

"I have to talk to Adam," she hissed back.

"You can talk to him all you want at the reception. People are getting antsy."

"I can't marry Adam."

"What!"

Erin glared at her brother. "Will you keep it down?"

"Have you gone out of your mind?" he protested.

She shook her head. "This is a mistake. I don't want to spend the rest of my life with Adam."

Brett looked confused. "I thought he was perfect. Nice guy, doctor, happily-ever-after."

"I was wrong," Erin said on a sob. "I was so wrong."

"Okay, then," Brett said, and put an arm around her. "Don't cry. We'll work this out. He'll have to understand that you've got to do what's best for you. And if he doesn't I'll beat the crap out of him."

Poor Adam. This was going to be hard on his pride. But, "It's best for him, too," she whispered. He never would have been happy with her, not really.

"You go back to your room, sis. I'll tell him," Brett offered.

Erin shook her head. "You know what Mom always said: if it's your mess, you clean it up."

Brett studied her. "You sure?"

"I'm sure." Finally, she was sure of something.

"Okay. If he gives you any grief I'm right here."

The door opened and there stood Dave, Adam's best man. "Are we ready?" he asked.

"Not quite," said Erin. "I need to talk to Adam."

Dave stood aside and motioned her in.

"Alone," Erin added.

The best man exchanged puzzled looks with the other grooms-men, but they slipped out to stand in the foyer.

"I'm right here," Brett reminded her, and gave her arm a sup-portive squeeze.

She nodded, slipped inside, and closed the door after her.

Adam came up to her, took one look at her and grabbed both her arms. "What's wrong?"

Of course she'd still have splotchy skin and red eyes from her crying jag, and her makeup was probably a mess. But that was the outside of her. The inside felt cleansed.

"We can't get married."

"What? What's happened?"

"I've just realized I can't marry you."

"Look, if this is about what I said back there at the gazebo I didn't mean it. Really."

She shook her head. "It's not that. Adam, we're not a match."

"Of course we are," he insisted, and pulled her to him. "We love each other."

She looked up at him and shook her head. "Not really. We just want to."

He stared at her like she'd lost her mind.

"Think about it. Think about how much we've fought ever since we got engaged."

"Every couple fights."

"Before they're even married, when they should be enjoying the happiest time of their life?" She shook her head. "We're not right for each other. And I'd rather admit that now and wreck a party than have to admit it a few years from now and wreck a marriage." He was still staring at her as if she was speaking another language. "Do you want to spend the rest of your life tripping over my shoes, getting frustrated because I've spent money on something you don't think we need, trying to make me stick to my diet?"

"I was only helping you," he muttered.

She put a hand to his cheek. "I know. You love to help. You're a natural-born rescuer and you love to be in charge. You'll make a great doctor. But you won't make a great husband, not for me."

"That's not true," he protested, gripping her more tightly.

"Yes, I'm afraid it is. I've been using you like a crutch. That's not a good foundation for a relationship. You needed a true Mrs. Adam. Not an Eve who's going to be letting snakes in the garden," she added with a wistful smile.

He dropped his arms. "I can't believe you're dumping me."

"I'm not dumping you. I'm setting you free," she said. She slipped her engagement ring off her finger and offered it to him. "Keep it for the right girl."

Looking chagrined, he held out his palm and she dropped the ring into it. "I guess I should tell your uncle that there won't be any ceremony today," he said stiffly.

She nodded. "Thanks."

Without another word, he slipped out of the room.

Erin surprised herself by not crying. She had just broken up with the man of her dreams. She should be devastated. Instead, she let out a sigh of relief. She felt lighter, better than she'd felt in months. She couldn't help shaking her head. All that dieting and she'd hardly lost anything. Now, just like that, she'd lost one hundred and seventy pounds. And it felt great.

The door opened. She turned, expecting to see Brett. Instead, she saw Dan, wearing a Hawaiian shirt and jeans.

Her lower lip started to tremble. She held up her naked ring finger. "You wasted a lot of money on fish."

He didn't say anything. Instead, he took her by the arms and pulled her up to him, and kissed her. And every nerve inside her went off like the Fourth of July. *Zing, zing, zing, zing!* By the time he let her go she felt like a pinball machine. "Oh, Dan," she cried. "I was so wrong, about so many things. I feel like such a fool."

He smiled at her and tapped her nose with his finger. "You've been trying to find your way. That's all. Now, come on. We're going to miss the wedding."

"There is no wedding," she protested.

"Oh, yes there is," he said. "And you're not marrying a doctor or a J. Crew fashion model. You're marrying a man who'll spend his last cent to make you happy, and who will love you fat or thin." He gave her one more kiss, then said, "Get your bridesmaids back in here and fix your makeup and let's get this show on the road."

Now it was getting really interesting. Gregory's wife tapped his thigh and nodded toward the back of the chapel. Here came the groom, marching right up the center aisle, stomping all over the white carpet where the bride was supposed to walk. Behind him came the minister, looking determined. Gregory and his wife gaped at the sight, then at each other. What could have happened?

The groom marched past them and up to his parents. He bent over and whispered something to them. Gregory could see the woman stiffening. "Oh, dear," he murmured to his wife.

"Exactly," she murmured back.

The parents of the groom left their seats and traipsed down the center of the aisle, further marring the white carpet, and followed the groom, whose face was now quite red, out of the church.

The minister ran a finger inside his collar and cleared his throat, preparing to make some sort of announcement. As if anyone with a brain couldn't guess what it was.

But now, what was this? Here came a woman running up, God help us, the center aisle. Ah, well, it probably wasn't going to be used anyway. She tugged on the man's coat sleeve and whispered something. The man looked at her as if she'd gone insane. She nodded, then trampled back down the white carpet. *Someone* needed to straighten that before a guest tripped and sprained an ankle.

The minister cleared his throat again. "Friends of the groom, I'm sorry to have to inform you that Adam and Erin won't be getting married today. After a heartfelt discussion, they have decided it would be a mistake. We must applaud this kind of maturity. We do hope this hasn't been too great an inconvenience for any of you. Adam and Erin would like me to assure any of you who have already sent wedding presents that they will be returning them soon. Any of you who would like to stay and enjoy the grounds are welcome to," he added.

The soft murmurs rose to a dull roar and the minister had to raise his voice to be heard over the din. "Those of you who are friends of the bride, we ask your indulgence for just a few moments. If you wouldn't mind, please remain seated."

"Well," Gregory said to his wife. "I'm going to straighten out that carpet."

A small crowd stood gathered in the ladies' dressing room. "This is insane," Uncle Jake informed them. "Erin, I don't understand what is going on in your head."

"I know it looks crazy," she admitted. "And believe me, there's been plenty going on in my head, and all of it messed up. What I need to listen to is my heart."

Her uncle cocked a skeptical eyebrow. "And just like that your heart now knows exactly who you should marry?"

Erin smiled at Dan. "As a matter of fact, it does."

Her uncle looked sternly at the pair in front of him. "This is not a game, you know. This is serious business. How can you possibly justify dumping one man and marrying another in the same day?"

"Because one wasn't right for me and the other is." And it was that simple. Embarrassing, but simple.

"He's a good guy, Uncle Jake," put in Brett. "You know that." He turned and pointed a finger in Dan's face. "If you ever make my sister unhappy."

"Not gonna happen," Dan said cheerfully, "and you know it." He smiled down at Erin. "I knew she was the woman for me the first time I kissed her. Even if she was just a kid," he added with a grin.

"How can I marry you two? You don't have a wedding license," said Uncle Jake.

"We'll go down to the courthouse and make it legal as soon as we get one," Dan said. "Meanwhile, can't you do a provisional wedding ceremony?"

"Like a mock trial," added Megan.

Uncle Jake looked horrified.

"I knew a guy who married a South American chick, and they had a church wedding and a courthouse wedding," Dan pressed.

"Please, Uncle Jake," begged Erin.

"Erin, people came here to see you marry Adam Hawthorne and now you expect them to stay and watch you marry Dan without a wedding license?"

"Why not?" put in Aunt Mellie. "That's what they did in *Philadelphia Story*."

"Oh, for Pete's sake, Mellie," said Uncle Jake in disgust.

She put a hand on his arm. "Sometimes there's nothing wrong with bending the rules a little. Like we did," she added, raising an eyebrow.

Uncle Jake's cheeks reddened.

"Please, Uncle Jake," added Erin.

He heaved a long-suffering sigh. "All right. We'll do . . . something."

And so, with the white carpet barely set to rights, the bride finally walked down the aisle.

Her groom stood waiting for her resplendent in jeans and a Hawaiian shirt, beaming like a man who had just won a million-dollar lottery.

"Do you take this woman to be your lawfully wedded wife, as soon as you get a marriage license?" asked Uncle Jake.

Dan smiled down at Erin. "I do."

"And do you take this man to be your lawfully wedded husband? And don't think I'm not going to march you two down to city hall first thing Monday to get that license, young lady."

Erin grinned. "I do."

Next to her, Angela started crying.

Uncle Jake took a deep breath. "Then by the powers vested in me, I now pronounce you man and wife. Almost. Go ahead and kiss her."

The remaining guests cheered and clapped as Dan pulled Erin to him and went at it.

"Go for it," called Lionel, and everyone laughed all the louder.

The kiss ended, and Erin opened her eyes and looked up at her new husband. She saw the boy who had teased her, the youth who had wanted her, and the man who had loved her enough to let someone else have her if it would make her happy. He spent money like he was Donald Trump and they'd probably never have a cent to their name, but she knew he'd always make her feel safe. And she hoped she'd be able to make him happy. She was sure going to try.

"This was quite the wedding," Erin's boss told her later as he and his wife went through the reception line.

She smiled up at Dan. "It was perfect."

Twenty-six

$\mathcal{I}$t was the Fourth of July, and the Bikinis stood cheering as Kizzy, now lighter by forty-five pounds, swam up to them from the opposite side of the lake. She was breathing hard by the time she climbed up onto the dock, but she was smiling from ear to ear. "I did it!" she gasped. "I thought I was going to die, but I did it."

Lionel, who had been swimming right behind her, came up the ladder next. "Way to go, Kizzy girl," he said, and kissed her.

"We need a picture," Angela said, grabbing her digital. Lionel kept his arm around Kizzy and they stood, smiling for the camera, a couple happily on their way to getting fit.

"Okay, now we need one of all of us together," said Angela. "Lionel, will you take one?"

"Sure," he said. He took the camera and backed up.

"Don't forget the trophy," Angela said, and handed it to Megan, who had lost the most—an amazing sixty pounds.

They placed her at the center of the group with Kizzy next to her, helping Megan hold up the No-belly trophy like she was a newly proclaimed boxing champ. "Here's to continued victory over fat," Kizzy crowed.

Angela, slimmer by twenty-five pounds and still working her way to hot, hugged her from the right, giving Lionel a Marilyn Monroe pose in her yellow polka dot bikini.

She raised her glass of lemonade in salute. "Here's to getting hot."

"To learning to listen when our bodies speak," said Erin, leaning over Angela and hoisting her martini glass. The weight she'd been so worried about had finally fallen away as she enjoyed life with Dan, working on fixing up the lake house where they had decided to live and raise a family. Today she was showing off her new figure in a hot-pink suit.

"And to hanging in there," added Megan. She had showed up in a one-piece and a cover-up, promising that by next summer she'd be bikini ready. "If I keep up the good habits I started, the old Megan will be a thing of the past," she'd predicted.

"She already is," Angela had said, and hugged her.

"Okay, ready?" called Lionel. "Say cheesecake."

"Cheesecake," they chorused.

The moment recorded for posterity, Lionel disappeared into the house to dry off and change. Later in the afternoon he'd fire up the grill and Dan and Brad and the girls would join the party.

Kizzy wrapped her towel around herself like a cape and turned to smile at her friends. "Well, girlfriends, we did it. And I'll have you know not only has my weight dropped but so has my blood pressure. My doctor says I'm not the same woman I was six months ago."

"None of us are," said Megan. "Thank God."

"I'm so glad we didn't break up the club," said Angela. "I couldn't have hung in there without you guys."

"I still can't," said Megan. "We have to keep this going forever. I still have pounds to lose. And starting a new law firm, I'm really going to need moral support."

"That's what friends are for," said Erin, "to hang in there with you."

"Through thick and thin," added Angela. She raised her glass. "Here's to girlfriends."

"I'll drink to that," said Erin, and they all did.

Good EATING

Recipes from the Bikinis

Changing lifelong eating habits can be hard. Believe me, I know. So that's why we wanted to share some of the recipes we made up. Hopefully, you'll enjoy them as much as we have and maybe they'll inspire you to start your own Bikini Club. —Kizzy

Megan's disclaimer: *Food values were figured to the best of our abilities. If you have any doubts or concerns, double-check all values to make sure they are accurate. Check with your doctor before beginning any diet/exercise program. If you don't lose weight, if you choke on a piece of asparagus, if your bikini doesn't fit by next summer—don't sue the Bikinis. They have a very good lawyer.*

ANGELA'S ASPARAGUS ANTIPASTO

(COURTESY OF THERESIA BRANNAN)

·····························•···

1½ pounds asparagus (best when still in bud)
1 (8-ounce) bottle light Italian dressing
1 pound presliced Black Forest ham
1 bunch green onions

Wash asparagus. Cut off 1½ inches and peel off bottom outer skin (about 2 inches) to eliminate tough fibers. Blanch asparagus in boiling water for 1½ to 2 minutes. Place asparagus in Italian dressing and marinate for at least two hours. (You can leave overnight in refrigerator. If you do that just blanch for half the time.) Remove the onion bulbs and blanch the green leaves. Set aside for later use. Cut ham pieces in half. Remove asparagus from dressing. Wrap ½ piece of ham around each piece of asparagus and tie it with a piece of green onion. Serve on oval or rectangular platter. *Serves: 8*

Nutrient value per serving: 150 calories, 12 g protein, 10 g carbohydrate, 5 g fat, 1 g fiber, 3 Weight Watcher points

MEGAN'S FETA CHEESE VEGGIE DIP

(COURTESY OF KATHLEEN HALE)

....

1 (6-ounce) (170 grams) container of crumbled feta cheese
2 ½ tablespoons light mayonnaise
½ teaspoon curry powder
¼ teaspoon dill weed

Mix all ingredients together well. Serve with raw veggies. *Servings: Makes 1 cup of dip (serving size 2 tablespoons). For parties, double the recipe.*

Nutrient value per serving: 57 calories, 3.7 g protein, 1 g carbohydrate, 4 g fat, 0 fiber, 1 Weight Watcher point

KIZZY'S CABBAGE SALAD

½ of a large cabbage (or 1 small cabbage)
½ medium-sized onion
2 large stalks of celery
1 green bell pepper
½ pound of small frozen cooked shrimp
½ cup light mayonnaise
Parsley, for garnish

Chop the cabbage, onion, celery, and green pepper and mix together in a large bowl. Drain shrimp and add. Stir in mayonnaise. Put in salad bowl and serve with a parsley garnish. *Serves: 6 to 8*

Nutrient value per serving: 80 calories, 6 g protein, 6.2 g carbohydrate, 2 g fat, 1.8 g fiber, 1 Weight Watcher point

MEGAN'S PRACTICALLY PERFECT
CARROT SALAD

6 carrots
1 green bell pepper
½ medium-sized onion
½ cup light mayonnaise
Salt and pepper to taste
½ cup crunchy Chinese chow mein noodles

Peel carrots and coarsely grate. Finely chop pepper and onion, and mix with carrots in large bowl. Mix in mayonnaise and salt and pepper to taste. Right before serving, add Chinese noodles and transfer to salad bowl. *Serves: 6 to 8*

Nutrient value per serving: 60 calories, 0.8 g protein, 2 g carbohydrate, 1 g fat, 0 fiber, 1 Weight Watcher point

ANGELA'S TOMATO AND MOZZARELLA SALAD

....

8 Roma tomatoes
1 green bell pepper
1 pound mozzarella cheese
1 medium onion
1 package (2/3 ounce) fresh basil
1 (6-ounce) can of black olives
1 to 2 tablespoons light Italian dressing

Cut tomatoes, green pepper, and cheese into bite-sized chunks and put in a large mixing bowl. Chop onion, basil, and olives and add to bowl. Mix in just enough Italian dressing to coat everything. *Serves: 8*

Nutrient value per serving: 220 calories, 15 g protein, 10 g carbohydrate, 15.5 g fat, 0.5 g fiber, 6 Weight Watcher points

AUNT MELLIE'S SEAFOOD SENSATION

½ pound frozen precooked small shrimp, thawed
½ pound crab meat (can use imitation)
1 red bell pepper
½ medium onion
½ cup cilantro, finely chopped
½ teaspoon dill weed
1 avocado
Dash of lime
¼ cup low-fat mayonnaise
Lemon wedges, for garnish

Drain shrimp and crab and put together in a bowl. Dice red pepper and onion and add to seafood, along with cilantro. Remove avocado skin and pit and cut into small pieces. Add dill and dash of lime then fold in mayonnaise. Put in serving bowl and garnish with lemon wedges. *Serves: 6*

Nutrient value per serving: 132 calories, 10 g protein, 10 g carbohydrate, 6.2 g fat, 1.5 g fiber, 3 Weight Watcher points

ANGELA'S ITALIAN STIR-FRY

....

    1 zucchini squash, well washed and sliced diagonally
    1 yellow summer squash, well washed and sliced diagonally
    1 red bell pepper, cut into bite-sized chunks
    2 carrots, peeled and sliced diagonally
    1 onion, cut into bite-sized chunks
    1 to 2 tablespoons oil for frying
    ½ of a pesto–dried-tomato cheese torta (you can find this in the
        specialty cheese section of your grocery store)

Cut up all the veggies, then fry in the oil in a large frying pan for about
5 minutes, stirring frequently to avoid burning. (Note: if you want the
carrots to be less al dente, fry them for a minute first, before adding
the softer, quicker-cooking veggies.) Add cheese torta and stir until
melted, about 1 minute. *Serves: 4*

Nutrient value per serving: 165 calories, 1 g protein, 3.3 g carbohydrate, 11 g fat,
21 g fiber, 4 Weight Watcher points

2 (14.5-ounce) cans Mexican-style stewed tomatoes
1 (15-ounce) can garbanzo beans, drained
1 (15-ounce) can black beans, drained and rinsed
1 (15-ounce) can kidney beans, drained and rinsed
1 (15-ounce) can Mexican-style whole kernel corn
4 cups water
1 package prepared taco seasoning

Combine all ingredients in a large soup pot and simmer 10 to 15 minutes. *Serves:* 8

Nutrient value per serving: 212 calories, 10 g protein, 35 g carbohydrate, 1 g fat,
1 g fiber, 4 Weight Watcher points

KIZZY'S PULLED PORK

(COURTESY OF NORMA SMITH)

....

1 pork butt or large lean pork roast (6–7 pounds)
1 tablespoon zesty steak seasoning (Kizzy uses McCormick Grill
Mates Montreal Steak)
3 to 4 peeled and crushed garlic cloves
1 small green bell pepper, diced
1 small onion, diced
1 cup chicken broth
6 ounces calorie-free or reduced-carb barbecue sauce

Lay meat on heavy-duty foil (or double-layer regular) in a roasting pan. Cover with seasoning, garlic, green pepper, onion, and broth, then fold foil over meat, sealing tightly. Roast at 300 degrees for 4 to 5 hours till very tender (internal temperature of at least 190 degrees). When done, you'll have lots of liquid in the pan. You can chill that, then skim off the fat and freeze for soup stock or to use in making baked beans (see next recipe). Remove meat to platter and cool. When able to handle the meat, shred with a fork, discarding any fat. Mix in 6 ounces calorie-free or reduced-carb barbecue sauce and serve with baked beans. You may eat this meat plain or served on a bun or low-calorie bread. *Serves: 12 half-cup servings*

Nutrient value per serving: 185 calories, 21 g protein, 0.5 g carbohydrate, 10 g fat, 1.5 g fiber, 1 Weight Watcher point

KIZZY'S BAKED BEANS

(COURTESY OF NORMA SMITH)

1 (12-ounce) bag white Northern beans

Juice from pork

1 quart chicken broth (or enough to cover the beans when cooking
with an inch to spare)

¼ to ½ cup ketchup, chili sauce, or barbecue sauce

¼ cup zero-calorie brown sugar, such as Sugar Twin

Salt and pepper to taste

Put beans in medium pot, cover with boiling water and simmer for 5 minutes. Let beans sit covered for 2 hours. Drain and rinse. Add juice from pulled pork recipe, leaving in onion, pepper, etc. Don't strain out. Add chicken broth and other ingredients and simmer until beans are tender and juice is mostly gone. Salt and pepper to taste and serve with pulled pork. *Serves: 12 half-cup servings*

Nutrient value per serving: 82 calories, 5.5 g protein, 2 g carbohydrate, 0.6 g fat, 7 g fiber, 1 Weight Watcher point

KIZZY'S CHOCOLATE RUM HEAVEN

....

*1 small package (1.4-ounce) sugar-free instant chocolate pudding
   mix*
1 cup whipping cream
1 cup cold water
2 teaspoons rum extract
1 (3.5-ounce) (100g) dark (72% cacao) chocolate bar, chopped
1 cup of whipped cream for topping
Dash of vanilla extract

Mix pudding with whipping cream and cold water until thick. Fold in
rum extract, then put in a fancy serving bowl and let sit in refrigerator until set. Finely chop up the chocolate bar and sprinkle over top
of pudding. When ready to serve, garnish with whipped cream flavored with vanilla. *Serves: 4*

Nutrient value per serving: 350 calories, 3.7 g protein, 15 g carbohydrate,
2.5 g fiber, 8 Weight Watcher points

KIZZY'S CHOCOLATE RUM HEAVEN, VERSION 2

. . . .

For less calories, substitute ¼ cup cocoa powder for chocolate bar (reserve 4 teaspoons for garnish), and 1 cup chilled evaporated skim milk for whipping cream.

Mix pudding with cold evaporated skim milk and cup of cold water until thickened. Fold in rum extract and cocoa powder and put in serving bowl (or individual parfait glasses). Refrigerate till set. When ready to serve, top with whipped cream flavored with vanilla and sprinkle with reserved cocoa powder. *Serves: 4*

Nutrient value per serving: 90 calories, 6 g protein, 19 g carbohydrate, 0 g fat, 2 Weight Watcher points

ANGELA'S LEMON PARFAITS

(COURTESY OF NORMA SMITH)

1 (3-ounce) package sugar-free, lemon-flavored gelatin
1¼ cups water, boiled
3 tablespoons lemon juice
1 teaspoon grated lemon peel
2 cups vanilla ice milk or carb-free ice cream (Angela uses Dreyer's
  Grand Light)
Dash nutmeg
Nonstick cooking spray, butter flavored
⅓ cup slivered almonds

Dissolve gelatin according to package directions but using only 1¼ cups boiling water instead of two full cups. Stir in lemon juice and peel. Add ice milk by spoonfuls until melted and smooth. Add dash of nutmeg, then pour into individual parfait glasses and chill. Spray almonds with butter-flavored nonstick cooking spray and toast till light brown in skillet, stirring often to prevent burning. Set aside. When ready to serve parfaits, top them with slivered almonds. *Serves: 4*

Nutrient value per serving: 145 calories, 5.75 g protein, 3.4 g carbohydrate, 9 g fat, 1 g fiber, 3 Weight Watcher points

NOTE: Nutrient values were taken from package labeling, United States Department of Agriculture *Handbook of the Nutritional Value of Foods in Common Units*, Netzer's *The Complete Book of Food Counts*, and Weight Watchers *Pointsfinder*.